3.99

The Magic Fart

PIERS ANTHONY

The Magic Fart

Mundania Press

The Magic Fart copyright © 2003,2005 by Piers Anthony Jacob

A Mundania Press Production

Mundania Press LLC
6470A Glenway Ave #109
Cincinnati, Ohio 45211

To order additional copies of this book, contact:
books@mundania.com
www.mundania.com

Cover Design © 2005 by Stacey L. King
Book Design and Layout by Daniel J. Reitz, Sr.
Book Production and Promotion by Bob Sanders
Edited by Daniel J. Reitz, Sr. and Audra A. F. Brooks

Trade Paperback ISBN-10: 1-59426-008-7
Trade Paperback ISBN-13: 978-1-59426-008-7

Hardcover ISBN-10: 1-59426-007-9
Hardcover ISBN-13: 978-1-59426-007-0

eBook ISBN-10: 1-59426-009-5
eBook ISBN-13: 978-1-59426-009-4

First Edition—August 2003
Second Edition—September 2005
Library of Congress Catalog Card Number 2003108296

Production by Mundania Press LLC
Printed in the United States of America

0   9   8   7   6   5   4   3   2

Contents

Part 1: Challenge

Chapter 1 – Œ Mission

Prior was bored. It had been a year since his great adventure on Mt. Icecream, where he had challenged the five deadly branches of the Cherry Tree, won the remarkable Spire, and finally recovered his small natural penis. He would hardly care to do that again, but had to admit that ordinary existence was downright dull in comparison.

Well, there was nothing wrong with dullness that couldn't be cured by a good outrageous fuck. He would have to go out to the slots, though he really craved something a bit more romantic. But he had no girlfriend, and high quality call girls were beyond his means. So he girded his loin for something considerably less enticing.

His doorbell rang. He sighted through the peephole and saw a comely but moderately severe young woman holding a rich bouquet. What was this? He hadn't ordered any flowers. It must be a mistake.

He opened the door. "I think you have the wrong—"

"Prior Gross?" the woman inquired crisply.

"Yes, but—"

"From a secret admirer," she said, putting the bouquet into his hand. The blooms had a strong aroma that threatened to intoxicate his outlook.

He saw no identifying card. "*What* admirer?"

She wedged by him and stood inside the room, closing the door behind her. "Me."

This was highly flattering, but surely still a mistake. "Do I know you?"

"Just call me Suzie."

"Look, Suzie, I'm just an ordinary guy with no money to spare, so if you figure to charge me some outrageous fee for a spot dalliance, forget it."

She gazed at him, her eyes turning round. Then they brimmed. "Oh!" she sobbed. "You think I'm one of *those* types." She hid her face in her hands. She looked younger than he had taken her for, and far less composed.

Prior felt like a well-worn heel. "I'm sorry," he said. "Of course you're not."

She continued to sniffle into her handkerchief, which seemed to have appeared from nowhere. "I just wanted to please you with my, my flowers, because you're such a nice man, and you hate me."

"I don't!" he said, putting his arm around her heaving shoulders. "I don't know what got into me. How can I make it up to you?"

"I just want you to like me," she said tearfully. "You're so wonderful."

What could he do? "Of course I like you," he said gallantly. "I just think you've got the wrong, um, address."

"But aren't you the great man who conquered the Cherry Tree and won the Spire?"

Had she been reading his private thoughts? "Well, yes. But aside from that, I'm nobody."

"You're still my hero!" She looked up at him, her eyes seeming larger and brighter. "I just know you're the one."

There was still something missing here. "The one for what?"

"The one to take my innocent maidenhood and make me a real woman. I so much want it to be you. Promise me you'll be gentle."

This put a different complexion on it. "You came here for your first sexual experience?"

"I just know it will be better with you than with anyone else. Because you know it all, and I know nothing. Please say you'll do it."

Yet this was remarkably sudden. What was the catch? "I'm not sure this is smart."

Her eyes filled again. "You think I'm repulsive!"

"No, you're not!" Indeed, her figure under her dress was robust, with her breasts swelling eagerly.

"Oh, thank you, Mr. Gross! Tell me what to do."

"You really want this? Sex with me?"

"With all my heart!" Indeed, her pulse was showing in her neck, making her breasts quiver under the tight nightie.

"In that case, all right," he said with enthusiasm. "First, take off your clothes and lie on the bed."

Her remaining clothing vanished as she appeared on the bed, one bare leg lifted. "Like this?"

"Exactly like that," he agreed, scrambling out of his own clothing. He got on the bed beside her. "Now first I'll kiss you."

"Like this?" she asked, suddenly up against him full length, her lips pressing against his.

"Close enough," he agreed. "Next, I'll stroke your breasts."

"Oh, yes," she agreed, catching his hand and guiding it to her warm full bosom.

"Right. Finally, I'll—"

"Put on a condom."

He paused. "What?"

"A condom. Don't you know why?"

He hardly paused for reflection. He did know why, and it wasn't for any reason anyone else would understand. "Um, yes." He began to get off the bed, when a condom appeared in his hand. Oh, of course. He put it to his stiff penis, and it spread itself over it to the base.

He got above her. "Now spread your legs."

She spread them, lifted them, and wrapped them around his hips. "Like this?"

"It will do." He angled his sheathed member, guiding it down into her open vulva. She lifted her bottom to meet him, and in a moment he was deep inside her and pumping furiously. The condom masked the sensation somewhat, so he had to work harder to get there.

"Don't forget the rest," she said, reaching up to catch his head and bring it down to her face. She tongued him in time with his thrusts, and her vagina squeezed his member rhythmically.

He came with rare power, wondering whether it was possible to blow out a condom by the force of ejaculation. That was probably just a male conceit, but it was the way it felt.

"Oh!" she gasped, milking him with her cleft. "Great! You really showed me how."

He hadn't shown her anything, but it had nevertheless been great, as she said. He collapsed on her resilient breasts, letting her strip the rest of his semen from his system. "Yeah."

"When did you catch on?"

He played the game a moment more. "Catch on to what, Suzie?"

She laughed. "You know I'm demonic, and not capable of caring much about any mortal. But I think I care for you, Prior. You treat me like a real person, and you play the game. But I know I made some mistakes. What was the first?"

"Your clothing. First you were in a female suit, then a dress, then a nightie, then nothing. Without having to do any of it by hand." He withdrew from her and lay on his back.

"I got carried away by the role," she agreed. "Was that all?"

"Apart from the fact that no woman or girl is that hot for me, you were too proficient. You would have been better with a hymen and some awkwardness."

She sighed. "My nature defeats me. But I'll keep working on it. I was afraid it was the condom."

"No, sensible girls do prefer it, so they won't get pregnant or catch a disease. They don't realize that my smegma cures all venereal diseases, even AIDS. Of course when you conjured it right into my hand and it put itself on me, that would have been a giveaway."

"I just couldn't wait any longer. I had to have your delicious little peg in me. I'd rather have skipped the condom, but then I'd have had to change to incubus form and find a woman to screw."

"I understand," he agreed, removing the condom. "This enables you to remain female longer. Do you want this?"

"Of course I want it!" She took it from his hand. "Just not in me, yet. I'll save it for another load. Tonight I mean to get more from you."

"Welcome to stay the night."

"I'll try. But I'll probably get too eager, and take a load direct, and then I'll have to go."

"It's your nature," he agreed tolerantly. The succubus had first approached him one day on the beach, seduced him, and discovered that his smegma had anti-venereal disease powers. She had introduced him to Tantamount Emdee, a lovely female doctor who had seduced him, drugged him, and stolen his penis for research. That had been the real start of his adventure: to get his natural penis back. Since then she had dropped by occasionally, to pick up a load, as she called it, and sometimes to talk. So they had become friends in a fashion, or at least lovers of convenience. It wasn't as if he had any better use for his semen, and she could be a most evocative sexual partner when she tried.

She put her hand on his penis, giving it an exploratory squeeze. "By the way, I have a message for you."

"Oh? Why didn't you just tell me?"

"And miss a fine fuck? What do you take me for?"

And of course the fuck was everything, for a succubus. "What message?"

"It's about your ideal woman."

He laughed. "I thought *you* were my ideal woman."

She rolled into him and kissed him. "You're sweet. I don't get much of that. No, this is the one you are destined to love, marry, and raise a dull family with."

"I'd love that. But I don't even have a girlfriend. Girls just laugh at my little member."

"3.97 inches erect," she agreed. "But you can put on any size you want."

"But they're all artificial. I prefer to stick with my original."

She gave it a tweak, and it started to come to life. "Can't blame you. It's a little darling. And that smegma is something else."

"So how can my ideal woman have a message for me, considering I don't have any woman?"

"Oh, the message isn't *from* her. It's *about* her." She kneaded his penis. "But first let's see some more action here."

His curiosity had been aroused more than his member. "First tell me about this woman."

"No, first give me a load."

"I'm spent, remember? Tell me."

"Maybe some variety," she said. She turned her back to him. "Put it in my ass."

"You're a demon. You don't necessarily have a rectum."

"I'll make one for the occasion." She nudged her plush buttocks against him. "Come on; it's tight and hot. Shove it in there."

Prior was tempted. He had never had that kind of sex with a woman who desired it, and wondered what it was like. Of course Suzie wasn't exactly a woman, but she could certainly pass for one. Still, he didn't want to be distracted from her tantalizing message. "Compromise," he suggested. "I'll put it in while you tell me."

"Done." She wiggled her bottom encouragingly.

She was right: variety was stimulating. His member had stiffened again. He took it in his hand and guided it to her nether crack, finding the pucker there. He pushed, making a dent. And paused.

The succubus got the hint. "She was abducted and shanghaied to Fartingale."

He poked the head of his penis in a fraction. "Farthingale?"

"Well, they do wear them there, but that's not it. It's fart-in-gale."

He laughed, and that made his member pound farther into her tight aperture. "That's a place? What do they do there, fart?"

"Yes. And she's a woman of fine sensitivities, so you'd better go rescue her before she expires of embarrassment. As a matter of fact, there's a time limit; you have to do it within one week, or lose her."

Jokes could be dangerous when they turned literal. "So where is this smelly place?"

She pushed her rear at him, taking him all the way into her as her nether cheeks flattened against his groin. Her rectum felt pretty much like her vagina, which it probably was; she had merely tightened it up and faked it. It hardly mattered at this point; she had hold of him and wouldn't let go until she had his ejaculation. That, again, was her nature.

But he held back, knowing that the moment she got the ejaculate she would depart, converting to incubus so as to seduce some hapless maiden. That, too, was her nature. He needed to get the information first.

"So how can I find this land, and find her? I don't even know her name." Because the idea had really taken hold of him. To rescue his ideal woman! She would surely be most grateful.

Her channel massaged his member, evoking its urgency. "The Eeg-trail leads to it. She's called the Prize Maiden in the Tower. Something like that. She'll be easy to find."

The Eeg-trail. He had taken that to get to Mt. Icecream. "You sure? I never found a place like that."

"It leads where're you're going, if the statues help. That's all I know." Now her bowel writhed peristaltically, forcing his orgasm.

He gave up his resistance and went to it with a will, withdrawing and thrusting, jetting his essence into her chamber. The feeling was intense despite coming so soon after his first effort.

"Ooo, that's good," she said. He knew she could literally taste the ejaculate. "Now get going on your mission, lover."

"My e-mission," he agreed, satisfied. He knew nothing about the woman, but was halfway smitten already.

Chapter 2 – Fartingale

She found herself sitting on a floor, naked, holding her son protectively. Where was she? What had happened? The last she remembered, a strange man had knocked at her door while she was nursing her baby. Impatient to get rid of him, she had opened the door and told him: "Whatever you're selling, I don't want any."

"I have come to take you away from all this," he said. He was short, fat, homely, half bald, and oddly garbed in pleated pantaloons.

"Well, you can just take yourself away. I'm not interested." She started to close the door.

The man turned around as if to depart. Then he bent forward, presenting his posterior to her. She realized with disgust that the pleats in his pants were actually strips of nothing; his pale bulging buttocks could be seen between them. There was a swishing sound, and the pleats fluttered.

Her mouth fell open in astonishment. The jerk was breaking wind at her!

Then a hideous odor assaulted her like a noxious cloud. She took a breath to protest, inadvertently inhaling the gas.

Now, suddenly, she was here. She had been gassed into unconsciousness by a rude crepitation and abducted. Now she was—where?

She looked around. She was in a chamber with curving reflective sides, so that she saw distortions of her body in floor, walls, and ceiling. This was like a glass lined cave, certainly an oddity. Why would anyone want to put her in a place like this?

She pondered why. She had been abducted. The man hadn't asked her identity; he had simply come to her door and gassed her. It was possible that this was a random act; some terrorist organization needed a hostage and took the first that offered. Perhaps the first shapely woman that offered, at any rate; there was no guessing how many doors the man had knocked on before reaching hers. Was her identity known? It could have been garnered from her address or her papers, but for now she would assume that it wasn't. Therefore she would do her best to remain anonymous, not even thinking of her identity, so that no ransom message could be sent to her family. It was a thin chance, but possible. So perhaps if she seemed to be of no value to her captor, he would in due course let her go. Meanwhile he had dumped her here in this unusual cave, out of sight.

She would be better off if she could escape before he returned. Of course she would be an obvious target naked; she had to find clothing. It was surely too much to hope that any had been left here, but at least she could look.

She got up, carrying her baby Chance, so named because she had conceived him by no planning on her part. He remained asleep, perhaps affected by the same gas that had knocked her out, but was breathing normally. That was just as well, as she didn't want to alarm him. He was only three months old; the alarming aspects of life were best postponed until he was better able to handle them.

Now she got a better look at her reflection, and paused with surprise. It looked as if she were wearing a hood over her head, that completely covered it. Of course that wasn't the case. She touched her face with her hand; there was no barrier there. Yet in the reflection her hand disappeared into a dark globe. Somehow there was the appearance of a comprehensive hood, as if her head were in a bag that concealed her face and hair, without any substance actually being there. How could this be accounted for?

Then she realized that the hood that veiled her face was illusion, and therefore probably magic. She had had little direct contact with magic, but had no doubt of its power. She had been magically hooded, to conceal her identity. That added a dimension to her predicament.

The chamber narrowed into a closure somewhat like a sphincter. In fact this seemed a lot like a huge bowel or intestine, and that could be its exit: the anus. Uncomfortable image. She turned away from it and explored the other direction. The cave twisted around and back on itself, narrowing and expanding, forming another chamber. Here was a rack on which hung clothing: a blouse, and a centuries out of date skirt, extended into a bell shape by a framework of hoops. And a pair of glassy slippers below.

She was supposed to wear this weird outfit? It seemed she had no choice, though whoever had set it out must have been a man, because the underwear had been forgotten. She really could have used it, because her pregnancy and nursing had made her a full-breasted woman, and the spreading skirt provided no protection from below.

She laid Chance carefully down, and donned the clothing, which fit well enough. The slippers were comfortable, but the skirt was like wearing a barrel: she couldn't sit or lie down in it, or even get too close to a wall. Both blouse and skirt were made of the same glassy material as the slippers, flexible, comfortable, but translucent. She would hardly care to appear in public in such an outfit. Which was perhaps the point; she would be a marked woman the moment she departed this intestinal residence. She was stuck with it, for now.

There was a smaller outfit that fit Chance: a shirt, diapers, and pullover pants, also glassy. So the clothing had not been selected randomly; it was definitely for them. She wasn't reassured; this suggested that her abduction wasn't random; it had been planned.

She moved on, and found a bathroom area with a sink, shower, and toilet, all translucent. And beyond that was a kitchenette, with food on a counter. The food was a package of sausage that looked unpleasantly like dog turds, but she was hungry, so she heated some on the stove and ate it. The taste was better than the appearance; it seemed filling. It wasn't actually sausage; more like a bean concoction.

In more ways than taste. Soon after eating, she felt her gut blowing up with gas. She hurried to the toilet to let it out—and the toilet turned out to be so constructed as to amplify the embarrassing sound. She was alone, except for the baby, but she found herself blushing.

Chance woke, and she nursed him. Before long he was gassy too; she was passing it along in her breast milk. What ill fortune, to be allergic to the local food.

In due course she came to the last chamber of her convoluted prison: a family room. It contained a translucent stuffed chair before a television set. She pondered briefly, then removed the unwieldy skirt and sat bare-bottomed in the chair. It was a relief.

The set came on, showing a printed screen. WELCOME TO FARTINGALE.

"Farthingale!" she exclaimed, recognizing the name of the ancient hoop skirt.

An announcer came on, wearing a costume similar to the one her abductor had worn. "That's Fartingale without the letter H," he said, as if answering her. "Fart-in-gale, the land of fabulous farts."

She sat frozen, hardly believing what she was hearing. A land where they gloried in flatulence? This seemed impossible.

"This is an introduction to our windy culture," the announcer continued. "Intended for tourists and other visitors. We certainly hope you will enjoy your stay here."

"I am definitely not enjoying my confinement here," she said severely. But of course the video didn't care.

"Some folk from other regions regard us as primitive," the announcer said. "But we prefer to think of ourselves as basic and friendly. Some call us poverty stricken, but we merely prefer not to waste resources on nonessential things. Consider, for example the matter of sanitary facilities. Why waste time and money building a toilet into every house, when it is so much easier to make one superior public privy for all to use?"

"A public privy!" she exclaimed.

"Consider the advantages," the announcer blithely continued. "The central privy becomes the public gathering place, where news is disseminated, acquaintances are renewed, and wares are traded. What could be more convenient and compatible? Everybody has to shit, so it is guaranteed that every person will make an appearance in due course."

"Sh—" she started, but was unable to say the coarse word. "Defecation." This had to be a joke—a dirty joke.

The announcer gave way to a village scene. The houses looked like huge piles of animal manure, and perhaps that was what they were made of. She knew that in third world countries they often used dried ox manure for many things. People thronged the central street, the men in shirts and pantaloons, the women in blouses and farthingales. When two people met, they paused for brief dialog, but individual words could not be heard in the general hubbub.

"Here is a typical polite encounter," the announcer said. The scene zoomed in on a man and woman meeting on the street.

The man bent slightly and his pleats whiffled. "May the farts be with you, sirree."

The woman bobbed, and her hoop skirt amplified her own gastric effort. "And with you, sirrah."

"I like your smell. Let's fuck."

"You're pretty strong-winded yourself. Perhaps tomorrow."

The man nodded and moved on, as did the woman.

"His invitation," the announcer explained, "is rhetorical; he doesn't really want to fuck every woman he meets on the street. But he compliments her by suggesting that she is attractive enough to make him desire her. She in turn is not interested in fucking every man she encounters, so she demurs by suggesting a later tryst. Both understand that it is unlikely to take place."

Despite her abhorrence, she was intrigued. As it happened, she knew something about sexual intercourse. "Suppose the man really does want to have nuptial relations with the woman?"

She had thought the video was one-way, but to her surprise it responded. "Then the man makes a counter-offer, suggesting immediacy. 'Let's fuck now, lovely sirree.' If she is genuinely interested, they go into the public privy together and do it." The picture showed the couple entering a genuine old fashioned privy structure, blowing out a couple of loud farts, and going at it. "If not, she demurs again: 'Some other time, sirrah.' He can not press the matter further without social awkwardness, so must bid her good farting and depart."

"You answered my question!" she said, her amazement for the moment overriding her disgust at this dirty culture.

"Well, I'm magic, of course," the announcer's voice replied. She realized that it was the video set talking, not a human person just off-camera. The man she had seen before had been just a model to show the outfit. "Now we come to the matter of food, as our couple eats out on a date. Most of it is ordinary, but some like it exotic." The picture showed the man and woman sitting down to a meal of sausage. Except that closer inspection revealed that the sausages looked like nothing so much as human refuse. The rolls resembled blobs of horse manure, and there was a pitcher of what she hoped was lemonade, but looked like urine.

"That food," she said.

"Ah, you noticed! Yes, this delicacy is crafted to resemble assorted turds in appearance and taste. It is of course wholesome and nutritious, but can hardly be distinguished from—"

"Next topic," she said tightly.

"The food is gathered by specially trained workers." The picture showed an old man with a shovel scooping up poop in an alley frequented by dogs. He delivered it to the cook, who fried it in a pan with seasoning. It looked exactly like small sausage, similar to what she had recently eaten.

She got up to turn off the set. "My little joke," the announcer said. "That isn't really the source."

"Then quit with the food," she said grimly.

"After their delicious repast, they go on a sleigh ride." The picture showed them on an open sleigh hauled by a single naked woman. There was no snow, but somehow the runners slid along the ground without apparent friction. More magic, of course. The woman had heavy breasts and stout thighs and seemed competent to haul it along. She wore a headband with the word PROSTITUTE. "The runners are lubricated by a film of soap," the announcer explained helpfully.

"Oh, this really slays me," the woman on the sleigh exclaimed. "What a great ride!"

The man burst into song. "Oh what fun it is to ride on a one whore soap an' slay!"

That did it. She got up and marched on the TV.

"There is more you need to know," the announcer said quickly. "I will continue my orientation presentation."

But she had had more than enough for the present. "Perhaps tomorrow," she said, and turned the set off.

She had learned that her abduction was probably not coincidental. She was here for a reason, and she wasn't eager to learn that reason yet. She was pretty sure she wouldn't like it. So if she could get away with delaying the presentation until she had a better strategy for escape, she would do it.

Meanwhile her baby needed nursing.

Chapter 3–Spire

Prior woke with his decision made: he would go to rescue his ideal woman, whoever she might be—The Maiden in the Tower. The succubus might not really care for him as a person, but she had no reason to deceive him in something like this. He would be satisfied with even a less than ideal woman, provided she was shapely and obliging.

But first he would fetch the Spire, the cosmic dildo or phallic horn of plenty. Because it had enormous power and information, and armed with it he should be able to handle just about anything. He knew better than to go into a land accessed by the eeg-trail without solid protection. There was no telling what magical hazards there would be along the way.

He drove to a section of town he hadn't visited in a year, and to the house of the lady penis doctor named Tantamount Emdee. He parked several blocks away, as he wanted to remain anonymous, and walked to the house. That was because he suspected he would not be welcome at that address.

It wasn't there. Instead there was a huge dirty-white mound of gunk. Oh, yes—he had set the Spire on his formula of smegma and left it to jet full-blast. Tantamount had stolen his penis to study his anti-VD smegma; he had repaid her by giving her more of it than she could use. He was the only one who could turn it off. Evidently it had overflowed and buried her house in the intervening year. Served her right. But by this time her joy with all that research material might have become something akin to annoyance at its unremitting volume.

There was a steam shovel there, scooping out great chunks of solidified smegma and dumping it onto a truck. The mound had a gap in one side where the shovel had excavated, but the house still didn't show. It was hard to keep up with the output of the Spire. Even if they got it all trucked away, how would they salvage the house? It would stink forever of spoiling smegma. His revenge had been more than adequate.

But now he needed to take back the Spire. That would cut off the flow and allow them to clear the property, in time. A year seemed sufficient to have made his point. If he ever encountered Tantamount again, she would surely be careful not to cross him anew.

He approached the truck driver, who was lounging in his cab, paging through a girlie magazine. "What's up?"

The man glanced down at him. "You don't know? You must be new to these parts."

"I am," Prior agreed. No sense in trying to explain his real connection; he might get arrested for creating a public nuisance. "This looks like an ambergris mine."

"Richer than that. This stuff's a universal cure for venereal disease. The doctor leased the rights to a drug company and moved out six months ago. The royalties must've made her rich by now."

So Tantamount had gone commercial. Naturally she had appreciated the value of such a supply of such a substance. She must have retired and moved to a big-city penthouse. So his revenge had not been complete; instead of destroying her, he had made her wealthy. Well, that was the way it went.

But under that mound was the Spire. He had to get in there and fetch it. How was he to do that? The pile seemed pretty solid.

Still, there had been caves in Mount Icecream, and there could be caves here too. He walked around the mound, examining its surface. Sure enough, he found cracks in the hardening stuff. The constant addition of new smegma would be pushing up in the center, squeezing out to the sides, like lava in a volcano, forcing the outer layers to fracture and separate. He should be able to wedge inside, though he would get thoroughly grimed. Well, so be it.

He found a large vent and squeezed into it. The smell was not pretty, but he would wash when he was done. The crack twisted, narrowed, then widened as it came up against a wall of the house. The house had burst asunder, the walls shoved outward by the pressure of the burgeoning stuff within, and was now a wreck. But he was able to traverse the cavelike gaps and make his way to its one-time laboratory area where the Spire was mounted.

Except that the smegma had hardened into a vault covering the area, with only the continuing surge of new smegma at its apex. How was he to get past this? It seemed as hard as granite.

Then he saw a keyhole in the side. Unfortunately he didn't have a suitable key.

Or did he? After a moment he realized that the region resembled a human vulva, with the hole where the vagina would be. That suggested a key of a special nature.

He checked his collection, and brought out a penis of the right configuration. He screwed it onto his socket. Then he imagined Tantamount with her skirt off and her bare legs spread. That brought his member stiffly erect.

He guided it into the crevice. It fit comfortably, but nothing happened. Oh. He thrust, withdrew, and thrust again, until he managed to produce a jet of semen. That softened the hole, and it melted. It continued to dissolve as he cleaned off his spent member and put it away.

Soon there was a door-sized opening in the vault. He climbed through. As he did, the vault collapsed; it had been defeated, so had no further reason to exist.

There it was: a device shaped like a foot-long horn, upright, with white fluid jetting from its tip. The force of the jet was sufficient to send it up several feet, where it caught on what remained of the upper story. There was just room to wriggle up to where he could put a hand on the shaft.

Prior did so. His fingers circled it. "Spire, desist." he said.

Nothing changed. The off-white jet continued with unabated force.

He tried to pull it off its mounting. It wouldn't budge.

This was an unexpected problem. The Spire had obeyed him after he defeated the demons of the Cherry Tree and took it. Why wasn't it doing so now? Did it not recognize him?

"Spire, I am Prior Gross. Desist the jet and come with me."

There was no effect.

He realized that he was not communicating in the manner it understood. The Spire spoke only in gouts that entered the body of the one it addressed. He would have to do what he hated, and get a mouthful of smegma.

He nerved himself, then shoved his hand over the apex, blunting the power of the jet, put his mouth over it, and removed his hand.

The gout rammed into his mouth and down his throat, inflating him, it seemed, all the way to his anus. Yet it was a delightful infusion, for the Spire was the essence of potency. **I AM THE SPIRE, CREATED BY EGG, THE ELDEST GOD OF THE GALAXY.**

Precisely. *I am Prior Gross, who captured you at Mount Icecream a year ago.*

Another inspiring gout distended him. **I REMEMBER.**

Prior removed his mouth from the tip, and it did not resume jetting. He cleared his throat with some effort, swallowing some smegma and spitting out the rest. "I need your service again." Then he put his tongue back on the tip.

This time the gout was smaller, a mere token. The Spire was evidently interested. **YOU MUST EARN IT.**

"But I conquered you. You belong to me now."

CORRECTION, MORTAL MAN. I AM THE TOOL OF EGG. YOU MERELY OB-TAINED MY SERVICE FOR A SET PERIOD, NOW EXPIRED.

So it was like that. He would have to deal with the Spire on its own terms. "How can I obtain your service for the next month?" For that should suffice, whatever the outcome of his quest.

I CRAVE A BIT OF MORTAL EXPERIENCE.

"But you generated all the mortals of the galaxy, or at least their ancestors."

AND ALL THE MATTER TOO. BUT THAT WAS SOME TIME AGO.

"About twelve billion years," Prior agreed. "I can see how it might have gotten dull in the interim."

MORTALS HAVE FLEETING EXISTENCES. BUT THEY COPULATE FREQUENTLY. I WANT SOME OF THAT. I LACK A MORTAL BODY. LEND ME YOURS.

It occurred to Prior that they could establish some overlapping interest. "You mean I should screw you onto my socket and have at some women."

COPULATE WITH SOME FEMALES. AMONG OTHERS.

Uh-oh. "*Only* females," Prior said. "I won't fuck males."

AGREED. I WILL ASSIST YOU AS REQUIRED FOR THE DURATION OF OUR ASSOCIATION. YOU WILL INSERT ME INTO ANY AVAILABLE FEMALES.

Prior caught another problem. "But you are endlessly potent. You'll want to spend the whole time, day and night, fucking women, and I won't be able to get on with my quest. There has to be some limit."

HALF TIME.

"So I must chase women during virtually all my waking hours? That won't work either. How about one hour a day?"

AGREED.

That surprised him. "What's the catch?"

ONE HOUR CUMULATIVE. IT CAN BE SPREAD OUT ACROSS THE DAY. A FEW MINUTES AT A TIME, FOR DIFFERENT FEMALES.

That did make a difference, but seemed fair. "However, women don't come to me a dime a dozen. In fact the only good fuck I've had in the past month was with a succubus. I won't be able to provide you with any except whores."

PROSTITUTES WILL DO, BUT ARE NOT SUFFICIENT IN THEMSELVES. MERELY TOUCH ME TO THE LIVING SURFACE OF A FEMALE AND I WILL RENDER HER CONDUCIVE.

"I suppose I could hold you in my hand for that."

NO. KEEP ME SCREWED ON FOR ACTION. I WANT TO EMBRACE THEM IN MORTAL FASHION AND FEEL THE LIVING FEELINGS.

"But that would make it too obvious. I'd get arrested for indecent exposure."

I WILL PROVIDE THE ILLUSION OF COVERAGE. TOUCH FLESH AND PROCEED.

Prior remained dubious. "Well, I can try. But don't blame me if it doesn't work. Women can be very touchy—no pun—about public contacts. They don't like getting groped."

THEY WILL LIKE THIS, the Spire gouted confidently. **DEAL?**

"Deal," Prior agreed, because he did need the Spire. He hoped he wouldn't regret it.

PUT ME ON.

Prior opened his trousers and unscrewed his keyhole penis. This was the legacy of his association with Tantamount; her sister Oubliette had fitted him with the socket and set him up with the alternative equipment. He shook it out and put it in his member pocket. He had a number of artificial penises to go with his natural one, of different sizes and types, all of them with nerves so that they provided full sensation. He would hardly need them, now that he had the potent tool of the Eldest God of the Galaxy.

Then he lifted the Spire, which now came loose readily, and brought it to his crotch. It had a screw-on base that matched his socket, by no coincidence, because he had carried it that way before. He screwed it on. It projected rigidly a foot in front of him. "You need to shrink."

DONE. This time the gout nudged into Prior's urethra just enough to convey its message. The long horn diminished and became flexible so that it would fit inside the trousers. He would use it for normal urination, but when the time for fornication came, it would provide its own potency. His flesh had grown around the socket, so that when a penis was attached, the connection was not apparent; any member he wore seemed to be his own. Not that he got a chance to show any of them off to women often, other than the succubus.

Now he had to make his way out of the pile, which was already settling down somewhat with the cessation of the Spire's output. As he crawled, the Spire made a small gout of query. **WHAT IS THIS QUEST FOR WHICH YOU NEED MY ASSISTANCE?**

"My ideal woman has been abducted to Fartingale. I need to rescue her. Do you know anything about that land?"

EVERYTHING. FARTS ARE THEIR UNIT OF CURRENCY. YOU WILL NEED TO PUT ME IN YOUR RECTUM ON OCCASION SO I CAN GENERATE WIND WITHOUT AROUSING SUSPICION.

"Up my ass!" Prior said, not pleased. But if this was the way of Fartingale, he was stuck for it. "They fart a lot there?"

YES. STATUS IS JUDGED BY PROFICIENCY. YOU WERE WISE TO ENLIST MY AID. I WILL MAKE YOU THE BLOWHARD CHAMPION.

"I just want to rescue my woman."

THAT, TOO, the Spire agreed, emitting a small sample fart that startled Prior. But of course the Spire could emit anything, literally, in any quantity. **THIS WILL BE A NICE CHALLENGE EVEN FOR MY POWERS, CONSIDERING THE NEED FOR SUBTLETY.**

Oh, great! Subtle farting. By the time Prior wedged his way out of the mound, he had a much better idea of the challenge ahead.

Chapter 4—Prize

Next morning she showered, donned the only outfit available, nursed Chance, and considered breakfast. There was oatmeal, milk, eggs, juice, and fruit in the refrigerator. No dog-poop sausage or cowflop pie. Relieved, she ate well. The magic hood remained around her head, completely obscuring her features and hair. There was an additional oddity: when she wore it loose, as it was now, her hair was well beyond waist length. Yet none of it showed. She had rinsed it in the shower, and dried it with a towel; there was no doubt of its continued existence. And it was there, brushing past her bottom. But it was invisible. Many women could be identified largely by their tresses, and so could she; her captor had made sure this was ineffective.

Then the gas attack came. She rushed to the toilet to let it out, and again the sound was magnified unconscionably. She had no further doubt: the food was spiked to generate wind in the bowel. This was the land of Fartingale, where nether emissions were proudly advertised. She hated that, but seemed to have no choice: she had to eat. So she concentrated on releasing the air silently. The trick was to let it emerge without pressure, gently pulling on a buttock if necessary. Unfortunately the widely flaring skirt made it difficult for her to touch her posterior, so that some sounds squeaked out.

Chance, in contrast, was soon firing away with gusto. He seemed to think that a fart was an act of creation. Maybe she could drown him out with the TV. She turned it on.

Words appeared on the screen: NAME.

What was this? It hadn't done this yesterday. Was her captor trying to trick her into identifying herself? Why conceal her face and hair, making her anonymous, then try to make her spoil it? It was almost as if her captor was teasing her. Well, she would use a nom de plume to foil whatever ploy he had in mind. If he wanted her identity, he would have to get it without her help.

What would do? She considered her situation and it came to her. "Veil," she said.

"Thank you," the announcer's voice came, startling her again. "Now it is time for you to know your place in this scheme."

"You actually admit it's a scheme!" she exclaimed. "Indeed, I would like to know the reason for this atrocity."

"We are a culture that loves contests," the announcer continued imperturbably. "Anything will do, but those involving natural functions are particularly diverting. Folk don't merely relieve themselves, they make a game of it. For example, pissing contests."

She should have known this would quickly get ugly. "Thank you, I'm not interested."

He ignored her. A picture came on the screen, showing two men standing before a slightly slanted, marked alley. "On your mark," one said. "Get set. PISS!" And both aimed their penises, whose tips barely protruded from their pleated pantaloons, down the alley and let fly with strong streams of urine. The man on the left's effort arced a good five feet before splashing on the pavement. The man of the right nevertheless had a stronger urge; his urine struck several inches beyond.

"Damn, you win again," the first man said. "Lunch is on me."

"You just need to tighten your bladder," the other said as they completed their voidings, pulled in their members and walked away.

Veil had watched the disgusting exhibition despite her best intention. "Men will be little boys," she said.

"And women," the announcer said. "Often they can arrange for male sponsors. Here is a more advanced contest."

"I'm not interested." But she was; there was a subterranean fascination in this gaucherie.

Two pretty women walked to an elevated pedestal, lifted their skirts high, sat on the pedestal, leaned back, spread their legs, opened their clefts, and let fly with twin streams of urine. Everything was visible from clitoris to anus. This time the one on the left jetted farther. There was applause, and now the scene widened to show a ring of men watching.

The women finished their voidings, wiped themselves off, and stood, letting their farthingales drop back into place. "I choose—you," the winner said, pointing to the handsomest of the men. "And you go with him." She pointed to the ugliest man. The other woman grimaced.

"I don't understand," Veil said.

"The contest was for dominance," the announcer explained. "The women are rivals, so they settled it the conventional way, with a contest. The winner gets to have sex with the man they both desired. The loser is stuck with the one neither desires. All the men are amenable, of course; they are stimulated by the sight of women urinating."

Veil knew a good deal more about sex than she cared to advertise in this situation, and agreed: the sight of women's bare spread thighs excited men, and female urination could be a phenomenal male turn-on. Such contests were thus designed to ensure that the spectators would be eager for sex.

The victorious woman took her man's arm and guided him into the public privy. "I expect the best fucking of my life," she told him as they disappeared.

"Come on honey," the ugly man said, approaching the losing woman. She sighed and got back on the pedestal, her skirt lifted. It was high enough so that his standing crotch was the same height as her seated one. He pulled his hard penis through the slit in his pantaloons and wedged it into her open vagina. He shoved, and it penetrated visibly. In a moment he was at full depth and pumping vigorously. The woman made no pretense of enjoying it; she leaned back, bracing herself with her hands behind her. The man climaxed, breathing hard, almost knocking her back with the power of his thrusts. Soon he was spent, and pulled out, his member disappearing in his pantaloons. The spectators applauded again, clearly appreciative of his performance. Then the man walked away, and the crowd dispersed.

"I don't—" Veil began.

"The loser might renege," the announcer explained. "So she has to perform in public. That's part of her penalty for losing. She doesn't have to pretend to like it; in fact she is expected to show resignation or aversion. Men like seeing that too, and it makes the stakes sufficient to guarantee that each contestant puts forth her best effort."

"It's legalized rape," Veil snapped.

"Precisely. Were you in such a contest, you would surely do your best to win."

"I would never indulge in such an atrocious exhibition!"

"Assuming you had a choice."

She didn't like the sound of that. "What do you mean?"

"In a moment. There is more to clarify about the contests."

"I don't care to hear it."

"You will nevertheless hear it."

"And if I simply turn you off?"

"You won't do that."

Veil reached forward and turned the switch. Nothing happened; it had been overridden. So it was like that. "And if I go into another room and cover my ears?"

"Allow me to pose an academic question. How much do you value your son?"

So Chance was hostage for her cooperation. They could readily gas her again and take him. Her freedom was sharply limited. "Clarify the contests," she agreed grimly.

Another picture appeared. This time a man and a woman were bending down to touch the pavement with their hands, their posteriors exposed. "We have seen pissing contests," the announcer said, reverting to lecture mode. "This is a shitting contest. The winner will get to dictate the type of sex they have this night. He wants friendly; she wants bondage."

"Defecation? This should surely turn both of them off."

"Not in Fartingale. Natural functions are a pleasant part of life. Fecal contests can be for volume, type, distance, or art. This one is for distance."

She refrained from inquiring about fecal art, certain she would not like the answer. "Distance! The material will simply drop to the ground."

"Not necessarily. Observe." The scene approached, until there was a close view of both puckered anuses. "Ready, set, fire!"

Two small globular turds shot out of the rectums. His struck the ground just over a yard distant, hers just under. The man had won.

Veil closed her open mouth. "Gas propelled," she said, catching on.

"Farts are legitimate propellant," the announcer agreed. "It requires internal skill to hold gas pressure behind a turd."

Obviously so. "At least it doesn't leave much of a mess," she said distastefully.

"There are mess contests too. Also shape contests."

"Shape?" Her question was out before she managed to stifle it.

A new picture appeared. A man bared his bottom, bent over, and strained. His anus eased open and a greenish brown turd emerged. This was no flying ball; it turned out to be a long one, tapering as it came, until it fell to the ground. It wriggled away, snakelike. "Animated turds," the announcer explained. "Most are snakelike, but some are like other animals, including small men. Girls really scream when a turd doll chases after them demanding a kiss."

Veil sighed. There was evidently no end to this disgusting nonsense. "What else are you determined to show me?"

"The third type of contest is the most popular: farting. It has the greatest number of divisions and classes. Champion farters are held in the highest popular esteem. Amplitude is measured on the Rectum Scale."

Like a gaseous earthquake. Another dirty pun. Veil sighed. "And you are going to see that I observe every type in action?"

"There is no need; you understand the principle."

She was surprised. "Now you will tell me what my place in this revolting scheme is?"

"In due course. First you need to become better acquainted with our culture."

"I am more than sufficiently acquainted with it already."

"You may think you are, but this could be like the woman who thought she was ready to have intercourse with a demon."

This intrigued her, irritatingly. "Oh?"

A picture of a slender young woman appeared on the screen. "Come to me, my demon lover," she breathed, removing her farthingale.

The demon appeared. He was big and muscular, but had a rather small penis. "At your service, mortal piece," he said.

The woman lay on a bed that appeared and spread her slender legs, revealing her tight genital region. "Put it in there, lover."

"Do you think it will fit?" The demon's member was growing.

She laughed. "Of course it will fit! Get on with it."

The demon obliged. But by now his phallus was huge, about eight inches long and broad in proportion. He put it to her slit, adjusted its orientation, and shoved, but the aperture was not large enough. "It's too big."

The girl had not looked at the implement since lying down, and evidently didn't realize how the situation had changed. "Nonsense. Just hammer it in harder."

The demon gave a powerful thrust, and the member forged in all the way, disappearing inside her. "There!"

And the thin woman split into two halves. There was one leg, hip, and breast to the left, and a similar set to the right, united only at her head. She had been cleaved apart by the wedge of his entry. She looked surprised.

Veil knew it was fake, because there was no blood and the cleavage was too clean. "Very funny," she said. "And do you have any jokes on men?"

Immediately a new picture came on. This was of a young man coming to a complex of clinics. "Time to get my teeth cleaned," he said. "I think this is the right address."

He entered the office. The woman at the desk looked up. "Yes?"

"I'm here for hygiene."

"You're in luck; we have an opening now." She showed him into the chamber and he sat in the reclining chair. "She'll be right with you, sirrah."

In a moment the sweet-faced hygienist arrived. She set out her instruments, making small talk. Then folded padded arm and leg clamps on the man's limbs and touched a button. The chair turned over so that he was suspended inverted. She opened a hatch that was now over his posterior. She pulled down his pants, baring his bottom.

"Hey!" he exclaimed.

"Have no concern sirrah," she said, taking a small brush to his puckered anus. "I am fully qualified for anal hygiene."

"But I came for *oral* hygiene!"

"Oh? That's the next office." She took a metal pick to his pucker, cleaning out a turd fragment. "You really should brush after every evacuation, so there's no chance for infection." She shot a jet of water into the hole, then took it back up with a suction hose. "You really need a cleaning, sirrah. Fortunately we have a special on enemas this week."

"But I don't want—"

She poked a larger nozzle in. There was the gurgle of soapy water. "You'll feel like a new man, once all that nasty old refuse is cleaned out."

"But—"

"Of course we'll clean your butt," she agreed, taking a shoeshine brush to it. In moments his buttocks shined.

"Enough," Veil said. "I believe I am ready to hear about my own situation here."

The picture faded. "You are in a contest. You are the Prize Maiden of the Week."

"Apart from the evident fact that I'm hardly a maiden, because I'm nursing my baby, what is this contest? I absolutely refuse to urinate or defecate before gawking men."

"Assuming you have a choice."

It sounded worse the second time. "What contest?"

"Each week a comely anonymous maiden is confined to the glass tower, the prize for the victorious contestant. She will be his or her sex slave for the following year."

"His or *her*?"

"We are an equal opportunity society. If a woman wants a woman, she is welcome to compete."

"And if the maiden declines to indulge in this—this sex slavery?"

"Few do. Most regard it as an honor. A significant portion of our roster is filled by local volunteers. If one gets pregnant, she has a claim of marriage on the man."

"And those few who don't consider it an honor?"

"They learn pretense, unless the man prefers unwillingness."

Legalized rape, again. They could drug her, or simply threaten her baby. She would cooperate, or else. "And you say I am this week's prize maiden?" She hoped she had somehow misheard.

"Correct. You are on display, and the first contestant has been selected."

"Already!"

"It started yesterday. Do you wish to see the man?"

"No!" But she knew it didn't matter. The mystery was clarifying. Each week they went out somewhere and persuaded or abducted a comely woman, and she was the current one. It seemed odd that they would take one with a baby, as most men preferred, as it had been put, maidens. Maybe it represented variety. Probably some were giggly teens, while others were mature women such as herself. She was 33, but had kept herself in shape with diet and exercise. Perhaps that had been her undoing. "There will be seven final contestants?"

"In a manner. Each will be a day's winner. You will choose one of them. That is why you might prefer to watch them contest; it may offer clues to their nature."

"I must choose one, to became a sex slave for," she said. "I am not allowed to turn them all down?"

"You are allowed, but then you go instead to the ogre." A picture appeared of a huge hairy apelike creature rattling his cage and fondling his enormous genital member. "You will be put into his cage. If you survive the year, you will be released."

She would choose one of the contestants. "Suppose I choose one, then discover I can't endure it?"

"You will be assigned to the runner up, and your year will begin again. If you have a problem with him, you will start a year with the third. If you should happen to run through them all, you will finish with the ogre."

It would be best to choose well the first time. They had their system pretty well worked out; maidens were not expected to balk. "You said I am on display?"

"In this manner." A new picture appeared. This one was of a standing woman, naked, her flesh translucent. As the camera approached, it became apparent that this was a glassy statue, with the innards visible. There were bones in the limbs and organs in the torso. And in the center, in the looping intestinal tract, was a suite of rooms. And a woman with a baby. Herself.

Appalled, she watched herself of the prior day, nursing her baby, dressing in transparent clothing, exploring the chambers, eating, hurrying to the transparent toilet. She saw her own bottom from below, and heard her amplified breaking of wind. She had no secrets from the public, other than her face. She was the prize maiden, on display for every man who might be interested, and evidently some were. Nobody cared about her background; she was comely and available, perforce. She would be completely amenable to whatever sexual inclinations the man of her choice had. She would also openly piss and shit and fart at his command, for this was the land of open natural functions. For a full year. Or else.

If this wasn't hell, it was a reasonable facsimile.

Chapter 5 – Now

Prior walked away from Mount Smegma, wanting a shower. It might be his own formula, but it stank. He'd have to launder his clothes, and maybe his car too.

There was a woman standing at a bus stop. **HER** the Spire gouted.

"But she's forty if she's a day," Prior protested. "And getting stout. You can do better." The truth was he wanted to clean up before getting into any complications.

SHE'S CLOSE.

"No, she'll have to wait. My stench would drive her away."

NOW. And the Spire gouted something into him that robbed him of his volition. He had to do it, on his own or as a zombie.

"Okay," he muttered, and his volition returned. "But she's going to flee, I tell you." He strode toward the woman.

She winded him and turned to stare disapprovingly. He nerved himself and spoke. "I—" he said, fighting his inclination to flee himself. "I want to— to have sex with you."

"Never, you stench that walks like an ape. Stay away from me."

"She doesn't want to—" Prior murmured.

NOW. The Spire was expanding to its full length, projecting from his clothing.

Prior stepped toward her. The woman, alarmed, stepped back. "I'll call the police!"

He reached for her. She turned and ran, but was hobbled by her high heels. He lunged and caught her from behind.

"Unhand me, you filthy pervert!" she cried.

Prior hauled up her skirt and jammed the erect Spire against her thigh.

She froze for an instant, then melted. "Quickly, please." She hoisted her skirt up the rest of the way and labored to get her panties down.

He was still behind her. It didn't matter. The Spire quested across her thigh, up into her stout posterior, and found her crevice. It nudged to her suddenly eager vagina. She leaned forward and shoved back as it did so, facilitating the connection. In a moment it was buried half its length, which was all any normal woman could accommodate. But she was still pushing, trying womanfully to take it all in. The Spire had a marvelously conducive facility.

Prior had full sensation. The woman's bottom was solid, but the anatomy was all there, and he felt the vagina closing around the Spire as if it were his own flesh. He also felt the Spire changing shape, shortening and thickening, so as to be able to fit all of itself into the woman. She was a bit loose, but the added thickness made her become tight. The tip nudged her cervix, massaging it; sensation was so specific that it was like a map of the interior.

"More! More!" she gasped, still shoving back as ably as she could manage in this standing position. Then she spied a telephone pole, grabbed on to it, and used it as a brace. "More!"

Prior was now into it himself, experientially speaking, and did his best to oblige. He reached around her, caught the pole, and hauled his crotch hard into her. Now, suitably anchored, the Spire did its business. It sent Prior a gut-wrenching orgasm and gouted so forcefully that the woman was lifted partway into the air. But she jammed against the pole and brought herself down to take it all in again. Only to be met by another gout, that not only lifted her, but squeezed seminal fluid out around the tight connection.

"Ooo!" she groaned, going into her own orgasm. Her vagina clenched spasmodically, squeezing out more fluid. But as it relaxed, the third gout come, distending it yet again.

This was too much. She rose right off the Spire and came down on her feet, the pale jelly pouring out. She had been heaved clear of the member. She scrambled to get back on it, her crotch dripping.

There was a honk. The bus was coming! "Oh, dear!" the woman said.

They hastily covered up. The Spire disappeared into Prior's pants, and the woman jerked up her panties and jerked down her skirt. Gunk was still drooling from her, pooling in the panties, but she didn't seem to notice. By the time the bus stopped, she was looking prim.

"We must meet again, soon," she whispered to Prior as she stepped into the bus. Then, to the front passengers who were staring, not quite sure of what they had seen: "I had a fainting spell. The kind gentleman managed to catch me and hold me upright. I'm all right now." She paid the toll and took a seat. Prior almost thought he heard a squish as she did so; the Spire had really filled her up.

SHE WON'T TELL. the Spire gouted. **SHE LIKED IT TOO WELL. I MADE SURE OF THAT.**

It had nevertheless been a close call, Prior thought as the bus pulled away. The Spire could have gotten him into real trouble.

Prior turned to go to his car, but the Spire made him pause. **WHAT IS THAT?** Apparently it could see through his eyes.

He looked. "It's a hospital. For sick or injured people. Nothing of interest there."

WE'LL SEE.

Oh, no! The Spire wanted to explore. "I really don't recommend it."

NOW.

So Prior walked toward the hospital. A businesslike nurse pushing a gurney intercepted him at the side entrance. "You can't come in here. Go to the front."

Prior stepped close to her. "It's my hand," he said. "Feel." He caught her hand and drew it down to his crotch.

"What are you trying to do?" she demanded outraged. Then her hand touched the Spire. "Come on in," she said, drawing him in through the door. The cosmic dildo really did have the magic touch.

"I was just going to look around," Prior said.

"Lie down on this," she said, pushing him onto the gurney. "They'll think you're a patient."

"But I'm not—"

She got him flat on his back, then climbed onto him, hitching up her uniform skirt. "Don't talk," she said. "Just do it. Fast."

"But—"

She stifled him with a fierce kiss, meanwhile squirming around to get her crotch against his. The Spire sprang up, a prehensile instrument, sliding between her legs and into her rear. It wedged past her underwear and into her cleft. "That's it," she said. "Put it right in deep. What a divine implement!"

The Spire obliged. It tunneled into her hole, and she held her place, making sure it had good lodging. The Spire had just spouted in another woman, but it was inexhaustible; it could do this, literally, indefinitely. And Prior had all its feeling. This vagina was tighter than the other, and firm throughout. This time the Spire had the wit to be smaller, so that it required no reshaping to bury itself to the hilt.

"Now! Now!" the nurse exclaimed, wriggling urgently, her effort to oblige the potent horn causing the gurney to start rolling down the hall.

Prior responded with a heave. He couldn't help it; the Spire was working him up to another orgasm.

"Yes! Yes!" the nurse said as the Spire commenced pumping. She contracted her bottom around it, getting all the feel of it she possibly could.

The Spire gouted. Prior felt the bolus pass through the penile length and pressure into the chamber like thick goo from a grease gun.

"What's going on?" a male voice demanded.

"Emergency mouth to mouth resuscitation," the nurse gasped, and pressed her mouth back on Prior's mouth.

"Uh, okay," the orderly said as the gurney rolled on past him. Fortunately the nurse's skirt was down behind, concealing the real action.

Meanwhile the Spire continued gouting, sending pulse after pulse into the hole. Prior felt each one as if it were his own, and perhaps he was contributing a driblet of semen, because he was certainly in the throes of an extended climax.

"Oh, I'm filled, I'm filled!" the nurse gasped in ecstasy. "What an eruption!" She was hardly exaggerating; the Spire must have shoved a pint of viscous elixir into her. It was squeezing out and soaking his crotch. He knew what she was feeling, because it had a warm rapture throughout, making his skin tingle with delight. The effect would be magnified inside her distended vagina.

The gurney came up against a swinging door and barged through. "Oh, God, we drifted into the morgue!" the nurse whispered. "Play dead!"

"Hey!" a man protested, appearing form a recess. "What are you doing?"

"Just delivering a fresh cadaver, doctor," the nurse said. She scrambled off Prior, drawing the front of her skirt down. "All yours."

"It stinks," the doctor said. "What did it die of, suffocation in Limburger cheese?"

The nurse forced a laugh. "Something like that." She shoved the gurney into a curtained alcove and drew the curtain across, hiding Prior for the nonce. "Do you have a moment? Let's take a break."

"From that stench? You got it." Doctor and nurse departed; Prior heard the door swing closed behind them. Women, he realized, were naturals at covering up.

He got hastily off the gurney, ready to make his escape in the time and privacy the nurse had made for him. Of course she was covering her own ass, so to speak; she wanted him to get out so she wouldn't have to explain anything. He was glad to oblige.

He didn't want to follow the route they had taken, lest he encounter them again, so he went the other way, though a door into another chamber. This one was cold, with several curtained niches. In each niche was a corpse. He didn't want to stay here long!

He was about to open the next door, but heard footsteps beyond it. He dodged back into the nearest niche and jerked the curtain across. He would hide, and resume his escape when the other person passed on by.

But the other did not go on. He—the tread sounded male—paused outside the closed niche. "What's up, doctor?" he inquired. Yes, the voice was male.

The closed curtain must signal that someone was there. "Just inspecting a new cadaver, doctor," Prior replied.

"Good idea." The doctor went to the next niche. "Might as well get a notion what we're in for, next dissection class. This one looks good; how about yours?"

Prior looked at the corpse. It was a naked young woman lying supine in death, rather pretty, like a princess in a century-long trance. "Good enough," Prior said.

NOW.

Prior froze for an instant. The Spire wanted to have sex with the cadaver? "No!" he protested.

"What's that?" the doctor inquired.

"Uh, nothing really," Prior said. "It's just that this is a young woman. It seems a shame to cut her up."

"I know what you mean. But all the cadavers are here for the demonstration lab. If we don't carve them, someone else will."

NOW. the Spire repeated, and sent back a small dose that forced Prior to climb onto the woman. He tried to fight it, but could not; the Spire had control. Prior set himself full length over the corpse and the Spire angled down, seeking her genital region.

"You okay there?" the doctor inquired. "Need any help?"

"No, not at all," Prior said quickly as his willful penis lodged in the cold cleft and heated it. "Just—just a moment of nausea. It will pass."

"Occupational hazard," the doctor agreed.

The tip of the member found the frozen aperture and squirted out a jet of hot fluid, thawing it. Then it wedged into the crevice, melting its way inside. Prior realized that the Spire was going to complete the act regardless of the complications this could make for its human host. He had to cover whatever sounds there might be, and keep the doctor distracted until it was done and he could escape.

So he talked. His mind scrambled madly for something to say that might divert a doctor. He remembered a joke. With luck the doctor wouldn't have heard it before. "Reminds me of a story," he said. "I don't know whether it's true. The Dean of Doctors called in a handsome young doctor who was new to the hospital. 'Smith,' he said, 'I have a special mission for you, if you are amenable.' 'Of course, sir,' Dr. Smith agreed, because he was as eager as the next for a promotion."

"Aren't we all," the adjacent doctor agreed.

The Spire was a good inch into the frigid woman, and such was its power of persuasion that she seemed to be thawing throughout. Prior could almost swear he felt a faint pulsing in her tight channel. But he had to focus on his story, because it would be utter disaster to be discovered doing what he was doing. He hoped the phallic horn finished before the story did.

"'As you know, we have a strict health policy here,' the Dean said. 'Every member of our staff must pass an annual physical. But some are resistive. It is notorious that doctors often take worse care of themselves than they do of their patients. I don't want disharmony, so rather than force the issue, I am resorting to a slight subterfuge. Do you know Dr. Jones?' 'The luscious lady internist?' Smith asked. 'I mean, the comely young doctor? We have a nodding acquaintance.' 'I am concerned that she has not performed her breast self examination regularly,' the Dean said. 'It is a matter I hesitate to broach to her directly, lest she assume I have some illicit motive.' 'Understandable,' Smith said, glad to agree."

"You wouldn't be referring to Miss Johnson, the sexy plastic surgeon, by any chance?" the doctor asked.

"I wouldn't think of it," Prior said piously. "'I want you to ask Miss Jones out,' the Dean said. 'Funds will be made available for a really nice dinner date. Dine her, wine her, and cap the evening with an intimate liaison. In the course of that, give her breasts a thorough checking for untoward lumps or any other indication of incipient cancer. With luck, she will never catch on to your underlying motive.' 'She'll think it's my way of lovemaking!' Smith said, understanding. 'What a novel idea! Of course I'll do it, for the good of the hospital.' 'Very good,' the Dean agreed. 'Report to me the morning after. I shall be most pleased if you accomplish this chore circumspectly.' 'I will do my best, in every respect,' Smith agreed, visions or rapid promotion alternating with visions of the lovely Miss Jones in bed."

"I wonder if that would work with Miss Johnson?" the doctor mused. "As far as I know, no staffer has bedded her yet. It seems a real waste."

Now the Spire had forged all the way into the frigid channel, and was buried to the hilt. It began working up for the first gout. Prior had to admit that the shapely cadaver seemed receptive. Her breasts were quivering. That was probably just the effect of the throbbing in her vagina, radiating out through her stiff torso, but he wondered. The Spire had phenomenal magical abilities.

But he had to keep talking. "A few days passed. Then Dr. Smith reported to the dean's office. 'You will be happy to know that there is absolutely no evidence of breast cancer in Doctor Jones,' he reported. 'I am gratified to hear that,' the Dean said. 'You have done excellent work, Smith, and I will remember.' 'You're welcome," Smith said. 'In fact it was a pleasure.' He paused. 'But I must say, she has a weird way of making love. It was fun, but a surprise.' 'We must learn to put up with oddities in the performance of our necessary duties,' the Dean said."

"If I got in bed with Miss Johnson, I wouldn't care how weird she wanted it," the doctor said.

The Spire gouted. The liquid pressured into the aperture, giving Prior another phenomenal orgasm. Even the corpse seemed to appreciate it, closing tightly around the erupting member, enhancing the pleasure.

"Pleased, Smith departed. Shortly thereafter, the Dean had another visitor. 'Why hello, Dr. Jones,' he said. 'To what do I owe the pleasure of this visit?' 'You will be happy to know that I have completed your assignment,' the shapely lady doctor said. 'There is no evidence of testicular or prostate cancer in Dr. Smith.'"

The adjacent doctor's laugh coincided with the Spire's final gout into the corpse. "Turnabout!" the doctor said. "I'll have to tell that one to Dr. Johnson. Maybe it'll make the luscious creature amenable." He hurried away.

That gave Prior the chance to withdraw from the corpse's heated cleft and get off her. She seemed to have a frozen smile on her face that he didn't think had been there before. Now he could finally make his escape. Then he paused, observing the pool of viscous substance oozing from her genital aperture. "They'll see that! It'll incriminate me. I've got to clean it up."

NO NEED. the spire gouted reassuringly. **I FILLED HER WITH EMBALMING FLUID.**

Prior had to laugh, somewhat shamefacedly. He found a sponge, mopped up what he could, tossed the sponge into a waste basket, and pulled open the curtain. He went out the door, and was soon out of the backside of the hospital.

And there was a uniformed meter maid ticketing his car for illicit parking. She wore full length trousers; no way to touch her thigh with the Spire.

TOUCH A DAB TO HER EAR the Spire gouted.

Prior reached down to catch the dab of goo at the end of the member, holding it on two fingers. "Don't give me a ticket!" he called as he approached.

"Tough beans, mister," the maid said. "It's done."

Prior extended his hand toward her head. She tried to pull away, uncertain of his intent, but he scored on her ear. The goo smeared into the auditory hole.

The change was instant. "Music to my ear," she said in wonder. "Come on, mister let's have it." She put her hands to her belt, dropped her pants and panties, and bent across the hood of the car with her bared bottom toward him, the labia parting to provide clear access. "Now."

That was the Spire talking. Prior put the tip to her open crevice, stroked it delicately along the channel, then paused. "About that ticket," he said.

She pulled it from her pocket and tore it in half. "What ticket?"

That would do. The Spire found the place and slid in halfway, pulsing like a motor on idle. "And no report on this incident."

"No report!" she said eagerly. "Give it to me!"

He rammed the member home. It was gouting even as he pumped, driving thick substance into her. "Aaah!" she said, transported. "What a magic rod!"

She was literally correct, though she didn't know it. Prior let her have it until the stuff was squeezing out as fast as it was gouting in, drooling down to soak her pants. Then he pulled out. The last gout spattered across her anus and slid down along her crack like corn syrup between steaming pancakes.

"There too!" she cried desperately. "Put it in, put it in!" She put her two hands back and pulled her buttocks apart, making her sphincter fully accessible.

Oh? Very well. He set the tip at the wet pucker and pressed it in just far enough to make the connection. Another gout pumped through the tight closure, shooting its ejaculate inside. Prior almost thought he heard a splat as it struck the farther wall of her chamber. The shaft followed it in, lubricated by its own production, until it was fully embedded, still jetting gout after gout. He held it there, waiting for her to cry enough, but she didn't; she would take all he cared to give. The rectum was far more capacious than the vagina, extending on back into the colon, and the stuff was infusing her lower intestinal tract. He was satisfied, because each gout was another surge of his own extended orgasm; the Spire was delivering the sheer joy of sex to both of them. Never before had he had a climax as long as this.

"Oooh!" she sighed as the deific spigot filled her up. Her anus clenched convulsively with her own continuing orgasm, swallowing the input, and her plump buttocks flexed as if she were running up an endless flight of steps. All of it helped his effort; this was a living, tensing ass. It was a pleasure to stretch it, quite apart from the long climax.

Finally it would take no more; driblets were squeezing out around the shaft. "Pucker it," Prior said. "I'm pulling out."

She did so, closing as the Spire slid slowly clear of the hole, and only a little was lost. "Thank you!" she gasped, and straightened up. Her belly was distended as though she were pregnant, from the sheer mass of protoplasm she had taken in, but she was smiling. "I'll never let this go!"

Prior suspected she would have to, eventually; her body could absorb only so much, perhaps digesting it, and the rest would come out in a series of exotic defecations. But she had certainly had her joy of the occasion; it was a fancy price for the destruction of one measly parking ticket.

She pulled up her pants, not even noticing their sopping condition. "What's your address? I want to spend the night with you."

"Sorry," Prior said. "I have to get home and clean up." He got into his car and drove off, leaving her standing there trying to get her belt to fit around her bulging midriff.

He was curious. "Will all that stuff make her sick?"

NO, the Spire gouted. **IT WILL LEAVE HER IN ECSTASY AS LONG AS IT LASTS. AND EVERY DEFECATION WILL THRILL HER ANEW.**

Prior was satisfied with that. He didn't wish the woman any ill. Let her have all the orgasmic shitting she wanted. But it was time to put his foot down, as it were. "You've had your fun with four women and gouted a lot of gout. Tomorrow we go to Fartingale."

AGREED. WE'LL FORNICATE THERE TOO.

Prior was sure they would.

Chapter 6–Plea

Veil struggled with herself. Now she knew she was on display all the time, day and night, her every action open to public view, even her natural functions. It was horrible, but she was stuck with it. She was the Maiden in the Tower, the prize for one of the men who won the privilege of taking her in sexual slavery for a year. What was she to do?

First she would stop putting on a show for the monsters. She had to eat, so as to be healthy enough to nurse Chance; she was not going to let him suffer. That meant she would continue to expel clouds of intestinal gas. But she could do that silently, and when she had something of greater substance to do on the toilet, she could make it quick and without any flourish. The rest of the time she would simply sit still.

Except that she had to exercise to keep her body fit. She had put on flesh during her pregnancy, and was carefully working it off. She had been blessed with a natural hourglass figure, and intended to keep it that way, even if it did make her more of a sexual object. She couldn't stand to become pudgy or even fat, whatever the cost. Like cleanliness, health was essential.

So she did her calisthenic routine, stretching and flexing. If this made her more appealing to sundry voyeurs, so be it; it was a necessary sacrifice. Because it was warm, and the clumsy clothing got in her way, she did it in the nude. That meant that the peeping Toms, Dicks, and Harrys would get some pretty special sneak peeks as she lifted her legs or bent over. Surely they already knew the nature of female anatomy. But this was the extent of the illicit treat she would provide them. With luck they would soon be bored by the repetitious nature of the routine.

Then she covered herself and sat with Chance in the easy chair. She turned on the TV. The announcer had been relegated to a separate channel; now she could watch what she wanted. So instead of a titillating Nude on Toilet, they would see a dull Woman Watching TV. It served them right.

But if she had been inclined to any smugness about her policy, it was soon vanquished. All of the channels featured programs she hardly cared to watch. One was herself, watching herself watching herself, her full breasts heaving gently beneath the black blob that masked her head. Another was news about the rivalry of men interested in the Maiden in the Tower. Another was pornography, with men endlessly plumbing women, women endlessly eager for the plumbing; the main variety was in the hairdos of the women and the positions of the sex. Another was children's stories, but not of the kind she cared to expose Chance to; they were filthy if not downright obscene.

Yet those were her choices. She turned it off. But then Chance starting fussing; the pictures, of whatever nature, were a distraction for him. So she turned it on to the children's channel, with bad grace. Her captors had her pretty well boxed in, leaving her choices between bad and worse. With luck, Chance would soon fall asleep, and she could ignore the screen.

"This is the story of the Littlest Turd," a dulcet female voice said. "He was unhappy, because every time the toilet flushed, the big turds jammed in and crowded him out. They made it to the Great Sewer in the Sea, where the stench was truly wonderful. He couldn't get flushed, and was left alone in the bowl. He hoped that maybe one of the people beyond the bowl would want to play with him, but they never touched him. It was awful, and he was very unhappy. He just cried all day."

The picture closed in on the toilet, magnifying the Littlest Turd until it almost filled the screen. There was a crude face at one end, with sad eyes crying urine-yellow tears. There was no explanation of how a turd floating in water could show tears; presumably children didn't care about such details.

Chance was watching with interest. She doubted he understood much, but evidently he identified with another baby, even one like this.

"How he wished he could be a Big Turd," the gentle voice continued. "He had a cousin who was so big he had had to be removed from the man's gut by a Caesarian section operation. It weighed twelve kilograms. That was surely the King of Turds! But the Littlest Turd was hardly more than a marble. He had emerged from the anus almost as an afterthought, unnoticed."

The turd floated in the water, looking miserable. "Then he realized that he would get nowhere, depending on others to treat him fairly," the voice continued. "He would never get flushed as long as he was the smallest piece of shit. So he resolved to do something about it. He realized that what he needed was more size, so that he could shove aside other turds and be first in line for the flushing. The only place he could grow was inside the colon of a living person. That was where the formative nourishment was. In there he could add layer on layer, steadily adding mass. He didn't have to make it to super-turd status, just to enough mass to be no longer the smallest. So he resolved to do something about it. He would go find a suitable colon to occupy."

The Littlest Turd smiled. He sprouted small arms and legs and swam to the edge of the water. He scrambled out, struggling to cling to the slippery side. Despite herself, Veil found herself rooting for the game little fellow to make it. Finally he did, and got on the rim of the toilet below the seat. He was so small he didn't need to climb over the seat; he simply rolled under it. He dropped to the bathroom floor, bounced, and extended his little legs again.

"The littlest Turd was on his way," the voice said. "Now all he needs is a nice warm colon to get into. Who is there out there who will help the brave little fellow?" There was a pause. Then the punch line: "How about you?"

Fortunately Chance had finally nodded off. Still, Veil had to admit that aside from the nature of its protagonist, the story showed the values of decision and action. It was, in its fashion, wholesome.

But it got her thinking. She was like the Littlest Turd, in that she was stuck in a virtual toilet bowl, unable to escape her fate. The Turd had grown legs; she would have to take a more figurative approach.

She changed to the announcer's channel. "I want your advice," she said. "How can I improve my situation?"

"I thought you'd never ask," he replied immediately, the picture showing a painted smiley face. It was clear now that there was a live person on the other end of this dialog, however much canned material there might have been before. "It's no good doing nothing; that attracts the interest of relatively few, the lowbrows who know they can't compete with better men. You need to catch the attention of superior men who are more likely to have good situations and pleasant dispositions. You could enjoy your year with one of those."

"My year of sex slavery."

"Of course. But a superior man is more likely to be gentle, and to consider your feelings. He would treat you more like a lady than a prostitute."

That did seem to be a recommendation. Of course what she really wanted was to escape this awfulness and return home, but she knew it would be unwise to say that openly. A sensitive man might be willing to allow her to go home, and possibly even to facilitate her return. She could certainly try her feminine wiles on him. These would exclude tempting him with sex, since he would have that already, and it would be essential that she never balk in that respect. But she was an attractive woman, and he might come to desire her favor as well as her body. It would help if she could show her face to him, instead of this dark blob of anonymity.

"The hood," she said. "When does it come off?"

"Normally, when you commit to a man, and he speaks your name. Then you cease to be the mysterious Maiden in the Tower, making way for next week's offering. He will know your full appearance. It is a gamble for him, of course, as you might be ugly in the face. There are no guarantees about the

Maiden; men must judge her by her body and her actions and speech."

"I am fair of feature."

"So you say. So they all say. Some men prefer to leave the hood on, so they can fantasize that the Maiden is actually a lost love. Your face will not be your fortune while you remain in the Tower."

"So what will be my fortune?"

"Do you have any talents?"

She had her professional talent, but she was not about to speak of that, lest it give away her true identity. "I am reasonably smart."

"That won't do. Can you piss, shit, or fart with authority—at least a 6.0 on the Rectum Scale?"

"Definitely not," she said, wincing inwardly.

"You can't juggle, or sew champion quilts, or cook gourmet?"

"None of the above."

He sighed. "Then smart has to be it, though that's a liability with some men. You must make a statement that will appeal to smart men."

"But I'm confined to this bowel tower."

"That is not a smart observation. You know that your every action and word is publicized. Your body may be confined, but not your words."

Veil was mortified. He was right. She had been stupid. She hated that. "I'll ponder a statement," she agreed.

"Do not take undue time. This is the third day of seven; two men have qualified, and the third is in process."

Ouch! The sooner she acted, the better chance she would have of getting more than one good man in the lineup. But as yet she had no idea of a suitable statement. Maybe it would help to see what was already in the queue. "Please show me the first man."

"Do you wish to interview him, or see him contesting?"

"I can interview them?" she asked surprised.

"Yes, of course. You can talk with them, question them, or have sex with them, whatever you choose, gathering information for an informed choice."

This seemed almost too fair. Then she caught on to the catch. "And everyone else will be watching and listening."

"Certainly. This is great entertainment for the masses. They will be judging you, and it could affect potential contestants, especially if you turn out to be sexually apt."

Veil knew she could be as apt as any woman, but that was not the way she wanted to choose. "Show the contest."

"A word of advice. You have been uncommonly silent of rectum. You will have to fart socially with any contestants you meet, or interviews will be pointless."

Veil realized that this was good advice. "Thank you. I will do my best to reform." She nerved herself and squeezed out an audible break of wind.

"Very good." The picture shifted to the base of the huge female statue. A sultry nude woman stood there. In a moment a halfway handsome naked young man approached. "Several have tried before, this day, and been rejected," the announcer's voice said. "This is the one destined to succeed."

"Actually he looks all right," Veil said. "But it's his mind and personality I'm more interested in."

"For that you will need the interview. The challenge is purely physical."

The man farted and put his arms around the woman, embracing her. She yielded to this, but did not smile. He whispered in her ear, but got no reaction. He stroked her body, cupping her full breasts in his hands. "You are the loveliest creature I have seen today," he said.

Now she smiled and emitted a small fart. "Thank you."

He let out a louder fart. "Your charms overcome me. I must caress you."

The woman merely stood in his embrace, neither speaking nor moving. He kissed her, and she held for the kiss, but did not do more.

"Something's odd here," Veil said. "She doesn't seem to be participating."

"She's a demon," the announcer said. "She is programmed to respond in a set way, and not to volunteer anything. He must make her climax within a set time, or lose."

Now it made sense. "Why did he whisper in her ear?"

"He was trying to make her laugh. That's a significant point; women like men who make them laugh. But his joke was old, so she didn't respond."

This contest was getting more interesting. The man laid the demoness on the bed behind her, lifted her legs, and did oral stimulation on her cleft. Veil noticed that her cleft was without pubic hair, clean in the manner of a child; that must be a signal of her demon nature, as she was clearly sexually mature. He licked her channel and tongued her clitoris. She reacted with a gentle sigh of pleasure. He was good at it; he had the right touch.

Then he licked her breasts and kissed her nipples. She reacted farther, visibly softening. He kissed her again, this time tonguing her. She sighed more firmly. Finally he got on her, inserted his hard penis, and drove it home. He thrust repeatedly, taking time to come. She writhed in ecstasy, and finally climaxed. Only then did he go into his own orgasm.

"If he had climaxed before her, he would have lost," Veil said.

"True; that's the trap. The point is to give her pleasure, rather than himself. He started slow, but improved, and brought her to a fair culmination. It can be done, played correctly. It is surprising how many men lack the skill or patience to make a woman react."

"Suppose he had failed?"

"Here is the case of the man before him, with this demon." The scene showed another moderately handsome man approach. He worked her up much as the other had, and penetrated her in good order, but when she started reacting it triggered his orgasm and he climaxed too soon.

At that point the demon's fair mien changed. She blew out a fart of conquest, caught his arms as talons sprouted, and wrapped her legs around him, locking him against her. She kissed him, and fangs appeared, latching on to his lips as she sucked his breath. Her breasts not only flattened against him, they spread out to adhere to his skin, abrading it as if feeding. But the main action was at his crotch. A close up showed her vulva lapping at his member like a hungry mouth, the labia actually smacking together where they didn't surround it. Then they closed firmly and sucked. The rest of his softening shaft disappeared into the hole, only to be pushed out again, then slurped back in. She was forcing thrusts, artificially engorging the member by means of the suction.

The man groaned as his second climax was drawn from him. But the demon didn't stop. She sucked his air until he was almost unconscious, then bit him again, injecting a sedative so that he was unable to move. Then she detached, rolling him off her; raw red welts showed on his chest where the carnivorous breasts had fed. Her vagina spat out his doubly spent penis, which flopped limply. She turned him over, lifted him to hands and knees, pushed down his head, and parted his legs so that he formed a crude tripod. Then she slid her tongue into his elevated anus. It was a long tongue, and it extended farther, snaking sinuously in. The scene closed on the region, showing his hanging scrotum and penis as her tongue still coursed into his colon.

The penis quivered. Veil knew what was happening; that prehensile tongue was massaging the man's prostate gland, squeezing it, forcing it to eject more fluid, and this was stirring the penis. It thickened in a weak erection, and finally jerked, dribbling out the product of another orgasm. The fluid was pale red.

The demoness reeled her tongue back into her mouth and pushed the man over. He fell, his face frozen in a rictus of agonized bliss. He was done for. It would take him weeks to recover potency, and longer to get over the memory of the experience.

"Why do they risk that fate?" Veil asked.

"For the prospect of winning a shapely maiden for a year of sexual bliss."

"Don't they know they lack the erotic skill to make the grade?"

"Every man thinks he's a champion lover."

"Every man is in denial!" She glanced at the scene, which had gone neutral. "So the ones that get past the demoness make it for the day. Are further applicants cut off?"

"No, if there is more than one in a day, they must face off against each other in a farting contest."

"I believe I'll pass over that exhibition. I will consider what I have to say."

She considered, and concluded that an appeal to the copulating, farting men who wanted her body would be less useful than a test of their mentality. She knew an intellectual puzzle that stumped most people who hadn't encountered it before. The first part was easy, the second hard. Only a smarter or better informed man would realize what she had in mind.

She stood and faced the mirror-wall, knowing it was transparent from outside. She doffed her clothing and did a few jumping jacks, knowing that they made her flesh bounce enticingly, especially her breasts. That should attract the attention of any men in range, and of course it was being recorded so they could watch it again. "I am Veil, the Maiden in the Tower," she said. "I will choose the man who correctly answers two riddles. The first riddle is this: Where in the world can a person walk south a mile, east a mile, north a mile, and be back where he started? The second riddle I will ask of those who answer the first, not announcing it in advance." Then she did a few more exercises, including leg lifts and bicycling on her back that proffered a good view of her genital region. She had the sexual equipment; she was making sure they knew it. Men were such fools about bodies.

"That should do it," the announcer agreed. "Top it off with a good fart."

Oh, of course. She had been automatically stifling her gas; now she blew it out as loudly as she could. It seemed that hearing a woman fart was similar to seeing her urinate, in this feculent culture.

Part 2: Contest

Chapter 7—Oubliette

Prior woke early next morning, invigorated. He had taken a thorough shower and cleaned up, but forgotten to remove the Spire from his groin. "Did you facilitate my rest?" he inquired.

YES, it gouted. **YOU FACE A CHALLENGE BEYOND YOUR MEANS. IT WILL BE EASIER TO SAVE YOUR SORRY ANUS IF YOU ARE IN GOOD HEALTH.**

"I appreciate the vote of confidence."

YOU WILL NEED TO WEAR ME IN YOUR COLON, SO THAT YOUR FARTS SEEM GENUINE.

That did not appeal phenomenally. "Let's wait until the time."

YOU MUST TAKE THE STATUE PATH.

"But that's three thousand miles away!"

WHAT IS YOUR POINT?

Prior sighed. He made the arrangements and shut down his house. He was fortunate in being able to catch a flight for the following day. He was afraid the Spire would want to seduce every woman they encountered along the way, but it, oddly, seemed as eager to get there as he was, and behaved.

In due course Prior arrived at the home/office of Oubliette Emdee, who had set him up with the socket and assorted prosthetic penises. It wasn't her fault that he had had little use for them the past year, because of lack of a girlfriend.

It was late when he arrived, even allowing for the time change, but there was a light on at her house. He knocked on the door, hoping she would not be annoyed by the intrusion.

She recognized him instantly. "Prior Gross! So good to see you. How's the plumbing?" She was as luscious and businesslike as ever, wearing a knee-length skirt and her halter formed from her own long tresses. That was a trick her sister Tantamount had had too. It was marvelous the way her fine breasts bobbed with the motions of her head.

"Uh, yes," he said, feeling awkward.

I WANT HER.

Oh, no! The Spire had come to life.

"What's the matter, Prior?" she asked, concerned. "Is there a malfunction? Let me see." She led him into the house and sat him on her patient's table.

"Not exactly," he said.

NOW.

Meanwhile she was opening his fly. The Spire sprang out, its full length standing tall.

"You have the Spire!" Oubliette exclaimed, delighted. "Oh, I must sample him!"

"But I'm here on business," Prior protested. "I need to walk the path."

"You can catch me up on everything while we share the Spire," she said. She touched the tip with a finger, and was rewarded with a trace gout. "Set yourself on slow small pulses," she said to it, and kissed the tip. "I'll be with you in a moment." She led Prior to a couch, pulled his pants off, drew her skirt down and off, and joined him on the cushions, expertly fitting her contours to his.

The Spire entered her immediately, sliding slowly into her deep vagina. It was a foot long, and broad at the base, so was more than any normal woman could handle. "Slowly dear, slowly," she said to it. "I'll accommodate." And she did. The Spire penetrated a careful nine inches, then commenced slow pulsing as her interior gradually adapted to its expansive pressure. She intended to take it all in, but would have to stretch somewhat. Prior suspected there was some softening element in the gout substance that enabled her to take it in without discomfort.

The Spire pulsed, like the beating of a heart, sending out tiny gouts, and each pulse delivered a surge of bliss to Prior and surely to Oubliette too; he felt her channel matching the cadence. "Oh, you darling creature," she breathed, still speaking to the Spire. "I have longed for you all my life, and now at last I feel your glory in my center. You are every woman's fondest dream, you most marvelous of members."

The Spire was pleased with the flattery; Prior felt its pleasure as his own. Oubliette wasn't just praising it; she was serious.

"Now tell me all, from the start," she said to Prior, kissing him. He knew the kiss was really for the Spire, but it was nevertheless wonderful. She was man's dream of a woman, and it was great to have her so affectionate and obliging, despite his knowledge that it was really his member she loved rather than him personally. The cosmic dildo. "Give it to me. Take your time." That was addressed to both man and phallic instrument. She surely knew that the Spire could communicate directly to her via its gouts, but was doing Prior the courtesy of letting him tell it. She was nice in a way her sister Tantamount hadn't been. She also wanted to extend her session with the magic phallus, knowing that he would soon be moving on.

So while the Spire pulsed and the woman's deep well responded, Prior talked. "The succubus who started it all a year ago has been visiting me every few weeks. I call her Suzie. She's been sort of a girlfriend, because she knows I'll deliver a load and not tell her supervisor that I wasn't asleep. She's not supposed to come to conscious men, maybe because then news of what her kind is doing would spread and people would be on guard. But we have an understanding. She gives me a really good time, and I give her a load or two, and we both pretend it never happened."

"Or two?" Oubliette inquired, internally stroking the organ within her while distending elastically to take more of it in. She had very special anatomy.

"She's learned to use a condom, so she can take my emission without having to change to incubus form and deliver it to a sleeping woman. That way she can stay the night, drawing a second or even a third from me in the course of a few hours, and I get the feel of a loving woman. Sure, I know it's pretense, but that's her role, to be my lover in exchange for the extra loads. It's not that she's nice, because she isn't, but that I recover faster and deliver more if I have the illusion it's a loving relationship. She's getting good at it; sometimes I do think she cares."

"A demoness? I think not. They have no souls, no conscience, no love. They do what they have to, to get what they need."

"They don't need love?"

"All the sexual demons need is semen. But they are good actors."

"Well, I guess it's an act I need. I really crave a woman to love, who loves me back. She makes a decent substitute. She assumes different appearances, pretending to be women or girls who find me irresistible. I go for that. It's an association of convenience."

"Poor man," she said sympathetically. "But with the assortment of members I gave you, you should be able to impress women."

"I want a woman who wants me for myself, not my fancy penis. A woman like you." He paused. "I mean, not you yourself, but—"

"One who matches my appearance, intelligence, and personality, but who isn't all tied up in her profession. Who would have time for you."

"That's it. I know it's a foolish dream."

She sighed, and the motion extended into her vagina, generating another wave of feeling around the Spire. "Prior, you're a decent man, and you have considerable courage, as your adventure on Mt. Icecream demonstrated. You'd make any woman a good if dull husband. If I were looking for a regular man, I'd consider you. But I'm not, and it wouldn't be fair to you to pretend otherwise."

"I understand. But decent men don't get the girls. It's the big, strong, handsome, rich men who have girl appeal."

"Yes, of course. It's our nature to desire that sort of thing, just as it is the nature of men to desire women like me and my sister."

"Tantamount," he agreed. "I could have gone for her, if she hadn't ripped off my penis."

Oubliette smiled. "But you repaid her for that, didn't you! She had to vacate her practice and relocate."

"So I gathered. There were trucks loading smegma at her house."

She smiled again, the expression seeming to reflect internally as her flesh caressed the member pressing into her. "I must confess it was a fitting revenge. She wanted your smegma, and you gave her more than she could handle. That did alienate her."

"I guess so. Maybe I overdid it."

"Put it this way, Prior: if you were the last man on Earth, and she the last woman, she would chain you to a wall, rip off your penis, stuff dirt in your socket, and do a sexy striptease just out of your reach. Then she would consider how best to humiliate you."

He nodded, experiencing a twinge of guilt. He had behaved badly. "Can't say I blame her."

"She swore me to secrecy about her situation, especially with respect to you."

He had figured as much. "So when Suzie said my ideal woman was in trouble, I just had to try to rescue her. It could be my only chance."

"Who is this ideal woman?"

"I don't know. Just that she's the Maiden in the Tower, in a weird land called Fartingale. I have a week to rescue her, if I'm going to. So I'm on my way."

Her body tensed, and not because she had taken the Spire in another inch. "Any clue to her identity?"

"None. I don't think Suzie knew either. But she wouldn't lie to me. My ideal woman, whoever she is, has been abducted and is captive, and I can rescue her if I act in time."

"I have heard of Fartingale. It's one of the worlds the Statue Path accesses. An uncouth place."

"The Spire told me. Farts are a way of life there."

"She would absolutely hate it. She must be rescued."

"You know the maiden?" he asked, surprised.

"I know her type. Every week they kidnap some innocent shapely woman and set her up for a year's sex slavery to the man who wins her. They don't mind if she's horrified; in fact they like to see a maiden react. It adds to the pleasure of the man who abuses her. Certainly you must rescue her and take her away from there."

Now he had doubts. "But you know, if she really is beautiful, she might prefer one of those other men to me."

"Not if you touch her with the Spire."

"But I want her to want me for myself!"

"Prior, Prior," she said gently as her avenue stroked the Spire with its special peristalsis. The godly spike was almost completely into her now; she had expanded enough to accommodate its full length and girth. She had truly amazing anatomy. "These things take time. Do you suppose you would have me like this at this moment if it weren't for the Divine Dildo? Capture her sexuality with the Spire, then maintain the association until she gets to know the rest of you. You will have to use the prime weapon, or you will inevitably lose her."

He wasn't sure how she could be so sure, but he trusted her judgment. "Use the Spire," he agreed. It was surely excellent advice.

"And practice your approach. The way you treated my sister is a fine example of how *not* to treat a woman whose favor you desire. Take that as a guide. *Don't* be yourself. After you tame her with the Cosmic Horn of Delight, focus on how nice you can be to her in other respects, and how decent you can be generally. That will give you at least a fighting chance to hold her when you no longer have the Spire."

Her estimate of his potential to charm a woman was not reassuring, but he knew she was being realistic. "Work on my decency," he agreed.

"Now let's see what we can accomplish here," she said. "Let's make some real love." She put her arms around him, drawing him tightly in to her so that her breasts flattened against him, and kissed him ardently as her vulva closed around and over his shaft. This was a piece of heaven; she was everything any man could ever desire. He responded, kissing her back, pressing his groin into hers, pretending she was really his woman.

But the real action was inside. She had entirely surrounded the Spire, and was squeezing it urgently. She was going into her orgasm, trying to take the divine phallus with her. Prior felt it all; it was like riding a storm that was centered on his embedded member. His own climax was coming; he couldn't have helped it if he had wanted to.

And between them, they got to the Spire. It was billions of years old, made to service the wives and mistresses of the Eldest God of the Galaxy; it could spout any substance in unlimited quantity. But it was of demonic origin; it lacked true feelings of its own. Until this moment.

Oubliette went into the full throes of her orgasm, drawing Prior along. She clutched him closely, kissing him fiercely, convulsing around his member. And the Spire responded. It built into its own involuntary orgasm, which was of course what the woman had been trying for. She wanted more than the keen pleasure of its touch and ejaculate; she wanted its own joy of union. She was getting it.

The Spire came. It erupted in an unbearably intense pulse of rapture, jetting with abandon. It exploded with the semblance of a supernova, flinging its passion outward. It was the éclat of the birth of the universe, with infinite energy and matter radiating out from an infinitely small center. The pinpoint swelled to a glob, the glob to sphere the size of a planet, the planet to a star, and the star to a nebula. This was the primeval pinwheel, the domain of the Eldest God of the Galaxy. Thereafter the galaxy expanded to a universe, but the terminology remained. The universe stretched out, cooling, until it was mostly vacuum, a relatively dull place. Out in the hinterland they hardly even knew of the greatness of EGG or of his divine copulatory pipe. But its power remained, for those few able to harness it.

Prior came out of his instant eon of orgasmic rapture to discover himself still embracing Oubliette, the Spire still nestled inside her, dribbling its last spasm of protoplasm. The two of them were floating in a viscous sea. The Spire's orgasm had pumped out enough juice to overflow her deep vagina and leak out into the room, which was now two thirds full.

"Spire!" Oubliette said in mock reproof as she tread thick water. "You overestimated my capacity."

APOLOGY. the Spire gouted.

She laughed. "I made you come, didn't I! Who was the last woman to accomplish that?"

EGG'S FAVORITE CONCUBINE. SEVERAL BILLION YEARS AGO. WHAT A CREATURE SHE WAS! A LOT LIKE YOU.

"I am surely her direct descendant," Oubliette agreed, not trying to conceal her satisfaction. "But you have ruined my carpet. Now clean it up this instant."

THAT'S WHAT THE CONCUBINE SAID. I SHALL HAVE TO WITHDRAW FROM YOUR DELIGHTFUL CHAMBER.

"Parting is such sweet sorrow," she agreed. "I would really like to keep you within me forever, you utterly divine implement, but to do that I'd have to retire and marry Prior, and the carpet would stink. I'm not ready for that."

"Let it stink," Prior muttered. But Oubliette was already releasing the Spire; he felt it easing along her channel, inch by inch, as the two of them continued to float connected.

"Farewell, dear," Oubliette said as the tip of the Spire finally slid out of her belly. Her labia closed on it in a parting nether kiss.

FAREWELL. DIVINE MORTAL. The Spire, also, hated to separate; it had not encountered a woman her equal in billions of years.

"How can you clean this up?" Prior asked it, stifling his unreasonable jealousy. "I thought you gouted only outward."

TRUE. I SHALL HAVE TO GOUT A CLEANER. POINT ME AWAY FROM THAT PERFECT WOMAN.

The Spire was out, but Prior was still embracing Oubliette, feeling her wonderful breasts against his chest within their mutual bath of thick fluid. "I have to let you go," he said reluctantly.

"Of course, Prior," she agreed. She kissed him again, and it seemed to make his head float better. She truly could have been his ideal woman, had she had the inclination. But he had always known she was well beyond him in every respect that counted. Which increased the mystery of the succubus' message: how could there be a woman anywhere near as good for him as this one, who would have any real interest in him? It seemed impossible.

Then they parted and floated separately. Prior turned around and aimed the cosmic dildo toward the center of the filled room. "Ready," he said, uncertain what was coming.

A weird bolus fired out of the member, churning the fluid in its vicinity. Prior couldn't see it through the opacity of the substance, but the surface dipped and formed a whirlpool leading into it. The level of the fluid descended. Soon they were able to stand, as the tide ebbed down past their chests to their waists. He couldn't help gazing at Oubliette's perfectly shaped breasts as they emerged from the bath; her hair halter had come undone in the throes of the rapture. They hardly needed such support, upstanding despite their mass. She saw him looking, and smiled understandingly.

The level dropped below their crotches, uncovering the Spire. It was flaccid, an unusual state for it; it truly had climaxed and was quiescent, apart from the bolus it had emitted. That continued to draw in fluid, making a sucking sound as air also went into it. "What is that thing?" Prior asked.

A SMALL BLACK HOLE. it gouted.

"A black hole!" Prior exclaimed. "That's dangerous."

"Do not be alarmed," Oubliette said. "The Spire knows what he's doing."

"I hope so." Prior retreated to the side of the room. He knew that a black hole had so much gravity that nothing escaped it, not even light, and indeed this one was a blob of darkness. Its event horizon was only about three inches across, but it was gulping in fluid at a phenomenal rate. It had been more like one inch before; it was growing as it fed.

Before long all the liquid was gone. The black hole started to consume the floor. "My carpet!" Oubliette protested.

"Do something," Prior told the Spire. "Before it comes after us."

AIM ME AT IT.

Prior lifted the limp member and pointed it at the black hole. Another bolus emerged, this one a blindingly bright pinpoint of light. It flew toward the black hole and circled it, caught in its gravity well. It spiraled in, ever more rapidly, until it disappeared into the event horizon. Then the black hole abruptly faded out.

"What was that?" Prior asked, amazed.

A WHITE HOLE. THEY MERGED OUT INTO NOTHING.

"I never heard of a white hole!"

YOUR CULTURE IS SCIENTIFICALLY BACKWARD. FORTUNATELY.

"I'll have to replace the carpet," Oubliette said crossly.

Prior had a bright idea. "Spire—"

AGREED. AIM ME.

Prior held it up, pointing it at the center of the room. It convulsed, and from it shot a mass of substance. The mass flattened as it extended, becoming colorful. It reached the far side of the room, then broadened as it sank to the floor, showing a furry surface. It was a new carpet!

The material kept spewing out, until finally it settled across the entire chamber. It wasn't just a rug; it was an enormously elaborate Persian carpet featuring an intricately woven picture of an ancient sultan making out with six luscious bare concubines simultaneously. That was quite a trick; his penis, tongue, both index fingers and both big toes were embedded in their open vaginas. Complicating the picture was a handsomely garbed woman just coming on the scene, surely his wife, who would demand equal service. What did he have left for her?

"That's the famous King's Dilemma carpet!" Oubliette exclaimed. "It was stolen a thousand years ago. It was reputed to be magic."

SORRY ABOUT THAT. the Spire gouted. IT WAS WHAT WAS AVAILABLE. YES. IT IS A FLYING CARPET.

Prior repeated its message to her. "I'll take it!" Oubliette said. "Oh, thank you, thank you!" She dropped to her knees and kissed the Spire. It quivered, recovering some erotic ambition. Perceiving that, she put her mouth around it and drew it in, farther and farther, while Prior stood in place, feeling rather left out. She kept working it in until almost the whole of it was down her throat. Only the thick base remained outside, too broad for her delicate mouth to compass. But she kept sucking and swallowing, silently urging it to perform.

The Spire was flattered; Prior felt its feeling. Oubliette truly understood it and liked it for its history as well as its capacity to deliver sexual pleasure. It gouted. Prior felt a surge of bliss jet from it and forge into her stomach. She had indeed evoked its potency again. Joy surged into her innards, so much better than the finest food or drink, transporting Prior as well in passing. She was getting a meal of divine seminal fluid, filling her stomach much as the meter maid had gotten her colon filled. It would surely last her a long time, giving pleasure as it progressed along her alimentary system in the course of the next few days.

The last gout faded. She drew her head back slowly, once again letting the long shaft slide out, adoring it on the way. Again, as the tip appeared, she kissed it. "Thank you, Spire," she murmured. "For everything."

It gouted again, sending a thin stream between her lips. WHEN I AM

DONE WITH PRIOR. PERHAPS I COULD RETURN TO BE IN YOUR LABORATORY.

"Oh, yes, yes, Spire!" she said dreamily, licking the goo from her lips. "Welcome anytime. My business is artificial penises; you are the ultimate in that respect."

OF COURSE.

It seemed they had made a date. Prior still felt somewhat isolated. "Maybe we should clean up."

Her fair visage clarified. She became aware of him. "Of course, Prior. This way."

She led him to her bathroom, where they had a steamy shower together and washed each other off. She paid him a lot of attention and hugged him several times, stroking her soapy breasts across him. He knew she was trying to make him feel better, and it was effective.

She also cautioned him again about dealing with the anonymous Maiden in the Tower. "She surely resents being abducted and put on exhibition like that. She may be angry at the man who wins her. That's understandable. Don't give her a chance to reject you; touch her with the Spire. She will then want sex, of course, and you will oblige her. But remember she is your ideal woman; you want to win her favor, not merely use her. Treat her as you would the woman you love, so as to win her love. Only then will she truly be yours."

"Uh, sure," he agreed, uncertain why she was orienting so firmly on this aspect. Why should she care whether he won his ideal woman? To make sure he didn't decide he wanted Oubliette herself? But she knew he knew she was hopelessly out of his reach.

"You seem doubtful of my motive," she said. "Perhaps this will clarify it: you are the one who carries the Spire. If you don't bring him back to me, I won't have him."

That did make sense. "I won't need it, once I have my ideal woman."

"Exactly. I want you to win her." She gave him a last luxurious embrace and kiss, then stepped out of the shower.

She had to find him new clothes, because his were sopping. Fortunately she had a fair supply, perhaps from male clients. "Maybe you should be anonymous, too," she said. "You have grown a mustache, which changes your face; that's good. Maybe some gray tint to your sideburns will make you look older."

"Why should I be anonymous?"

"Because it could be a trap. Maybe someone there knows you have the Spire, and wants to take him from you. You must not give them that chance."

That did make sense. He let her tint his hair, and cut it so that it changed the apparent shape of his face.

By this time it was late. "I shouldn't ask, I know it," she said. "But the

Spire is just so—so—"

He opened his new trousers and drew it out. She embraced him standing, feeding the Spire up under her skirt and into her pantyless cleft. It remained not fully erect, having been softened by her considerable prior attentions, but it stiffened as it encountered her flesh, and in a moment sent a nice gout up into her. She thrilled once more to its offering. Then she kissed Prior again and showed him to his room for the night.

Tomorrow he would set out on the statue path. That was bound to be its own challenge.

Chapter 8 – Farting off

Veil had seen more than she cared to of the ways of Fartingale, but realized that she had to learn more. The better she understood the contestants, the better equipped she would be to deal with them. So she would have to watch more of them coming up.

She got Chance squared away, then watched that day's contests. This time there were female challengers. The first one advanced on the male demon awaiting her. Both were naked, according to the competition rules. She was full breasted, actually more than full; her breasts sagged somewhat, borne down by their own masses, but were surely quite appealing to the male eye. She embraced him, pressing those big breasts against his chest. "You're such a virile hunk of a man," she said, farting enthusiastically. "I want to have a piece of you."

The demon's penis twitched as he let an answering fart; she had pushed a male button. But it did not become erect.

"Lie down here," she said, taking him by the hand. He obeyed, lying on his back. She kneeled beside him, her long black hair falling to cover him like a blanket, and stroked her hands across his chest and belly. "Oh, yes," she said. "You have a great big cock. I want to get it in my cunt."

Veil did not like the gutter terminology, but evidently it didn't bother the demon. His member swelled to half mast. Many men did like to hear women talk dirty.

"And handsome too," she continued, stroking his face. She kissed him on the mouth, lingeringly, her hair forming a tent across his face. The penis grew another notch. Yes, he was indeed programmed to respond to certain key stimuli.

The woman stroked his belly again, this time descending to his member. She lifted it in her fingers, admiring it, then put her mouth to it. She licked its tip, circled the glans with her tongue, and took it into her mouth. She sucked competently on it, and it swelled farther.

"Your virility has got me all worked up," she said. "Fuck me, before I die of deprivation." She lay on the bed beside him, lifting and spreading her legs invitingly.

The demon obliged. He got on her and inserted his penis an inch. "Oh, what a great pecker!" she said. "It just makes my pussy so hot. I've never had a better one in me. Give me some more, you manly man."

These were the correct words. The demon drove in another inch. Veil was impressed, not with the woman's too-obvious ploys, but with the precision of the control of the demon. He was doing exactly what the manual required for a given stimulus, not more, not less. He was now in about halfway, his member half visible.

"Oh, you're teasing me with that monster," the woman said. "Don't make me suffer longer! Shove your big lusty cock all the way into my hot wet cunt!"

The demon obliged. The woman moaned in simulated passion and wrapped her legs around him. "Fuck me harder!" she begged. "Pull it out, shove it in! Fuck me into my biggest orgasm. Jet your cum right into my eager crack!"

Again the demon obliged, thrusting repeatedly while she expressed continuing delight at his prowess. Veil nodded; the average man would do that, enjoying the experience even if he knew she was faking. The average man hardly cared whether the woman got any satisfaction out of the interaction, just as long as she was comely and willing. Or even if she wasn't willing. The mere availability of a vagina sufficed to put him into action.

The demon climaxed, pulling his penis out at the last moment so the spectators could see it jet. The woman had made him come within the time limit, and had qualified.

Except that there was another woman on the scene. She had long fair hair. That seemed to be a thing with the women of this culture: hair that was at least a yard long, worn loose. Veil realized that her own four foot long hair might have been an element in her desirability as a potential sex slave. Except that her captor had arranged to conceal it. That was an oddity; couldn't he have masked only her face?

Now the new woman approached the demon. "Normal sex is so boring," she said, farting sweetly. "I'll show you some kinky fun."

The demon merely looked at her. If she failed to make him climax on time, he would surely have some kinky fun with her. After seeing what the demoness had done to the losing male, Veil didn't care to guess what the demon would do to a helpless woman. So she found herself hoping that the woman would win through, despite her misgiving over the presence of any women in this contest. What would a woman want with another woman for a sex slave? She had to be an aggressive lesbian that other lesbians couldn't tolerate. Veil did not want to be the plaything of a brute man, but she was more averse to being the plaything of a twisted woman.

"Try some of this," the woman said, taking the demon's two hands. She planted them on her breasts, beneath her flowing tresses. "Squeeze them." He did. His penis thickened a notch; men did like to handle breasts. "And this," she said, taking his right hand and putting it to her mouth. She sucked on his thumb. His penis grew a bit more.

Now that was interesting, Veil thought. The thumb was an analogy of the penis; figuratively this was penis into vagina. The fact that it made him respond indicated that the demons were programmed for figurative as well as literal.

"And this," the woman said as she lay on the bed and lifted her legs. She brought his hand in to her genital region and slid his damp thumb into her vagina. "How's that feel, big man?" she asked as she worked it back and forth. She hardly needed to inquire; his penis had risen to half mast. The analogy was now only half analogy, as her vagina was the real thing. But where was she leading?

"Now let's get serious," the woman said. "Lie there." Obligingly, he lay on his back on the bed. She put her right thumb in her own mouth and worked it around. Then she put it to his anus, stroking it with saliva. "Loosen up that pucker, big man." He did, letting a fart swish out. She pushed her thumb into his rectum.

Well, this was different, Veil thought. But some men did like to be penetrated by women, in a kind of turnabout. Indeed, the demon's member stiffened the rest of the way. He was programmed for kinky sex too. But though his penis was now fully erect, she couldn't get it into her without removing her thumb.

She didn't try. Instead she bestrode him, facing away from his head, and brought his hand around and forced his thumb up her own anus. "Push it in there, deep as you can," she told him. He pushed, and it penetrated its full short length. Now they had exchanged asses, as it were.

Finally she put her head down and sucked on his phallus, framing it with her hair. At the same time her thumb was pumping in and out of his rectum, and his was doing the same with hers. She hollowed her cheeks, applying strong vacuum.

The triple stimulation was effective. In a moment the demon climaxed. His groin jumped as he thrust deeper into her mouth. His orgasm was manifest.

As his member spurted, she spat it out, so that it jetted on his own belly. She had made him come; this was the proof. But she left her thumb in his rectum, and kept his in hers for a moment longer, evidently enjoying the feel of both. Yes, she was into kinky sex. But she had defeated the demon.

Veil thought about that. The woman had never had the demon's penis in her vagina. She had put his thumb in her mouth, then in her vagina, and then into her rectum, and her thumb into his rectum. But she had finished him off with her mouth. This could mean that she didn't like having a man's member in her key orifice. Yet the way she had indulged in other interactions suggested that she was turned on by penetration. She might be seeking a woman to penetrate, in her peculiar fashion.

Veil had no intention of subjecting herself to that. Far easier to deal with a man, who generally lost interest after he jetted.

Now it was time for the two women to settle with each other. They would not be having sex, according to the rules, but a farting off, as the announcer explained. The winner would be the candidate for the day. Veil watched with a certain fascinated aversion.

They entered a spherical wire cage that rested on a wider floor. The door was latched. The two women faced each other, having room enough to stand but not to get more than an arm's length away from each other. They grappled. There was no scratching or hair pulling; this was not a fight but a competition. The first woman, who had seduced the demon in normal fashion, was of slighter build despite her larger breasts, and seemed to be at a disadvantage. Indeed, Kinky soon wrestled Normal to the floor, holding her upper body down by the weight of her body.

But neither was holding down the point. This was a farting contest, and Veil was more than curious to see how it proceeded. She knew there had to be some other move.

There was. Kinky, having pinned her opponent, wrestled around to get her posterior into place for an effective discharge. But Normal slid out from under, clasped her from behind, and rode her as she struggled to her feet.

After a moment, Normal dropped off and the two women faced each other again. "What happened there?" Veil asked.

"The prospective fart hold was broken," the announcer replied. "They wound up in a neutral position, from which neither could prevail. There's a fifteen minute time limit; if neither wins within that time, both lose. So there's no point in maintaining a bad position; they break and start over."

That made sense. Now came the second grappling. This time Normal made a sudden leap, caught the top of the cage, and swing her legs across to clamp on Kinky's head. That would put her anus directly into position. But Kinky countered by ducking down, and Normal missed the hold.

Kinky whirled and grabbed her from behind as she dropped down, swinging her around and lowering her to the floor. This time she had a better hold, and got her knees on Normal's arms so that her own arms could fend off Normal's attempt to bring her feet up for another head clamp. She slid forward, getting her bottom over Normal's face. Her anus dropped down close. It fluttered.

And Normal jerked her head up and plastered her mouth against that opening hole. She blew. Hard. Air pumped into the rectum, inflating it, diluting the fart gas.

"Nice ploy!" the announcer said enthusiastically. "Perfect timing."

Veil had to agree. But to put one's mouth tightly against another person's anus—that was dedication of a sort she herself would muster only with the greatest difficulty.

Kinky held her position, and in a moment Normal's lungs gave out and she had to let her head drop back to the floor. Now Kinky blew out her voluminously augmented fart, bathing Normal's face, and jumped off. The referee began the count. One. Two. Three. Four. Five.

Normal rolled to her feet and stood unsteadily. She had been stunned by the diluted gas, but not sufficiently to knock her out for the full count. Kinky did not go after her immediately, because she had expended her gas and needed time to regenerate. That gave Normal time to recover fully.

"Why didn't she hold her opponent down?" Veil asked.

"The requirement is that the fart alone must knock the other out," the announcer explained. "The count doesn't start until there is no body contact. That's why there are no fists or hard throws; they might contribute to the knockout, disqualifying it. This is a fart off, nothing else."

"But there is a time limit," Veil said.

"Yes, so they will go at it again soon. But now one has depleted her gas, while the other maintains hers. The advantage has shifted."

So it seemed. Normal stalked Kinky, looking for a takedown and hold. Then Kinky moved rapidly, catching her by arm and leg and pushing her to the floor. She dropped on Normal's belly so hard that the air whooshed out of her mouth.

"Trying to squeeze out her fart," the announcer explained. "It didn't work; she kept her sphincter tight."

Another interesting ploy. There was obviously some sophistication in these contests.

Kinky continued to hold Normal down, as she extended one arm and put her hand on the woman's crotch. She tried to get her finger into Normal's anus, to force it open so that it released its gas, but Normal locked her legs tightly together, preventing the other from achieving the necessary leverage. Meanwhile her own hands were moving around somewhat ineffectively.

Kinky gave it up and started to get up—and found herself entangled. Normal had knotted the end of her hair to Kinky's hair, and their two heads were linked together. Now Normal lifted one leg, passed her foot the other side of the hair connection, and brought it down again. Kinky's head was yanked down toward Normal's belly. Normal put her two hands onto the head and pushed it down into her crotch—just as she let fly with her fart.

Kinky was caught. She tried to hold her breath, but Normal tickled her ribs and she had to inhale to scream. She got a lungful and passed out.

Normal quickly untied the hair and got to her feet. The referee counted off ten seconds. She had won the fart off.

Veil concluded that she didn't want to be this woman's plaything either.

Chapter 9 – Trail

Prior set out along the Eeg trail in the morning. Oubliette had outfitted him with a knapsack and supplies, taking a solicitous interest in his welfare. He wondered why. She was a nice person, true, and she wanted to safeguard the Spire, but he knew she had little interest in him apart from that. There was something else. She had gotten an excellent sexual workout from the Spire, but even that did not quite account for her friendly attention. What else was she after? He trusted her; she would not do anything contrary to his welfare. But there was something.

WHAT A WOMAN, the Spire gouted.

"But what is on her mind?"

I REGRET I AM NOT A MIND READER. I CAN PICK UP YOUR THOUGHTS BECAUSE YOU ARE ATTACHED TO ME. BUT I COULD NOT PENETRATE HER UN-VOICED THOUGHTS. JUST ASPECTS OF HER MOOD. I AGREE THERE IS SOME-THING. NOT BAD. NO ILL WILL. JUST CURIOUS. THERE IS SOMETHING SHE WANTS ALMOST AS MUCH AS POSSESSION OF ME, THAT PERHAPS YOU CAN FACILI-TATE. THAT IS THE LIMIT OF MY UNDERSTANDING.

"Well, I hope I can facilitate it, and make her happy."

They came to the first statue. This was a lovely nude woman, her arms spread invitingly, her lips puckered for a kiss. He had seen that expression before; it meant she was expecting him.

"You know how to relate to the statues?" he asked the Spire.

OF COURSE. THEY ARE THE BASTARD OFFSPRING OF THE DEMONS OF THE FORMER CHERRY TREE, RENDERED INTO IMMOBILITY AND PLACED IN AS-SORTED PARKS.

"Yes, of course. I mean, according to Oubliette I need their help in finding the way to Fartingale. That means—"

CERTAINLY. THAT MEANS ANIMATING THEM, WHICH CAN BE DONE ONLY SEXUALLY. LEAVE IT TO ME. I WILL ANIMATE THEM AS NEVER BEFORE.

"Good enough." Prior unlimbered the cosmic dildo and let it project from the front of his trousers. He stepped into the lady statue. He kissed her stone cold lips, and they warmed slightly.

Then the Spire found the place and slid into her hard cleft, which instantly softened. It penetrated her melting vagina and gouted, once.

Suddenly she was fully warm and animate. "Oh, you marvelous man!" she exclaimed, kissing him fervently. "You have made a woman of me."

"It's the Spire," he said, knowing that the magic phallus had indeed done a job beyond the ability of any mortal man. When he had made out with her before, it had been a rather slow, difficult process, and she had spoken only one word before returning to stone.

"I know that, silly. I meant that you brought him to me. No one ever did that before. However can I reward you?" She hugged him closely, pressing her statuesque breasts against him.

"Just tell me the way to Fartingale."

She made a stony moue. "Stay here with me, and I'll give you much better sex than those smelly sluts."

"I have to go there to rescue my ideal woman."

"I could be your ideal woman, if you just keep My Lord Spire close." She guided one of his hands down to stroke her firm bare bottom.

She wanted to argue? "I'm sure you could, but I fear my destiny is there."

She pouted. "Oh, very well. I have put the path right. Go your way. But when you return—"

"You get another gout."

"Exactly." She kissed him again, ardently. It was almost possible to believe that she could indeed be suitable for him. Motivation was so important in a woman.

Then he drew the Spire out, and she reverted rapidly to stone. But there was a hint of rapture on her face; some of the Spire's gout remained in her crevice.

The trail did not seem to have changed, but Prior took it on faith. The next statue was a man, as he remembered, but he thought might be a different one. The other had wanted anal intercourse, which was not Prior's taste when it was his own anus in question.

I WILL DO IT. the Spire gouted.

Prior unlimbered the phallus of the Eldest God and approached the statue. He put the tip of the Spire to the statue's rear crevice. It found the place and nudged in, issuing a gout.

The statue came to life.

"I recognize that gout!" he said. "The Spire!"

"We're going to Fartingale."

"On your way," the man agreed.

The Spire withdrew, and the man became stone. His smile remained fixed as he reverted; his stone cold colon retained the hot gout.

The next statue was a female goat. Prior was sure it had been a sheep before, so the path really was changing. He stood behind the doe and inserted the Spire. In a moment the gout brought her to life.

"The Spire is the best buck fuck in the universe," she remarked, her interior squeezing it.

Prior was startled. He hadn't expected her to speak fully human. But of course she was really a demoness. "We're going to—"

"Yes, of course. It is there for you."

They moved on, encountering increasingly different statues; there was now no question that the path was changing. The original trail had led to the Eggers; this one led, he hoped, to Fartingale. And the Spire, with its eternal potency and conducive effect, was indeed making progress much easier.

Then they came to the mermaid. She was a stone statue with her tail immersed in a stone pool. How were they to get at her business end?

KISS HER.

He did, and her face softened and warmed. Then the Spire made a drop-sized gout onto the water—and it clarified, becoming transparent in a widening circle. Soon the mermaid was floating in real water. She remained stone, however.

Prior doffed his trousers and climbed into the pool. He found the place under water just below the beginning of her scaled tail and infiltrated the tip of the Spire into it. It forged slowly into the softening channel there until it reached minimum operative depth, then gouted.

The mermaid's tail flexed, and the member was suddenly forging twice as far into her. Her arms closed around Prior. Her lovely full breasts heaved. "More," she murmured.

The Spire gouted again. The mermaid kissed Prior. "Oh, it's been so long," she said. "Hardly anyone uses this trail these days. And you—you've got the Spire, you lucky man."

"We're going to Fartingale."

"Where?"

"It's a magic land where farts are common."

"How uncouth." She used her comb to straighten out his hair. "Whyever would a wonderful man like you want to go to a dreary place like that?"

Prior realized she was stalling, to make the Spire stay longer. But her breasts were very sleek and soft, her hands caressing his face and neck, and her hidden groin was stroking the embedded member. It was easy to allow this dialogue to continue. "I have to rescue my ideal woman."

She frowned. "Don't you realize that's a miscue? What can she offer you that I can't?"

"Legs?"

"Oh, who cares about legs! Nothing matches a great piece of tail." She squeezed the Spire again, evocatively.

"Well, I'm really not a great swimmer."

"I could help you there. Suck on my breasts."

"Excuse me?"

She caught his head in her hands and bore it down to her left breast, just above the water line, setting his mouth against the nipple. "Breathe."

He tried it, dubiously. Highly oxygenated air come into his mouth and lungs. He drew on it harder, and the breath of life flowed into him. This was wonderful!

She cradled his head with her arms. "All this can be yours, you nice mortal man. You can sleep in my loving embrace at the bottom of the sea, safe and warm and in perpetual erotic delight. What more could you ask?"

It was rather tempting. But he knew that the moment the Spire withdrew, she would become stone again. It simply wasn't feasible.

"I know what you're thinking," she said. "That I have a heart of stone. But if you can get your friend the Spire to give me larger gouts where I can keep them for a while, such as in my other aperture, I can last a day or so between refuelings, and be everything to you."

Is that true? he asked the Spire.

YES. it gouted, providing the mermaid with another thrill. **BUT YOU WOULD STILL BE LIMITED TO THE SEA.**

"But you'd be with *me*!" she protested.

He removed his mouth from her rich nipple. "And I couldn't breathe underwater unless nursing from you."

To his surprise, she nodded. "It wouldn't work, unless you transformed into a merman. Of course that would happen if you nursed long enough."

Her fresh air would transform him to half a fish? "Uh, thanks all the same, no."

She didn't fuss; she had expected his demurral. "But it's been great. If you should ever change your mind, I'll be here." She caught his head and kissed him again.

At that point the Spire withdrew, and her lips hardened. **NO DEMON CAN GIVE YOU TRUE HAPPINESS.** it gouted.

It was surely true. But Prior felt almost guilty about leaving the expressive mermaid.

They moved on, interacting with assorted statues. Then they came to a centaur filly. She was a problem, because her human fore section was well removed from her equine hind section. He wasn't sure a gout in the rear would bring her to life all the way to the front. How could he talk with her?

IT IS FEASIBLE. the Spire assured him. **IT WILL REQUIRE A FAIR INFUSION. BUT YOU WILL BE ABLE TO ANIMATE HER FACE.**

"If you say so," Prior agreed doubtfully. He approached the centaur's posterior.

It was too high for him to reach. He had to scout for some separate stones to pile behind the statue. He stood on them, and was able to get there. He fed the Spire under her tail and into her huge vaginal orifice.

A small gout softened the stone, allowing further entry. A second gout animated the interior, and finally the Spire penetrated to its full length. Prior stood there, his crotch up against the statue.

Now the Spire started gouting in earnest. It sent surges in, filling the chamber. There seemed to be plenty of room for more. The furry flank softened and warmed. Color came to the hide, coursing from the tail on up toward the front.

The centaur bent. The frozen human section was carried around to the left. With each gout it moved farther, until the torso formed a huge U. The stone forelegs, breasts, and face came around to face Prior. But the eyes remained blank.

Oh. He leaned to the side and into her and managed to reach her face with his mouth. His groin remained attached to hers, so the position was awkward, but feasible. He kissed her lips at a slightly skew angle.

They warmed. "Thank you, Prior," she said. "It is kind of you to animate me, however briefly."

"You know my name!" he exclaimed.

She laughed, her huge breasts bouncing. "The Spire told me, with his gouts. They can be very communicative. The news reached my brain before you freshened my face."

That seemed to make sense, in this context. "Then you know that we—"

"Yes, of course, and I have already fixed the path. Your next statue will be there. I do appreciate this visit."

"Uh, sure, welcome." He was at a lost for useful words.

She smiled and kissed him again. "You are so pleasantly naïve. Now if you will excuse me, I must return to form before the Spire withdraws, so I will be a presentable statue."

"That's fine," he said lamely. These statues had a lot more personality than he had anticipated, this time around.

She got straight, the Spire sent one more gout and withdrew. She smiled, then slowly congealed.

At last they came to a huge statue of a naked man sitting on a toilet, leaning forward in deep concentration. His right elbow rested on his right knee, his hand supporting his forehead. It was clear that he had some truly weighty matter on his noble mind.

THAT'S THE STINKER, the spire gouted. **HE GUARDS THE ACCESS TO FARTINGALE. YOU MUST PUT ME IN YOUR RECTUM NOW.**

Somehow this did not appeal to Prior. He didn't mind using the Spire to fill other rectums, but he preferred to keep his own clear. "I'll just walk past without activating him."

YOU'LL BE SORRY. But the Spire did not try to stop him.

Prior started to circle the statue. There was a sound like a cosmic section of cloth ripping, and a truly appalling stench wafted out from the toilet. Prior caught one whiff, gagged, and fell to the ground, retching.

After a while the potent gas dissipated, and he was able to recover enough to climb back on his feet. "I got the message." He dropped his pants, un-screwed the Spire, screwed a six inch circumcised member on, then gingerly poked the tip of the Spire into his anus.

NOT THAT WAY, IDIOT. it gouted, jetting a jot of goo on the resistive pucker. **I MUST POINT OUTWARD.**

Oh. Of course. He reversed the implement. But now he had another problem: its substantial base was far too wide to pass the sphincter. But then the Spire shrank to much smaller size, and he was able to slide it in. Once there, he felt it expanding again, shaping itself to his rectum so that it was firmly anchored, with the tip just shy of the anus. It was oddly comfortable.

NOW I WILL SALUTE THE STINKER.

Prior bent over so that his posterior faced the statue. The Spire emitted a whistling peal of gas that formed a small cloud and drifted up to puff into the statue's face.

The effect was immediate. The face came to life. "The Spire!" the Stinker said. "What an honor."

NOW TALK TO HIM.

Prior pulled up his pants, turned around, and spoke. "Uh, hello. I'm Prior Gross. I need to go to Fartingale to rescue my ideal woman."

"And the Spire farts for you," the Stinker said. "Of course you may pass." He eyed Prior. "But waste no time in getting appropriate clothing. The natives don't much like strangers unless they come bearing gold, sex slaves, or superlative farts."

"Thank you. I will do my best."

The statue solidified. Prior walked by it. This time it let him pass. He had made it to Fartingale.

Chapter 10—Interviews

It was the fourth day of her confinement, and Veil was not optimistic about her fate. She was unable to tell whether the fourth qualifying candidate, a man of middle age, was intellectual, as the contest did not test that quality.

But perhaps she could find out. She would interview the first four qualifiers, and discover whether any of them were remotely acceptable. She hoped for one she would be able to tolerate, as a fall-back choice in case the three qualifiers to come turned out to be even worse.

She tackled them in turn. The first was a rather brutish looking man with a huge gut capable of generating formidable gas, as she had seen in the playback video. She did not ask his name; she thought of him as Gut. He was admitted to the residential intestine with the understanding that the interview was under the control of the Maiden, and any untoward move could disqualify him.

"May the farts be with you," he said jovially, letting a moderately loud one out.

"And with you," she agreed politely. She doubted she would ever be entirely easy with this social convention, but it was necessary to honor the local forms. She forced herself, and managed to emit a ladylike break of wind.

"You're a great looking dame," he remarked. "Good boobs, good buns, great ass."

"Thank you." He was truly meaning to compliment her.

"I'll fart with you anytime."

It was time to get to business. "As you know," she said delicately, "I am the anonymous Maiden in the Tower. I must choose one of seven to be my sex master for the coming year. I wish to know more about you, to determine whether we might be compatible."

"Compatible, shmatible," he said derisively, blowing out another solid fart. "I got a cock, you got a cunt, we both got assholes. What's to compat?

My pecker'll fit, even if your pussy is small; I just have to jam it in hard enough."

This did not seem promising. But she was determined to conceal her private reactions. "True, and I'm sure the fit will be adequate to satisfy you. But there are other things in a relationship than sex and intestinal gas."

His jaw dropped. "There are?"

"I believe so. What do you propose to do after you have satisfied your lust on my limp body?"

"What'll I do? What kind of fucking question is that? I'll sleep, of course, then fuck you again."

"Would you wish me to reciprocate?"

"Huh?"

"To have enjoyment of the act too."

He was baffled. "Why would I want that?"

"It is thought that a man's pleasure is greater if the woman shares it."

He pondered. "Yeah, maybe worth trying, once, just for the feel. You could sit on my cock and jack yourself off, and your clenching would make me come. Might be fun."

"It might indeed," she agreed, and terminated the interview.

The second man was halfway handsome and certainly manly. He understood the meaning of the word 'compatibility' but felt there would be no problem. "I don't need or want your interest," he said. "Merely your acquiescence. You obviously have the body. I would have no trouble getting off with you. But mainly it's your prospective appeal to other men that I want. I could make some handsome money farming you out, especially considering your notoriety as a Tower Maiden."

She was appalled. "You wish to prostitute me?"

"Yes. I figure you could take on maybe a dozen men in a day, each of them paying well. Of course you would have to satisfy them, or I would revoke the deal."

"But what of the risk of venereal disease?"

"What of it? If you got it, I would not let you tell the clients, though I would have to stop patronizing you myself. It's a calculated risk; chances are I would have had enough of you by then anyway." He farted indifferently.

Somehow she was not any more eager to go with this man than the first. "Thank you for clarifying that. May the farce be with you." She couldn't bring herself to say it properly. Fortunately she got away with it; he heard what he expected to hear. Perhaps her accompanying flatulence masked the word.

The third candidate was the woman Normal. "No, actually I'm not lesbian," she said, after they had exchanged greeting farts. "I have an apt husband."

Veil was surprised, but not yet relieved. "Then why do you want a sex slave?"

"It's like this: he's manly and gentle, the perfect lover, and he takes good care of me. But just straight sex doesn't turn me on. He likes a turned-on woman, so I'm not very good for him. But he has excellent qualities, and I want to keep him. When I caught him seducing one of the maids I had a revelation."

"That he was unfaithful," Veil agreed.

"That, too. But it didn't really bother me, because I knew I wasn't giving him what he needed. That servant girl was only sixteen, and not really well endowed, and frankly rather homely of feature, but she put a lot of enthusiasm into it. It was obvious that she really liked sex. She just couldn't get enough of his penis. In fact he just lay there, and she played with it, sucked it, and finally impaled her hole on it just before he spurted. She wrapped her legs around him and kept kissing him, even after he had spent. And do you know what?"

"It must have given you some excellent ideas for your own performance."

"Yes, but not in the way you might think. I was horribly turned on, watching it. So much so that I sent the maid to her room and addressed him myself. He was amazed, and it took about fifteen minutes to work him up, because he had expended his semen. But I was so avid that he recovered, and then we had a great mutual climax. The time it took was just enough for me to achieve my own orgasm, and he loved having it with me."

Veil nodded. "Normally it's the man who gets turned on by watching his wife have sex with another man, but it can work either way. That seems to have solved your problem."

"Yes and no," Normal said candidly. "I had to fire the maid, because I can't have my husband sexing around promiscuously; he might decide to leave me for a more turned-on woman. Yet I also need him to do it in my presence with another woman, for the stimulation it provides me, and for the time it enables me to have him. He is unable to do it in a minute when he has just spent, enabling me to address him in leisurely manner. So I need a woman with no ambitions of that nature, who is aesthetic, and under my control. Thus my interest in you."

Now this was an interesting prospect. "Would you wish me to have sex with any other man?"

"Heavens no! You must be only for my husband, and only when I am present. You would be required to rebuff him if he wished to have sex any other time. The rest of the time you could do whatever you wished, being fully cared for, provided you kept yourself clean, comely, and mannered. No servant duties. For the year. Thereafter if I wished to maintain the arrangement, I would have to pay you a standard mistress wage."

This seemed to be a prospect. But Veil was not keen on playing such a role if she could avoid it. "Thank you," she said, concluding the interview.

The fourth candidate was a man of about her own age, muscular, healthy, and well spoken. "Compatibility hardly matters," he said after their social farts cleared. "I will provide you with your own suite and servants. Your baby will be well attended. I do not wish to socialize with you. I need you only for sex."

"With you alone?" she inquired cautiously.

He considered. "Well, I suppose if you wished to have a boyfriend on the side, that would be satisfactory, provided he did not intrude on my time."

"I mean, you would not expect me to prostitute myself to make money for you."

"Horrors, no! I have no need of money. I am wealthy. I merely will need you to be sexually available to me at all times, day and night."

"This is my understanding of sex slavery."

"Perhaps. Here is the constraint: I am highly sexed. I have worn out two wives, because they could not keep up. I dislike using prostitutes; they can be uncouth or unclean. I need a constant woman."

"Just how often were you thinking of?"

"Normally, four times a day and once at night. It is difficult for me to go more than six hours without sex, and shorter periods are preferable. Thus it would be morning, noon, afternoon, evening, and midnight. Sometimes more often, as anything can set me off. My second wife departed after I required sex of her three times within a ten minute span while we were watching an erotic play. That's why you would need to be steadily on hand. There may be only a minute's notice; you must be ready at all times."

"But when not with you, I could do what I want, provided I remain close enough to join you immediately?"

"Correct. If you wish entertainment, I can't allow you to depart the house unless it is in my company—and there will no foolishness about refusing sex in a coach or a concert booth or even standing in an open field if that is where the call comes. The entertainment will be brought to you, and perhaps I will share it with you if it interests me. You will not be denied anything. Neither will you be bound; if you have genuine need to travel, such as to attend an ill relative, you will merely so acquaint me, and I will accompany you there. I mean you no discomfort. I merely must know that your sexual favor is never denied me."

Veil happened to know something about sexual precocity. There were indeed highly sexed men, but normally their urges abated somewhat when reliably and competently accommodated. Frequent repetitions occurred when the sexual episodes were less than satisfactory. She could make them satisfactory. This might be as good a way to spend the year as any. She saw that the man's pantaloons were bulging; the mere discussion of sex had stimulated him, as was the case with many men. That gave her a notion.

"I am minded to give you a try," she said. "Without as yet making any commitment, as three candidates remain to be selected. Do you wish sex at this moment?"

"I do." As if there could be any other response.

"Then join me now on the bed." She had learned from the announcer that this too was permitted; it was considered an optional part of the interviewing process. She stepped out of her farthingale, baring her nether region, blew out accumulated gas, and lay supine on the bed.

He joined her immediately, his penis springing erect from his pantaloons. She was relieved to see that it was an ordinary member, not oversized or misshapen. He got down on her and guided it to her vulva, then plunged it into her vagina. She felt his emission on the first thrust.

Then he withdrew and stood again, putting his spent member away. "Much appreciation," he said.

It had been so fast she had hardly gotten her bearings. It had been like a hypodermic injection, in, discharge, and out. She quickly mopped herself and donned the skirt again, returning to perch on the farthingale stool. "This is your normal mode?"

"Yes. I do not waste time."

"Let me know when your desire rises again."

"Thank you. I will. It is kind of you to accommodate me." He issued a gratified fart.

She wanted to discover whether he slowed, after relieving himself, and whether he truly recovered swiftly. She needed to know whether his four or five times a day would ease off to once or twice, once the edge was off. She questioned him on details of his household.

Then, barely five minutes along, he expressed his renewed interest. "By all means," she agreed, removing the skirt again. This time she did not take the couch, but stood waiting for him, to see how he would handle it. He had after all mentioned doing it standing in a field.

He didn't hesitate. He bent his knees, produced his erect penis, and wedged it up into her moist cleft. He penetrated her with a single trust, jetting as he did. And withdrew immediately.

She mopped herself again; there had indeed been an emission. This time she left her skirt off, and sat on the couch, crossing her bare legs.

He looked. "If you would be so kind—"

That was only about one minute. Was he bluffing? "By all means." She stood.

He was into her again, and jetting, and withdrawing.

Intrigued, she continued to question him, while quietly assuming provocative poses. They were effective. They had sex three more times in fifteen minutes. The last one was slower: it required two thrusts, and the emission was only a token. But it had definitely occurred.

"I must say, you are very understanding," he said. "You are a most attractive and accommodating woman. I would like very much to have you with me for the year."

"How did you make it past the demoness? I watched the video, and you did not seem to spurt prematurely then."

"That's the key: she *is* a demoness. Not a real woman. Such an emulation does not turn me on, whatever her appearance. No more than a statue or a man turns me on. I was able to get an erection by laboring diligently to pretend she was real, but I could not climax. The rest was merely a matter of going through the motions. The point, after all, is that *she* climax, not the man."

That was a subtlety she hadn't properly picked up on before. "Do you ever actually make love?" she asked. "By that I mean, taking time for a single incident of sexual expression, not with a demoness, but with a real woman. Kissing, stroking, embracing."

"No. That is impossible for me. I climax too soon. If I do not get inside the woman, I spend into the air, which is frustrating and embarrassing."

She could appreciate that. It meant that sex with this man was indeed only that, and only for him; the woman got nothing from it because it was too fast for her to respond. Did she want that for a year, even if everything else was nice? Only, she concluded, if she had no better alternative.

"I think I know enough," she said. "Let's do it once more, so that you can make it home without frustration, and end this interview."

"Gladly. He jammed into her, jetted, and departed.

There would be three more candidates. She hoped at least one was better, but knew there was no guarantee.

Chapter 11—Fartingale

Prior reached the village of Nude-on-Toilet shortly before dusk. This featured a statue vaguely similar to that of The Stinker, but smaller, with a nude young woman sitting on a toilet. She was pretty, with well formed breasts, a small waist, and very nice slightly-spread thighs. From the toilet bowl came a melody fashioned from delicate farts of different pitches. There was an odor of sweet violets.

The statue was at the community center, which of course surrounded the public privy. Folk were gathering for the evening socializing. The men wore colorful pantaloons, the women farthingales. Many of the latter were bare breasted.

THAT MEANS THEY'RE AVAILABLE FOR CASH OR BARTER, the Spire gouted quietly in his bowel. **YOU WANT TO FART FOR FOOD AND FLAT, NOT FUCKS.**

"Ah, right," Prior agreed, half reluctantly. Some of the revealed upper sections were fetching, and the nether sections too, when the women happened to pass between him and a light so that the bell-shaped skirts became translucent, verging on transparent.

A lovely woman approached him, her full breasts playing peek-a-boo behind her veil of hair. She issued an inviting fart. **NO GOOD,** the Spire gouted. **SHE'LL ROLL YOU.**

Prior turned away, letting out the Spire's negative fart, and the woman retreated.

A second beauty oriented on him, wafting a fart that smelled of roses. Her breasts were painted silver with bright red nipples. **NO GOOD.**

Prior wasn't sure how the Spire knew, but had to trust its judgment. He faced away, blowing aversion.

I CAN SMELL THEM, the Spire explained. **I ANALYZE THEIR FARTS AND ASCERTAIN THEIR PERSONALITIES.**

There was more to farting than Prior had realized.

A third one came, hesitantly. **HER.** Prior did not turn away.

"May the farts be with you, stranger," she said politely, letting out a small ladylike fart.

"And with you," he replied, doing the same in a more masculine tone. He found this social custom quaint.

"You look in need," she remarked. Her breasts were full and bouncy, making up for an ordinary face and hair that was less than lustrous, though it did reach to her bottom. "You must be here for the fair tomorrow. I am Smellie."

There was a fair? He wasn't here for entertainment. He needed to locate the maiden in the Tower as soon as possible. "I'm Micro." That was the name he had decided to use here, as part of his anonymity. It referred to his small natural penis, though he wasn't wearing it now. "I just need food and lodging for the night."

She considered. "I have food and a bed. You have gold?"

"No," he replied, embarrassed.

"Then what do you have to offer, Micro?"

A MAGIC FART.

"A magic fart," Prior echoed, not certain what it meant.

"Magic in what manner?"

"It will put you into delight for the night," he said, prompted by the Spire.

"I'll risk it. But if it doesn't, you'll have to scrub the floor."

He followed her to her house, which was nearby. Inside, she shut the door and faced him. "Demonstrate."

The Spire let out a squeaker. It spread into the air of the room, with a faint musty odor. This wasn't promising.

But the woman smiled. "A joy fart! You've got a joy fart!"

YOU ARE IMMUNE TO ITS EFFECT. the Spire explained. **PARTLY BECAUSE OF YOUR SMEGMA (WHICH YOUR REMAINING GENITAL FLESH STILL PRODUCES DESPITE THE FACT YOU ARE NOT NOW WEARING YOUR NATURAL PENIS). MOSTLY BECAUSE I AM IMMUNE TO MY OWN EMISSIONS, LEST THERE BE PARADOX. AND THAT CARRIES ACROSS TO YOU. PRETEND YOU'RE FEELING GOOD.**

Prior smiled. "As I said, magic."

"Well, you'll certainly do. I haven't smelled a joy fart in years. In fact we don't see a lot of magic here in the hindland." She bustled about, rousting up a meal for them. "You just sit down and keep that hot air coming while I set up."

He sat the indicated chair, and the Spire continued a moderate emission. Smellie hummed a tune as she worked. It was halfway familiar, but he couldn't quite place it. "What is that melody?"

"My theme song." She sang the words of the refrain: "And 'twas from Aunt Dinah's farting party I was seeing Smellie home."

Now he placed it. The variant he knew referred to a quilting party and

Nellie.

They had a meal of beans and cabbage juice. It was what she had. His gut roiled up, but of course all the food in this land did that. Just so long as he could pass his natural gas without blowing the Spire out. It seemed okay; the Spire continued a low volume emission of joy farts, and that kept Smellie smiling. Her life remained bleak, but she was on a sustained high.

They talked, and he learned that the village had a monthly fair for entertainment, contests, and business. It was designed to attract tourists, so that the village could profit.

"I'm just passing through. I need to find the Maiden in the Tower."

"Oh, for that you need to go to the Maid-in-Tower Village. They have a new Maiden every week."

"Every week? What happens to her?"

"Each day there's competition, with one candidate qualifying. On the seventh day she must choose which one will be her master for a year."

"Her master?"

"She's his sex slave. They generally have good-looking anonymous Maidens who have been abducted for the purpose."

"Abducted!" he exclaimed as if surprised. "You mean this is involuntary?"

"Of course. That makes them more appealing. But it's a recognized device; they have no choice but to carry through."

"I should think there would be outrage by their families and friends."

"Sure. That's why they aren't taken from the local village unless they volunteer, as some do. They are fetched in from far away."

Prior saw how it could have happened to someone from his realm, if that was the case. Was she really his ideal woman, or was that just propaganda spread about to many men to garner more interest? He would simply have to rescue her and hope for the best. "Where is the Tower Village?"

"That's three days trek from here, unless you have a fast steed or magic."

Three days! That gave him barely enough time, as he had only a week to rescue the Maiden. "I don't have a steed or that kind of magic. Is there any shortcut?"

"Sure. Win a ride on the Fart Blimp. It can take you there in one day."

THIS IS FEASIBLE. the Spire gouted.

"Thanks, I'll do that."

When they had eaten, they repaired to the public privy, entering it together and taking adjacent holes. Smellie let out quite a load, by the sound of it, clearing her body for the night. Prior eased his gas and turds out around the Spire, discovering that there was no difficulty; the magic implement knew how to stay in place.

People glanced at them, paying no special attention. Crapping together in the public privy was a signal that they were a couple, at least for the night. **FOLK WHO SHIT TOGETHER, FIT TOGETHER,** the Spire opined, evidently quoting a local maxim.

Prior glanced at the statue of the nude. "She's beautiful. Was she modeled from a real person?"

"Yes, of course. Every year we have a contest for comely young women posing bare on the toilet, and the loveliest wins the title of Mistress of the Village and the statue is sculpted to conform to her image. It's a great honor, and more."

"More? In what sense is she mistress?"

"Every sense. She becomes the leading citizen, making key decisions for the village, with a stipend so that she does not have to work at any other trade. She also has her choice of men, single or married, a different one each night if she wishes, for that year's fucking. The men are normally glad to do it; it's not considered a breach of their marital state, but a civic duty, and their wives are honored. She also entertains traveling men who pass this way; it brings a number who might otherwise select a different route, and the village gets their business. When her year as Mistress expires, she may choose any one of the men she has fucked to marry. Oh, I would have loved to be the Mistress, as any girl would, but of course that was a laughable dream."

Prior avoided the need to agree. "I'm a traveler. She didn't choose me."

"She's ill and wants to retire. Soon there'll be another contest to select her replacement."

"Ill?"

Smellie smiled. "Euphemism for knocked up. It happens. She can't marry her lover until she steps down."

"Now I understand. Don't girls have ways to avoid pregnancy?"

"There are spells. But sometimes they forget."

They settled together on her bed. He saw that it was bumpy, with a ragged blanket. It was what she had. She did not complain, but it was clear she had reason to prostitute herself to traveling men; she needed to survive.

"How would you like me?" she asked, with a petite fart of invitation. "I can do it any way you want."

"Actually, all I need is food and board, and you have provided that. You don't have to have sex with me."

"Oh no! You're gay!"

"No, just trying to be reasonable. All I paid for was food and bed—and I fear you have little in either respect."

"Oh, please, don't leave now! I know it's not great, but it's all I have. I can make it up by giving you great sex, so you'll have no complaint."

She thought he was seeking a pretext to go elsewhere. Rather than argue, he clasped her. She met him eagerly, and they proceeded to the best natural sex he'd had in some time, because he wasn't using the Spire for it. Nothing fancy, just a simple stroking of her nice breasts, kissing her face, easing his member into her receptive cleft, thrusting, and ejaculating. All perfectly ordinary, but nice.

Then he realized that she had not joined him in the climax. He had come to depend on the Spire to thrill the women it touched, but he wasn't using that now. "I'm sorry; I was forgetting your share. That was selfish of me."

"Oh, I should have faked it," she said, chagrined. "It was so nice having unkinky sex for once, I forgot."

"You're not frustrated?"

She laughed. "I never come. It would distract me from properly catering to the needs of my guests. If you want to do it again, I'll make sure to give a better performance."

"No need. You were good as you were."

"It's nice of you to say that. You're a nice man."

As he sank into sleep, against her obliging body, he addressed the Spire: *She's a good person, doing what she has to. I want to help her.*

YOU ARE BECOMING SOFT HEADED. SHE'S A WHORE.

Maybe so. But also a decent human being. What can I do for her?

ENTER SOME CONTESTS TOMORROW AT THE FAIR. WIN HER SOME STAPLES.

I will. Then, satisfied, he slept.

In the morning he saw that his clothing was undisturbed; she had not sought to steal anything. She served him gruel: all she had. "I have paid you with joy farts," he said carefully. "Now I am minded to hire you to show me around the fair tomorrow. I will pay you in goods you need, that I can win in contests."

She looked at him. "Why?"

"I appreciate being treated decently. You didn't try to rob me or cheat me, and you gave me more than I paid for. I will stay another night with you, and try to leave you satisfied that I was here."

She shrugged. "All right." He knew she was trying to figure the catch.

The fair was impressive. There were impromptu singing groups doing feeling renditions of "Fart of my Fart" and "Beer Farts and Gutsy People." There were acappella farting groups. There were sexy bare-bottomed dances.

"Everything's here," Smellie said. "Depending on your taste."

"Blankets."

She guided him to a stall where many excellent blankets were available. "What blanket would you take for yourself, price no object?" he asked.

She laughed, think it a joke. "That one."

Prior addressed the proprietor. "May the farts be with you," he said, emitting a small fart. The Spire had prepared him for this. "I wish to purchase that blanket. I offer a jug of Joy Fart."

"You have magic?" the man asked, squinting.

"He sure does," Smellie said. "I boarded him last night, and he kept me happy the whole time."

"Give me a sniff."

"One sniff," Prior agreed, turning around and bending over. The man put his nose down near his pantaloons. The Spire emitted a tiny fart.

"That's Joy!" the man agreed immediately. "But that's my best blanket. Three jugs."

"Two," Prior said, knowing that bargaining was expected.

"Two. But they have to sniff good."

Prior put his anus to a two-spouted jug. His fart went into one spout, forcing air out the other. When the Joy started coming through, the man clapped caps on both spouts. "How much time do you need to recharge?"

"I've got a good load of gas. I can do it now." He filled the second jug.

The man gave him the blanket. Prior gave it to Smellie. "Take it home, then return to me here. We have more shopping to do."

Amazed, she accepted, hurrying home with the blanket.

"You got it for her?" the man asked, surprised.

"She's a good woman."

"Sure, but her face is plain."

"So is mine."

Soon Smellie returned. "Now food," Prior said.

"But you've already paid me far more than I deserve."

"I'm paying you for your guidance. It's a day's work."

Still dubious, she took him to a stall where there were many kinds of beans. Prior bought several packages with more joy farts, and helped her carry them home.

"I don't get it," she said.

He told her as much more of the truth as he thought was wise. "I'm here on a personal mission. I have special magic for this occasion. Once it's done, I won't have it any more. So I might as well use it to help a nice woman. It's free, for me."

"You can get a slew of beautiful women, for what you're giving me."

"Can I trust any of them without watching them?"

She was silent a moment. "No. But how did you know you could trust me?"

"It's a magic sense I have. You proved out, and I appreciate it."

She shook her head. "I've never been rewarded for being trustworthy before."

"And maybe never again. But this time you are."

She considered. "May I kiss you?"

"We kissed often enough last night."

"I mean in public, so others see."

Ah. "Sure."

She did so, and there was a stir. Others had been paying more attention than he had realized. Probably news of his magic farts had gotten around.

"But you know I'm moving on to rescue the Maiden in the Tower," he reminded her. "I'm not staying here."

"Yes, of course. Who would want to stay with me?"

"I didn't mean it like that."

"I know. But it's true. I'm strictly a waystation woman. That's why I appreciate being treated like a person. It doesn't happen often."

"You're a nice person. You could make some man a good wife."

"So can any number of women with prettier faces."

Can we help her? he asked the Spire.

YOU'RE AN IDIOT.

Answer the damn question.

YES. I COULD GENERATE A MAGIC FART THAT WOULD MELT HER FACE AND SET GUIDELINES FOR A BETTER ONE. SHE'D HAVE TO PROTECT IT FOR SEVERAL DAYS. BUT THEREAFTER SHE'D BE BEAUTIFUL.

Prior nodded. He'd make the offer when it seemed appropriate.

"Now let's tour the fair," he said.

She hesitated. "Everything's centered around the privy. You can find whatever you want without my help."

"I thought I was buying your service as a tour guide. Are you reneging?"

"No! It's just that—well, I'm a—you know. Everyone knows it. To have me with you, treating me like a date, that could fart off your reputation in a hurry. You've been so good to me, I don't want to do you ill in return."

She was definitely not cut out to be a mean whore. "What do I care? Tomorrow I'll be gone."

"You *should* care." But she dropped the subject.

They toured the fair. They stopped to eat fartburgers, drink fartfrappes, and nibble on pot cheese. All these generated generous quantities of gas, which they blew out with abandon. Prior saw a poster saying THE FAMILY THAT FARTS TOGETHER, STARTS TOGETHER. They were honoring its windy spirit.

There were shows galore. One was a little play featuring a man with a tremendous penis. "I'll marry any woman who can handle this," he proclaimed. One woman tried, bending over so he could penetrate her from behind, but barely half the member got into her before it balked. Another tried, and a bit more than half got in.

The third woman was more confident. "Sit down and lean back," she said. He did so, and she stood over him, then lowered herself onto his member so that her own weight bore her down. Inch by inch she took it in, until at the end she reached down, grabbed his thighs, and hauled herself onto the last two inches. "There!" she said victoriously.

"No fair," someone called. "She's using leverage. Make her let go." Reluctantly the woman did—and she flew up off the phallic pole, propelled by the recoil.

"That's all right," the man said. "It was the force of my ejaculation that did it, she's such a good fuck."

There was applause for the act. Obviously no ejaculation could have thrown her whole body up like that; she had jumped. But it was a nice punchline.

"Actually I once had a harder fuck," the woman said, going into the next stage of the act. "My boyfriend didn't have the biggest cock, but he was really enthusiastic. He fucked me so hard that when he was done, he had to pull out his cock, both balls, and half of his asshole."

Laughter. Two more people came on stage. "You never fucked *me* that hard," the new woman to her man.

"Well, I would have, but my farts would have blown you up like a balloon." More laughter, as they had topped the prior joke by suggesting that not only could the man have thrust so hard as to get his entire rectum into her, he would then have farted and inflated her. Realistic anatomy be damned.

"Then there's the time I had constipation," the woman on stage continued. "For two months I couldn't pass anything, not even a fart. So finally the doctor gave me a pill. Not just any pill; it was the hydrogen bomb of laxatives, with a count down of exactly twenty four hours." She looked at her watch. "Come to think of it, that was yesterday. You'd better fuck me within the next two minutes and get out of here, because you don't want to be at ground zero when it detonates."

"I don't believe it," the man said. "I'll fuck you any time I want." He unlimbered his large member in leisurely fashion.

"One minute," she said, her eye still on the watch. "Maybe you'd better postpone it, because I can't be responsible for what happens at zero time."

"Forget it," he said, pushing his penis slowly into her as she bent over to accommodate him. Their positions were carefully structured to provide the audience a clear view of the genital contact. Prior realized that the jokes were merely the pretext for the sexual display. It was working; he was turned on.

"Thirty seconds. And don't pump, because any little vibration could set it off prematurely."

"You can't scare me," he said, and made a huge forceful thrust.

There was a bright flash, a crack of noise, and a thick cloud of smoke. By the time it dissipated all that remained on the stage was a head-high pile of fecal matter.

More applause. That had been a fine act. They must have used the smoke to clamber through a trap door, and shoved out the pile. It had also been one fine fuck while it lasted.

Prior and Smellie moved on. There was a seduction contest, where the men stood on one side of a glass wall, their limp penises poking through suitably placed holes. Each woman did a strip-tease dance. The winner would be the one who managed to make a penis spurt without touching it. The audience was mostly women; it occurred to Prior that they might be studying technique.

Several women were able to make the members stiffen admirably, but none jetted. Finally a truly sexy creature came on the scene and performed a dance of such passion that Prior himself was stimulated painfully. "Um," he murmured.

"Got it," Smellie said. She hoisted up her farthingale, stepped into him, turned, and got his stiff member into her cleft just in time for it to spurt. Then she pulled herself off, dropped her skirt, and stood as if nothing had happened. No one had noticed; they were watching the dancer, who finally did make a penis spurt without touching. She had won.

Now the women of the audience forged in, advancing on the remaining stiff penises. Each of them turned and backed onto one, efficiently absorbing its triggered jet. "It's a tradition," Smellie explained. "The spectators get to tap the leftovers."

Next was the stench trench, where the most feculent guts let fly. The aroma was truly awful, but there were those who were breathing it in like misty elixir. "Stink addicts," Smellie murmured. "Last one left standing wins."

They moved on to the main event: the champion fart-off. This was the one Prior meant to enter. "Now you know, joy farting won't do it here," Smellie warned him. "These aren't feel farts, they're cloud farts, so they can be seen and judged. There will be some pretty tough contenders."

"I can handle it," he said confidently. "I have more than one kind of magic fart."

"You're really a wonder. May I—"

He embraced her and kissed her on the mouth. She looked about ready to swoon with delight. In this culture, a fast fuck in public was nothing, but she felt obliged to ask permission for a kiss?

Two fat men got up on the stage. They turned together, bent over to present their plump rears to the audience, and blew out a fanfare of several tuba-like notes. This was the signal for the start of the event. People gathered around to watch.

An announcer appeared. "As you know, this event attracts competition from fart and wide. I'm sure most of you are familiar with the rules, but just in case any aren't, here's a reprise: Each farter will fart alone, into the central cavity, where his fart must form a visible cloud. Our panel of judges will measure this cloud for duration, determining when it has faded too far to qualify. The longest duration will win—" He paused for effect. "A day's ride on the Fart Blimp tomorrow!"

There was applause as he waved toward the anchored brown blimp floating at the village's edge. That of course was the prize Prior needed to win.

"Now the call for contestants. Please step up to the stage and give me your names so I can announce them."

"Wish me luck," Prior murmured as he started forward.

"Oh, I do, Micro, I do," Smellie said, and seemed to mean it. He liked that.

Three men and a woman were lining up as Prior came to join them. They all had huge bellies for the generation of champion farts. They glanced at Prior briefly and dismissively; his gut simply wasn't big enough to host a serious contender.

"Our first contestant," the announcer said, "is the WindBreaker, from the windswept plains to the north. He holds three awards for fartsmanship. Here is his opening effort."

The first man faced away from the arena, so that Prior got a good look at his ugly face. He bent grandly over, and emitted a long slow peal of a fart that pulled itself together into a globular brown cloud about a foot in diameter. It roiled and turned as if some demon were inside trying to get out. It floated slowly upward, fissioning off curls of smoke, gradually shrinking. Finally it imploded, leaving only a fading wisp of vapor. "Time!" a judge exclaimed. "Seventy three seconds."

There was applause. It had been a good effort.

"Now we have the ButtGuster from the gassy fumaroles to the south," the announcer said. "He has competed in more cloud fartings than any other man, including last year's Super Bowel, and is just hitting his second wind."

The second man approached the arena and turned about. His face looked like a fart that hadn't yet finished coming out. He bent over, concentrated, and blasted out a huge yellow cloud with tan specks. It sailed upward, expanding, until finally it thinned to the point it lost cohesion and got torn apart by the breeze. "Time! Eighty one seconds."

There was louder applause. This was indeed a excellent emission. The big-name farters were coming through with a fine show.

"And our entry of the fragrant gender is Whoopee, runner-up in our contest last month," the announcer said. "We have real hope that she'll be our first local female champion."

The woman approached the arena, lifted off her farthingale, and stood with a broad bare bottom. She pirouetted, squatted, and let fly a modest pink cloud that rotated like a football. It hovered, valiantly retaining its shape, until it flattened, buckled, and gave up the ghost. "Time. Eighty two seconds."

There was considerable applause. Whoopee's effort had taken the lead, however narrowly.

"Now Blowtorch, a convert from the firefart division. Last month's time was sixty nine seconds, enough to place. He says he's improved his wind since then." The fourth competitor stepped up, almost as ugly as the other men. His gut could be heard rumbling from a fair distance. He pushed out a swisher of a reddish cloud that did indeed vaguely resemble the flame of a blowtorch. It coruscated into the air, shimmering with power. But it burned out too swiftly, and was only seventy seconds, not in the running this time.

"And finally we have a new face, as it were," the announcer said. "Micro, for his first competitive effort."

The audience was silent. The people were waiting to see this thin-bellied amateur make a fool of himself. Prior hoped they were in for a remarkable disappointment. It was up to the Spire.

He approached the arena, turned, and bent over, orienting the Spire. *Do your stuff.*

The Spire issued a rushing jet of black gas. It formed into a spherical mass that sparkled like a dark star. It floated in place, neither shrinking nor expanding. A murmur spread through the audience as it hung on past a minute. This was no amateur effort! Slowly, reluctantly, it thinned, until at last it sank to the ground and dissipated into a trace of goo.

"Time," the judge said. "Ninety seconds."

"The winner," the announcer said, amazed. "Micro."

Prior relaxed in relief. The Spire had come through.

I COULD HAVE MADE IT TWO MINUTES, BUT DIDN'T WANT TO BE OBVIOUS. A NEW RECORD WOULD HAVE BEEN SUSPICIOUS.

Thank you, Prior thought as he walked away from the arena. People were closing in on him, eager to learn more of him, now that he had made his sudden fame as a worthy farter. The other contestants looked on, scowling. They didn't like being bested by a rank amateur.

Smellie hugged him and kissed him impulsively. "You were great!"

"Just get me out of here. I don't want to answer questions."

She took possessive charge. "Micro is tired from his great performance. He needs to rest now. I'm sure you understand." She took Prior's hand and hauled him away.

When they were safely in her house she kissed him again. "Oh, Micro, that was absolutely wonderful! You showed them all."

"You helped," he said.

"I was glad to. Oh, this village has never seen a fart like that! Hardly anyone can do a black one, and they mostly poop out in a few seconds. What a spectacle!"

She served him a nice meal made from her new supplies. The time seemed right to broach his special idea. "Smellie, if you had a pretty face, you could land a good man, right?"

"Oh sure. Men care about faces almost as much about bottoms, once their edge is off. But what's the use debating that? I'm a realist."

"I may have a way to give you that face. But it would not be an easy process."

"What are you talking about?"

"As I said before, I have a magic fart. It can be turned to several different things. I could make a fart that would melt your face and allow it to heal in a prettier image. But you would need to keep it swathed for several days, and there might be pain. Thereafter your face would be as nice as your nature."

She sat down, awed. "You can really do this?"

"I believe so. But it could be risky. Magic can be dangerous in the hands of amateurs, and I'm an amateur."

"Let me think about it."

As they settled down to sleep, after making their evening excursion to the public privy, she hesitated, then spoke. "You've been so good to me, I really shouldn't ask anything more."

"Ask."

"Last night we clasped, and you were concerned because I didn't climax with you. Tonight I can put on a show that—"

"No. I don't want fakery."

"That's what I thought you'd say. So my idea is, maybe I should try it for real, this one time. Let you simulate—as if we're—that much would be an act, of course but—"

"In love?"

She blushed. "In pretense. So I can fool myself into letting it happen. Forgetting myself. I know it's a lot to ask."

"I've never had a woman to love me. That's why I'm going after the Maiden in the Tower. She's supposed to be my ideal woman, and my hope is that she'll truly come to feel it. It's the biggest thing I've missed in my life."

"Yes, and I wouldn't even think of interfering with that. Tomorrow you'll go to her, and I hope you succeed. But tonight, in pretense—" She broke off. "Maybe it's a stupid idea."

"I like it. We can say the words and do the acts, knowing it's only for tonight. Completing our association."

"Oh, thank you," she breathed.

When night came, they joined each other in the bed, in darkness. "I—I don't know what to say," Prior said, feeling awkward. "I've never—"

"Just hold me, beloved."

Relieved that she knew how to proceed, he put his arms around her. She was all warm woman. He kissed her, and she was all melting love. It was so nice that he just kept holding and kissing her for a while, then stroked her hair. "You're beautiful."

"I have dreamed of this moment."

She was better at this than he was, but he was learning. "I never had the wit to dream of love, just sex."

"And I want it with you, dear."

It was stupid, but that word "dear" sent a wash of pleasure through him. "Oh, this is great!" He hardly cared whether they had sex; it was just so nice loving her. "Darling," he added belatedly.

She kissed him more ardently. She caught one of his hands and brought it to her breast. He had stroked breasts before, but this time it had more meaning. He put his face down and kissed it. She shifted just enough to slide the nipple to his mouth, and he kissed that too, feeling it swell. She held his head to her bosom, breathing harder, and each breath pressed it firmer and softer against his face.

"I'm getting warm," she murmured. "But not there yet. Can you enter me without ejaculating right away?"

As it happened, he had jetted that afternoon, and his response was a bit slower than usual. He got in position and entered her carefully, and it was all right. He did not thrust, but just held position, kissing her mouth again.

"Oh, my love, my love," she said. "I love you so much."

"I love you," he echoed, feeling it.

Her vagina softened around him, and tightened. He repeated the words, and got a similar response. She was sexually turned on by words of love. Soon she came to the climax, and clasped him tightly, kissing him constantly, while her vagina convulsed.

It was too much. He had to thrust, and thrust again, his orgasm overwhelming. She clung to him, meeting him with her closure, taking all that he had to give. He felt himself spurting, felt her accepting it, in a phenomenal mutual climax.

Yet it was not the end. He kept kissing her. "I love you, I love you!" His penis was diminishing, but not his passion. He couldn't let go of the feeling.

"Yes, yes," she breathed, meeting him kiss for kiss.

But finally they relaxed. "Yes, that's what I never had," he said.

"I neither." Then, after a pause: "In the morning, before you go—I'll take that fart."

They relaxed into sleep, embraced. It was wonderful.

Chapter 12–Curse

Veil watched the next qualifier. He tackled the demoness orally, turning her on with kisses of the face and breasts, then licking her vulva expertly until she climaxed. He was good enough so that it made Veil react; she could live with that kind of sex. But there was bound to be a catch.

There was. "I am impotent," he informed her when she interviewed him.

"But then what would you want with me?"

"That is why I want you. I have a strong desire for sex, and my doctor says I have the physical capacity for it. But I can't get an erection in the presence of a woman. It's psychological, perhaps the result of some early episode I can't remember. I believe that if I once have real sexual experience with a woman, the barrier will be gone, and I will then be able to do it with other women."

"I'm not sure how I can give you that experience. It would more likely be an exercise in frustration for you."

"Not necessarily so. You will be committed; you will neither laugh at me nor avoid me. Your interest is in having sexual experience with me. That should make a difference."

"My interest is in getting out of here and going home with my child."

"And your surest means of achieving that end is to make me potent. You will address me, use your female wiles to arouse me, and finally bring me to copulation with you. You will have no other purpose. I believe that there should be some progress in the course of a year."

"May I see your penis?"

"Welcome." He doffed his pantaloons and stood with his nether portion exposed.

His penis and testicles looked completely normal. She squatted and took hold of the member, peeling back the foreskin and inspecting the glans. Nothing wrong there. She massaged it with her fingers. It was ordinary throughout, but did not react. "May I make an oral approach?"

"You may."

She touched the tip of the glans with her tongue, then licked it. There was no increase of its size or hardness. She licked the stem just behind the glans, the highly sensitive equivalent of a woman's clitoris. Still no reaction. She put her mouth over it and sucked gently. Nothing. She took the whole limp penis into her mouth, not difficult at all in this small state, caressing it with tongue and lips.

"You are wasting your time," Impotent said. "Other women have tried."

So it seemed. "Would you care to try it on me?" For the average man got just about as much sexual titillation from licking a woman's vulva as he did from having a woman swallow penis.

"If you wish."

She doffed her farthingale and lay on the couch, spreading her legs. He got down and addressed her cleft. "Take me to orgasm," she said. But she reached down to put one hand on his penis, verifying its condition.

He was just as competent on her as he had been on the demoness. Soon he had her building to pleasure, and then to full climax, which she did not try to diminish or conceal. Her bare legs clamped his head as she writhed with the force of it.

But his member never budged.

This was a tough case.

"Have you tried a variety of women?"

"Every variety."

"Including very young ones?"

"I am not turned on by children. My desire is for comely grown women. I merely can not get an erection in the presence of one."

"What of violence?"

"Sado-masochism does not turn me on; it disgusts me."

"What of sexual demonstrations? Does watching others have sex turn you on?"

"No."

She was constrained to believe him. "What of romantic stories?"

"Those, yes."

Progress at last. "Do you get an erection when watching a romantic play or hearing a story?"

"Yes. But it fades in the ready presence of a woman. I can relieve myself only by masturbating."

But she was minded to test it, for this seemed to be a man she would be able to relate to comfortably. "May we experiment?"

"If you can find a way to make me potent, welcome."

"Then let us lie together, and I will tell you a story."

They lay down on her bed, side by side, naked, on their backs. She took hold of his penis so she could verify its state of arousal without looking or calling attention to it. She knew that he would forget the contact after a while, if she kept her hand quite still.

"There was once a young woman called Desiree," she said. "She was not particularly attractive, so was not socially popular. She wanted more than anything to have the kind of sex appeal she saw other girls practicing."

"I would like to encounter a girl with enduring sex appeal for me."

Veil knew it. "Desiree was walking home from her dull job when she was caught by a sudden shower. Half a torrent fell in a few minutes, and she was drenched. Water cascaded into the gutters of the street. Then she spied a little man caught in the flow, about to be washed into a deep culvert. She reached down and caught him by the collar, hauling him out of danger." As she spoke, she found herself getting into the story, and let it flow on its own.

'Thank you, plain woman,' the little man said. 'I regret I can not suitably reward you for saving my life.'

'That's all right,' she said.

He evidently felt guilty. 'I'm an elf. We come in two varieties. A wish elf could have granted you one wish. But I'm a curse elf.'

'A curse elf!' she exclaimed. 'I never heard of that.'

'We're not popular, so we keep a low profile. Now, unfortunately, I am required to curse you.'

She was curious. 'What kind of curses do you do?'

'Oh, there's an infinite variety. Do you have a preference?'

Desiree laughed. 'Curse me with sex appeal.'

The elf hesitated. 'Are you sure?'

'You mean you really can?'

'Indubitably. But you'd be better off with a minor curse, like a hangnail.'

'I'll take the sex appeal.'

'As you wish, so to speak.' He lifted his two little hands, spread his fingers, and made a strange gesture. She felt a weird tingle. She blinked—and the curse elf was gone.

Had he really cursed her with sex appeal? She doubted it. But she was curious to find out.

The rain abated, and she walked on toward home. A man was walking the other way on the sidewalk. He saw her, and paused, staring. She tried to skirt around him, but he put out an arm to intercept her. 'How much?' he asked.

'How much what?' she replied, confused.

'To have sex with you. Now.'

She thought he was joking. 'I'm soaking wet, and I'm not even pretty.'

He brought out his wallet and showed a twenty dollar bill. When she just stared, he produced another, then a third. 'That's all I have,' he said.

Bemused, she decided to call his bluff. 'Okay.' She took the money from his hand.

He immediately backed her up against a telephone pole, opened his fly, and hoisted up her skirt. Before she realized that he was serious, he had her panties to the side and his hot stiff penis was pushing into her surprised vulva. It jammed up somewhat painfully. 'Hey!'

He didn't stop. She tried to back off, but her back was against the pole and her wiggling only settled her vagina more firmly down on his intruding member. She was fairly skewered.

The man panted and thrust, and in a moment she felt the hot jet of his semen. It was way too late to protest; the deed was already in progress. He thrust several more times, spewing out what was in him, and subsided. Then he withdrew, pulled in his penis, and hurried away, looking somewhat shame-faced.

Desiree was left holding the money. It wasn't even rape; she had been paid. Stunned, she fumbled out a tissue, wiped her cleft, and put herself back together.

She took a moment to ponder, and realized that maybe the elf had not been joshing her. He just might really have given her the curse of sex appeal.

The episode had not been fun, but she did have sixty dollars she could certainly use. Still, it could be a fluke. The man she had encountered might have been so desperate for a woman that he simply took the first one he encountered. How could she be sure?

There was a pair of rather cute boys living a few houses down the street from her. She would have liked to have something to do with them, but they had never noticed her. They were decent types. She would ask them.

She walked to their house, went to the door, and knocked. 'Hi, Al,' she said when the door opened. 'I'm Desiree, down the street. I wonder if—'

'You're soaking wet,' Al said. 'You'll catch your death of cold. Come in.' He called back over his shoulder: 'Hey Bo, it's Desiree.'

'Well, there's really no need. I just want to know whether—'

Then Bo was there too. The two boys bustled her into their warm apartment and solicitously stripped away her sodden clothing. While Al dried her with a soft towel Bo fixed her a mug of hot chocolate. In moments she was sitting nude at their table, drinking it. It was wonderful.

'This may seem inopportune,' Al said. 'But there's something about you. Would it be too much to ask if—'

This was the test. What did she have to lose? 'Welcome, both of you.'

Suddenly she was on the bed with them, and Al was kissing her mouth and fondling her breasts while Bo was squeezing her buttocks and tonguing her cleft. Then Al's rigid penis was in her mouth while Bo's was plunging her vagina. They tried to be gentle, but were overcome by passion. They jetted almost simultaneously.

Desiree swallowed the coursing fluid, and rocked with the force of the eruptions. Her question had been answered: she had potent sex appeal.

The boys were embarrassed as they subsided. 'We've never been like this before,' Al said. 'I don't know what got into us.'

'I do,' Desiree said, satisfied. Innate caution caused her to avoid the truth. 'You just never saw me nude before.'

'We thought you were, well, plain,' Bo said. 'No offense. This was amazing.'

'Just my luck to get caught in the rain. I'd better go home now.'

'Of course,' Al said. 'But now that we know the real you, we'd like to—'

'How about formal dates with each of you, on alternate nights?'

They agreed. Soon she was on her way home, in borrowed dry clothing, carrying her wet things. She was well pleased with her supposed curse. Now she had two nice boyfriends.

But as she settled down to sleep in the evening, it occurred to her that it could be awkward at her job, where there were four men for every woman. Could she turn off the sex appeal? Would baggy clothing mask it? Or would she be stuck trying to fend off married men, including her boss?

Well, she would worry about that in the morning. She drew he sheet over her and dropped off to sleep.

She woke in alarm. There was a man in bed with her! Or something. He was trying to rape her.

She turned on the light. She stared. The sheet was squeezing her breasts, and part of it had somehow gotten wadded around her hairbrush, and the wrapped handle was pushing into her cleft. She realized with horror that she had so much sex appeal that the very things of her bedroom wanted to have sex with her. It was indeed a curse; how could she sleep if she couldn't trust even the sheets to leave her alone?

Veil paused in her narration. The man's penis had swelled in her hand with each recounted sexual episode, and was now fully hard. She sat up and mounted him, setting his member at her cleft.

The man looked at her, remembering where he was. And his penis shrank. Sex became impossible.

"Damn!" he said, blowing out a foul stench.

"I'm afraid I can't help you. You were potent only when you forgot you were with a woman."

"True. But you got farther than any other woman has. You could tell me other stories, and perhaps in time it would become possible."

"Perhaps," she agreed. But she was afraid it was a lost cause.

The next man was a callow youth with a dirty neck. How clean would he be where it didn't show? "I got two friends," he said, farting politely. "We do everything together. We swore never to let a woman break us up. So we figure to do it together. One for the mouth, one for the cunt, one for the asshole, blasting off together if we can. Between times you can scrub the floor, cook the mush, wash the sheets—you know, what women do. You understand?"

"Perfectly," she said. She had described two young men having simultaneous sex with one woman; this trio planned to go it one better, stretching all her orifices at once with their unclean instruments. She'd be better off with the impotent man.

One day remained, with one more man to qualify. She hoped he turned out to be a better prospect.

Chapter 13 – Tower

Prior woke with one hand on Smellie's breast. He wasn't sure whether it was accident, or he had been feeling her in his sleep, or she had placed it there. It didn't matter; it was nice. He rolled over, kissed the breast, and then her mouth. "It's been great," he said.

"The greatest," she agreed. "You've done so much for me."

"But do you want the last thing?"

"Yes. I have decided."

"You will be blind for a few hours, and you'll have to keep your face bandaged for days."

"I'm ready. Do it now." She put two breathing straws in her nostrils and lay with her eyes closed.

He straddled her on hands and knees, his rear aimed at her head. The Spire issued an almost liquid fart that settled across her face and around the straws. That was all; Prior, prompted by the Spire, moved away.

Her face was melting. It looked like a wad of taffy with two straws poking out. It was awful.

LEAVE HER, the Spire gouted. **SHE WILL BE UNCONSCIOUS FOR SEVERAL HOURS. THEN HER FEATURES WILL FIRM ENOUGH SO SHE CAN REMOVE THE STRAWS. ALL WILL BE WELL; SHE KNOWS WHAT TO DO. IN TIME SHE WILL BE BEAUTIFUL.**

Prior hoped so. He dressed, ate, and quietly departed. At least this abated any sticky farewell scene.

He made his way to the fart balloon. It was being filled by several men with so much intestinal gas the hiss of it was continuous.

A woman arrived. There was a provocative flirt to her hips as she walked; that, more than her pretty face, identified her. She was the winner of the seduction contest, who had made a penis spurt without touching it.

"Ah, the fart champion," she said, recognizing him. "We are to be travel mates. May the farts be with you." She let out a ladylike fart.

"We are?" he asked, surprised, as the Spire loosed a courteous response fart. "Travel mates?"

"I have kin in Maid-in-Tower Village, so I'm taking advantage of the transport there. I'm sure you won't mind."

Prior wasn't eager for such a distraction. "I, uh—"

"I promise to entertain you on high," she said, taking a little dance-like step that compelled his attention. "I am Seducia, mistress of masters." She farted again, with more authority, and removed her jacket so as to bare her breasts.

Nevertheless, he was determined to resist her blandishments, because he wanted to be at full potency for the Tower contest on the following day. It was bad enough to have to tangle with demons, without doing so depleted. "I am Micro, master of not much," he responded, and the Spire issued a social fart that smelled of honeysuckle.

Soon the balloon was full of gas. They boarded and it was cut loose. It floated into the sky.

"But how does it steer?" Prior asked, alarmed, for there was no visible mechanism.

"The wind takes it, silly," Seducia said, laughing. "The trip is timed for the correct direction." She farted humorously.

"Live and learn," Prior said, and the Spire let fly with a two note tweedle fart.

"Oh, you are good," Seducia said admiringly. "As we saw yesterday. You came from nowhere, but you farted in masterly fashion." She glanced side-long at him. "Shall we proceed?"

"Uh—"

She shook her midsection, causing her short skirt to flounce up, flashing her bare bottom as her breasts bounced jigglesomely. "I don't really know a man until I have had him in me," she said. "But it's more sporting if I make him spurt untouched."

"I saw, yesterday," Prior agreed, not wanting to admit that she had already roused his erection.

"But you have to bare your member," she said. "For fair play. I don't like working blind."

"I'd really rather see the sights," Prior said desperately, looking out from the basket to the landscape drifting by below.

"I'm trying to show them to you," she said reprovingly, with another evocative flip of her bottom. "Are you gay?"

"No. I just—have a challenge coming up."

"You're competing for the Maiden in the Tower!" she exclaimed.

"Uh, yes."

"Why? With your superior farts, you can win any woman you want. Me, even, for today. Why risk your health fighting the guardian demons? A fellow can get his ass reamed for keeps that way."

"I—I just need to do it," he said lamely.

"Now you have intrigued my feminine curiosity. First I'll make you spurt untouched, then I'll weasel out your secret. It's a double challenge. But we'll have to establish the rules of the game. Both naked, of course."

"I don't want a game," Prior protested. "I just want to get where I'm going."

"You're not from Fartingale, are you," she said.

"I'm from another country," he agreed. "I followed the statues to get here."

She nodded. "So you surely have motivation. I understand those statues can be demanding."

"Yes." He saw a cluster of houses surrounded by fields. Maybe he could change the subject. "What's that village?"

"Take off your clothes and I'll tell you."

He kept his eyes off her. "You're really determined, aren't you."

"Yes. It's a challenge."

And she would keep after him until she got her way. He doffed his clothes and stood with his moderately rigid erection.

"This is the village of Shit-for-Brains," she said.

"You're kidding!"

"By no means. All the villages of Fartingale have descriptive names. Didn't you notice Nude-on-Toilet, with its coed privy seats?"

"Uh, yes. I guess I didn't think about it."

"You seemed to adapt pretty well to the local scene, quick-sticking Smellie when I did my act. How come you picked her to shit beside?"

She had seen that? "She's honest."

That set her back for a moment. "Good point. You're smarter than I thought. Most men can't see far past a girl's face and figure. Smellie deserves better than she's had."

"She'll have better in future."

"That's nice. But now you're with me."

"I didn't choose to be. I'm just trying to travel."

"And I'm your travel mate." She glanced again at the village. "Shit-for-Brains specializes in quality manure that grows plants that are said to clarify the mind. There's not a huge market for that, compared to farting stimulants, but it does well enough."

"That explains the pile of turds in the center."

"Yes, that's their statue. It has a carefully cultivated odor."

Just then a whiff of it came. "What a stench!"

"The stenchiest," she agreed. "The villagers believe it makes them smart."

Suddenly Prior felt an urgent need to defecate. "Is there a—a potty on board?"

Seducia laughed. "Of course not. Just do it over the side. The smell is conducive, by no coincidence. It is considered good luck if you can score directly on the statue."

"You're fooling."

"Hardly. Hold me while I drop one." She got up on the rail, and he held her arms while she poked her bare bottom out and squeezed out a ladylike turd. Her position was such that he had the best possible view of her dangling breasts and flexed thighs, which were not far above his standing penis.

"Now I'll hold you," she said.

He didn't argue; he was about to let loose regardless. He got his balance, buttressed by her lock on his shoulders, and spewed out a string of loose turds, powered by considerable gas. They sailed gracefully down toward the ground, but missed the statue; the craft had already passed it. There was no urine; his hard erection prevented that. "Uh, thanks," he said as he finished.

"Welcome. Folk who poop together, whoop together. We have now shared shit." She blew out a short fart as punctuation as she drew her remarkable breasts away from his face.

And that, in this culture, was romantic. He was coming to appreciate it. After all, how realistic was it to think that women had neither gas nor feces? This culture celebrated every part and function, without illusion or hypocrisy.

The balloon moved on across field, river, and forest. "That's the Rootin-Tootin River," Seducia said. "One sip of that bubbly water and you're ready to inflate a dirigible. And the Feculent Forest, of which it has been justly said you haven't truly known feces until you've trodden there." The river was brownish, and the forest from this height looked like mold on manure.

Beyond the forest was another village, featuring a giant yellow fountain. "And that is?"

"Look at me and I'll tell you."

She was playing her game. He looked at her, and she did her dance while she talked. Any faint notion his penis might have had about subsiding was banished. "That is Piss-on-It, where they hold regular pissing contests."

"I thought those could be done anywhere."

"They can, and are, just like the farting parties. But for championship pissing, Piss-on-It is the place. They have divisions for distance, volume, color, and I'm not sure what else, and prizes galore. There's a story that once a thatch hut caught on fire, and there was no water near to put it out, but their champion pisser unlimbered his hose and pissed so powerfully that he put it out alone."

"Didn't it stink up the premises?"

"The whole village stinks of piss, so they never noticed."

The balloon drifted on by another village. This one had a huge statue of a woman lying with bare legs spread wide. There seemed to be activity in the vicinity of her crotch. "And that is—?"

"Look at me."

He looked. She intensified her dance, moving close to him but never quite touching. Such was her allure that his penis got overstressed and jetted its load into the air.

Seducia smiled, flush with victory, as she caught the flying fluid in her cupped hands and spread it on her thighs like lotion. "That is Fuck-It, where they raise and train the fucking demons for export."

"Copulating demons?" he asked nervously as his penis dribbled the last of its content and descended, untouched. He had encountered some of those demons in his day.

"They are very popular. Plain women buy the males and use them as indefatigable lovers. Men buy the females and share them with their friends. They are programmed for a set number of fucks before they have to be returned for refurbishing. Maid-in-Tower uses them as challenges for the contestants; didn't you know?"

The Spire had mentioned it, but it had slipped his mind. "I'll have to seduce a demoness to get into the tower."

"Correction: you'll have to make her climax. If you do it wrong, she'll run her tongue up your ass and pump your prostate until it's prostrate. So you don't want to have your orgasm first; she'll make you sorry. I'm really doing you a favor by harvesting your jism now."

That was one way of putting it. "Uh, thanks."

"Their main office is in the statue's cunt," she continued, looking down at the village. "You can see the people going in and out. Every evening they haul up a huge hard-on shaped battering ram and give the goddess a good fucking. It is thought that bad luck will fall on the village if they don't satisfy her. You can hear the whomping for miles around."

That thought made Prior's flaccid penis twitch. Seducia saw it, and nodded. She wasn't just talking; she had an agenda.

They floated over a fourth village. "That's Sorry Ass, where people go to address digestive complaints, such as inadequate gas in the gut."

"Wouldn't want that," Prior agreed, and the Spire emitted a melodious fart.

"Next stop will be Maid-in-Tower," Seducia said. "Now you can tell me your story, and I won't touch you as long as it interests me. But when it falters or ends, you're mine. See if you can hold me off until we arrive."

So Prior started talking, telling the story of the news of his ideal woman being abducted and in need of rescue. He omitted the details of his penis socket and the Spire. Unfortunately that abridged his narrative, and he ran out of it before the balloon reached Maid-in-Tower.

"Give it to me," Seducia said, clasping him and closing her thighs around his swelling penis. She pressed her breasts against him and kissed him as her buttocks massaged his member. Meanwhile the Spire let out a silent fart, almost unnoticed.

Prior's will to resist evaporated. He re-angled his rod and thrust up into her slick tube. On the second thrust he spouted, and he felt her climaxing with him, her whole body convulsing with her passion. It was like wrestling a panther, except that she was not attacking him but stimulating him to further emissions. Their tensing bodies squeezed out their reserves of gas, and they farted almost in unison, thrust by thrust.

Soon they collapsed together, panting. "Oooh, you made me come too, you amazing lover," she gasped. "That hasn't happened in eons."

Prior wondered, as he had not been trying to stimulate her. He had simply responded to his sudden need. She didn't normally climax in sex? Evidently the challenge was all. *Was that you, Spire?*

OF COURSE, the Spire gouted. **I ISSUED A PHEROMONE FART THAT TURNED HER ON.**

"You're some man, Micro," Seducia said. "If you don't get your Tower maiden, I'll still be around for a few days."

"I'll keep it in mind," Prior said.

Then it was time to get dressed, for the next village was approaching and the balloon was descending. It had been aimed and filled remarkably accurately; the windmakers clearly knew what they were doing.

The balloon drifted to the ground beside the tower, which was a huge translucent statue of a nude woman whose intestines could be seen within her belly. There was a person in there: the Maiden. He wondered who she was. Well, with luck he would find out tomorrow.

"If you'd like a roommate for the night..." Seducia said, with one of her special hip flirts.

He was tempted, but knew he needed to recover what sexual energy he could overnight. "I'll never be in condition to rescue the Maiden if I stay with you," he said.

"Naturally not," she agreed. "Well, your chances are only one in seven even if you win your day. I'll be watching." She turned and walked away, her rear view as intriguing as her front view, as she clearly knew.

He found lodging for the night, ate, and settled down to sleep. But there was something he had to settle with the Spire. "Where do I want you tomorrow?" he asked.

I CAN SEDUCE THE DEMONESS WITH ONE TOUCH, it responded. **BUT IF YOU HAVE A FART-OFF, I WON'T BE ABLE TO HELP YOU. FARTING FROM YOUR PENIS WOULD DISQUALIFY YOU. BETTER TO KEEP ME IN YOUR COLON.**

That made sense. "Fart me into a good sleep," he said, not depending on nature; he was too keyed up. He heard the faint hiss of gas, then was out. He knew that in the morning he would wake refreshed and potent; the Spire had marvelous powers of restoration. But he also knew that that did not guarantee him any victory.

Chapter 14—Choice

Veil watched the final contestants with a certain unease. One, Micro, was not a large or flashy man, and she didn't give him much of a chance. The other was a big brute of a man she detested at first sight.

Both seduced the demoness. Brute swung her about and thrust into her repeatedly without climaxing himself, until she yielded. Only then did he suffer his own orgasm. Might, it seemed, made right. Micro was far more sensitive, stroking the demoness and kissing her as if he really cared, working her up. It was of course an act, but Veil much preferred it. The rituals of sex might be scripted, but the urge itself was genuine, and what started as a script could readily become real.

Then the two men faced each other in the farting off. Brute soon wrestled Micro to the floor and positioned his big bare bottom over his face. Micro seemed lost. He was holding his breath, but eventually he would have to breathe.

Then a visible fart squeezed out of his rectum. It formed a small cloud and floated slowly up behind Brute, following his body contours. It expanded as it went, until when it reached head height it was large enough to enclose the man's head. "It's a magic fart!" the announcer exclaimed, amazed. "Micro won a magic farting contest in Nude-on-Toilet; he has a remarkable power. But can this prevail before he has to breathe?"

Brute, unaware of the mist closing in around him, did breathe—and fell over unconscious. Micro got to his feet, the winner. Veil was hard put to it not to applaud.

But the victorious underdog could still be a shit. She needed to know, so she could choose between the contestants. "Send Micro up for an interview," she told the TV.

Micro was just turning, about to return to his lodging, when her summons preempted him. She saw his look of surprise. "But I'm not dressed," he protested.

It didn't matter. He was borne upward into the tower, up one leg, past the crotch, and to the station at the anus. The sphincter dilated and he stood looking into her apartment. He was mussed and sweaty, looking as if he wanted to be elsewhere. That was fine with her; she could surely get a better measure of him while he was emotionally off-balanced.

"Do come in," she said, forcing a bit of a fart. "May the farce be with you."

"And with you," he agreed, stepping awkwardly in, emitting a meek answering fart. "I—I'm called Micro. I—"

"I saw," she said. "You powered your way to victory with a magic fart. It was a remarkable achievement."

"I do want to meet you," he said. "But I wanted to clean up and change first. This—I'm not ready."

"This is merely an interview," she said, taking his hand and leading him to the couch. It felt good to be in control, even to this limited extent. "As you surely know, I am Veil, the Maiden in the Tower. I am required to choose one of the seven daily victors to be my sex slave master for the coming year. I want my choice to be informed."

"Uh, sure, of course. But I wanted to make a better impression."

She smiled, though of course it didn't show through her shroud. She sat on her high stool opposite him and leaned forward so as to give her bare breasts better definition. She wanted to dazzle him if she could, again with the object of getting honest responses. "Why are you here, Micro?"

His eyes fixed on her breasts, as she had intended. "To rescue you, of course."

She laughed. "Rescue me? I assumed you wanted a sex slave."

"No. I mean, I'm sure that would be nice, but that's not why I came. I—I don't believe in slavery."

This was certainly different. "You don't even know me. Why should you want to rescue me?"

"I—it's awkward to explain."

Especially if he was lying. "Make the effort."

"Well, for one thing, where I come from, women aren't slaves."

"Where do you come from?"

"I don't know whether you'd understand. It's—it's beyond Fartingale."

"Try me."

"It's called America. It—"

"America!"

"It's like this, only with less, uh, farts. Not much magic at all."

"I know. I'm from America."

He stared at her veil. "You're from home!"

"I was abducted and brought here, with my son."

"Son?"

"You didn't know?" Chance was stirring, so she went to the crib, picked him up, and started nursing him. If this turned Micro off, that was something she needed to know. "My son Chance is three months old. So obviously I'm not a maiden in the archaic sense. I can't think why the beasts who run this ongoing lottery selected me to be their prize of the week. Maybe they didn't realize I wasn't alone, and then it was too late to find another. Is that a problem for you?"

"I, uh, I'm just surprised. I assumed—"

"That the Maiden in the Tower was a true maiden," she finished for him. "Normally I'm sure she is. If you're looking for a virgin, I'm not the one."

"I—I guess it doesn't matter."

"I can and will fulfill my obligation to be your sex slave, if you are the one I choose. Chance is well behaved, and sleeps more than he wakes. Any delays will be of short duration."

"No, I mean I guess you're the one, with or without a baby. It just takes some adjusting."

"The one for what?"

"Well, I was told my—my ideal woman was captive, and I had only a week to rescue her. So I got on it immediately."

This was curious. "Who told you that?"

"It doesn't matter. I believed it."

He was being evasive. "Who?"

"A—a succubus. A magical creature who—"

"I am familiar with the term. You had relations with a female demon, before you came to Fartingale?"

"Uh, yeah," he said, staring at his feet.

"Obviously you do not have a regular woman in your life."

"Yes, I don't."

"So you thought you'd like to have a sex slave for a year."

"No! I mean, sure, I'd like that, but that's not—"

"Not why you came here," she finished. "I believe we have already covered that territory. So the succubus told you where there was better sex to be had, and you decided on a rescue mission."

"I guess it does sound sort of stupid. Maybe it's a cruel hoax I fell for. I just thought—if it really was my ideal woman, how could I not try to save her, somehow?"

He seemed sincere. She softened. "At least you had to investigate the situation."

"Yeah." His eyes remained fixed on the floor.

"So am I your ideal woman?"

"Well, I don't know. In appearance, sure."

"You can't even see my face."

He blushed. "Apart from that, I mean. And I don't know your personality. So probably I shouldn't have come here."

He seemed to be an ordinary, fallible man, with some exceptions. He was from her homeland, which counted for a lot. But that raised a serious question. "How is it you have the ability of magical farting?"

"I—can't explain that."

"You're being evasive."

"Yes. I'm sorry."

Curiouser and curiouser. "You mean you could explain it, but you won't."

"Yes."

"How do you expect to win my favor if you aren't candid with me?"

"I guess I hadn't thought that far ahead. I'm not the brightest bulb on the chandelier."

She smiled again, though the expression was wasted. "Somehow you got hold of a magical ability and used it to get you here. Now you want to take me home with you."

"Yes, if you want to come." He shrugged. "I know there's not much chance."

"We could be totally incompatible."

"Yes, I suppose the succubus would really laugh if she got me hooked to the wrong woman. But I guess it's a gamble I'm ready to make."

"Because I have a good figure?"

"That, too."

Yet he was from her homeland. If she went with him, she could go home immediately. That truly tempted her. "Tell me about yourself. What do you do for a living?"

"I'm a file clerk."

"You expect to maintain a family on that level of pay?"

His eyes had strayed upward. Now they fell to the floor again. "I guess not."

"You know there's no market for magic farts where you live."

"No more farting," he agreed.

"Were I to choose you, we might be better off remaining here in Fartingale, where you seem to have some renown as a farter."

"I don't want to stay here."

"But back in America, I would have to support you."

He flushed. "I guess I see the joke. Maybe you're my ideal woman, but I'm not your ideal man. I guess I've made a real fool of myself."

He had, yet there was something endearing about it. There were worse things than being with a man she could manage. As a sex slave, she would have to support whatever man she selected, at least for a year. In that sense, Micro was no worse than the others.

Veil suddenly remembered that she had forgotten to follow up on her riddle challenge. None of the other contestants had mentioned it, and this one might not even know of it. Perhaps now it would help her make her decision. "Where can you walk south a mile, east a mile, north a mile, and be back where you started?"

Micro smiled. "I've heard that one. The north pole."

"Agreed." Now she sprang the second riddle. "Where else?"

"That one really stumped me when I heard it. I talked it over with my friends, and we finally figured it out: draw a one mile circle around the south pole, then start from a mile north of that. That will do it. Or draw a half mile circle, and walk twice around it, and back." He glanced at her hood. "Is this supposed to be a test? Because if it is, I flunked it. I know the answer only because my friends figured it out, and I remember."

So much for selection. Yet his candor appealed. "Tell me a story that will make me laugh." If a demoness could be won over by a man who made her laugh, maybe it would be true for a captive Maiden.

"You like storytelling?"

"Sometimes."

He pondered a moment, then obliged. "There was this famous, arrogant bachelor celebrity. A friend came to him and said 'Hey, Hal, I've set up the perfect date for you.'"

Veil listened as Chance nursed, letting her mind get into the story so it seemed she was seeing it first hand. She pictured herself as the date, mentally substituting her own name for the one in the story.

Hal was interested. 'Who is she?'

'She's called Veil. She's really a great girl.'

Hal was suspicious, because his so-called friends were always trying to fix him up with stray women whose faces and figures were not their fortunes. For some reason they thought that the best women for him were intellectual types. 'So how did this great date get set up?'

'Well, that doesn't really matter. You'll like her, believe me.'

'It matters. What brings her here?'

His friend fidgeted, then grudgingly came out with it. 'She entered this contest, and she did really well, but she didn't actually win. So she got the consolation prize: a date with you.'

'Consolation prize!' Hal exclaimed, outraged. 'Me?'

'It's not how it sounds. When she learned who you are, she was all for it. Eager, even. She—'

'Forget it!'

'But she's such a great girl! She'll be so disappointed if she can't be with you. You'll like her, I swear!'

'Absolutely not. Get out of here.'

His friend sighed. He walked to a cloaked woman standing nearby. 'I'm sorry, honey. He won't go for it. No date.'

'Darn!' Veil said. She threw off her cloak and stalked away, naked.

Hal stared after her, noting her hourglass figure and glorious tresses. 'Just what was this contest?'

'It was for the world's most perfectly developed body,' his friend said. 'But she didn't win. The judge's niece won. So Veil was runner-up.'

'I changed my mind,' Hal said. 'I'll date her.'

But it was too late. The rejected woman was gone. Hal had lost his perfect date.

"Served him right," Veil said, laughing. Then she paused, considering. "It's really not that funny, but I did laugh. You must understand me on some level."

"Well, woman like stories about arrogant men who lose out," Micro said.

"We do indeed. Maybe you'll do."

"Because I told a story?" he asked incredulously.

Chance had finished nursing and gone back to sleep. She set him carefully back in the crib. It was time to fathom the rest of this man, so she could make her decision. "Kiss me."

"Uh—"

She stood, leaned down toward him as he sat on the couch, and kissed him solidly on the mouth. He was clearly startled, but his lips firmed up; he did know how to kiss.

"How much sex would you require of me, for that year?"

"None! I mean, not if you didn't want to."

She removed her farthingale skirt and sat on his lap, surprising him again. She could feel his penis stiffening against her bottom. "None?"

"It's supposed to be mutual. Sure I want you, but if you don't want me, then it's no good."

"How quaint." She turned into him so that her breasts touched him, and kissed him again. "But I am required to desire you, in effect."

He was breathing hard. "You sure do turn me on. But I think you're playing with me. Maybe you should let me go and choose the man you want."

"Maybe I should," she agreed. "Why are you holding back?"

"Because I don't trust this."

Of course he knew she was playing with him. "How do you mean?"

"Why should someone abduct you and your baby, put you here for men to compete for, and send word to me about my ideal woman? It smells like a trap."

Her jaw dropped. She got off him and climbed back into her farthingale. "It certainly does. You're not the dullest bulb on that chandelier, either."

"Middle range," he agreed with a wan smile. "So maybe we should avoid the trap by not getting together, much as I hate letting you go."

"No, I prefer to spring the trap and find out what this is all about." She faced the TV. "I hereby choose this man to be my slavemaster for the year."

"I'm not sure this is smart," Micro said.

"You have chosen," the TV announcer said. "Now for your honeymoon in Eden."

Veil was about to say something else, but there was a hiss of gas, and everything changed.

Part 3: Honeymoon

Chapter 15—Eden

Prior looked around. He was standing in a lush garden replete with flowers, berries, fruits, and nuts. Before him stood Veil, head still hidden in a blob of darkness but otherwise quite naked, holding her baby.

That remained a point of difficulty. He had never dreamed that his ideal woman, if she existed at all, would be a mother. That meant that some other man had had at her first, and there had been enough of a relationship to produce a child. Was that man still around? She acted as if she were free, but it was a question that needed an answer.

"The Garden of Eden," Veil remarked. "It seems we are honeymooning as Adam and Eve."

The TV set had spoken of Eden. Obviously this was it. They must have had to clear out the Tower to make room for the next week's Maiden, who would be similarly put on display to attract contestants. He hadn't realized that there would be an interim setting. "I guess so. So we can get to know each other privately."

"With our privates showing," she agreed. She looked around. "Well, I chose you, so now it's time to deliver. Let me find a place to put Chance down, and I'm yours."

"I told you, I don't believe in slavery." But his penis thickened, desiring its lodging. He had intended to change to the Spire, but the immediate transition to the interview in the tower had prevented that. He still had Normal on, the nondescript standard model, while the Spire remained in his colon. That gave him considerably less control. Oubliette had told him to touch the Maiden with the Spire, to make her desire him; he hadn't been able to do that, but had lucked out when she chose him anyway. But if she was really his ideal woman, he didn't want to alienate her by making her a fucking object before she was interested.

"Are you sure?" she asked, glancing meaningfully at his lifting member.

"I wish I had a fig leaf!"

She laughed, and her breasts quivered in a way that hastened his erection. "Let me see if I have this straight: your spirit is trying to be decent, but your flesh is rampant."

"That's it," he agreed. He looked around. "Maybe there are some fig leafs, or the equivalent, that we can use to make skirts." But he saw none.

"There are two ways to handle this," Veil said. "Discharge your member, or ignore it."

"I can't ignore it." His way-too-obvious erection was an acute embarrassment, but it refused to subside.

"Then let's discharge it." She considered briefly. "I am not entirely ignorant of the ways of men, obviously." She glanced at her baby, who was now sleeping in a bed of leaves she had fashioned while talking. "A penis may be discharged by penetration or manipulation. Penetrable orifices are vagina, mouth, and anus."

"Uh, no. I said not unless you want it."

"Manipulation it is," she said. She dropped to her knees before him, took his penis in her hand, and squeezed it.

Before he knew it, his seed was jetting in an arc through the air, spurt by spurt. She had made it respond in a way he never had, knowing exactly where and how to press. "You've done this before," he said, amazed.

She shrugged as she returned to her feet. "So it seems. Next time it rises, I will abate it another way, if you prefer. The choice is yours."

"Uh, thanks," he said, embarrassed.

"But I will say that I appreciate your courtesy in not pressing the issue despite your right to do so."

His feelings were mixed. He was glad that she hadn't freaked out at sight of his involuntary erection, sorry that she hadn't wanted sex, glad that she had found a way to alleviate the condition, sorry that he had wasted his sperm on the ground, and glad that he had deviously pleased her. She was, it was turning out, some woman.

"I guess we'd better look around," he said. "Find a way out of here, maybe."

"I suspect there will be no convenient egress."

"I guess we're here to—to get to know each other better. As it was with the real Adam and Eve."

"To be sure. I wonder whether there is a forbidden tree."

"Forbidden?"

"One that bears the fruit of the knowledge of good and evil."

"Oh. Yes. I guess there could be. Maybe we'll have to eat of it to get out of here."

"Or to be cast out."

"Whatever. Let's look."

Veil picked up her baby and they browsed through the garden. They sampled the fruit, which seemed to be of every kind, all of it remarkably and tasty. They need never go hungry here.

But soon after eating, Prior found his erection forming again. Veil, too, seemed antsy. "I believe this fruit has aphrodisiac properties," she said.

"You too? I guess they meant it when they said honeymoon."

"You still prefer to avoid copulation?"

"I guess I look like a liar, with my dick rising. But I don't want it unless you do."

"The desire is upon me, but I confess I prefer to avoid it at this time, simply because I would prefer to know you better. A man can indulge in sex at any time, with any available woman, but a woman prefers to have more of a relationship."

"So you're in the same fix I'm in. Your flesh is rampant."

"Correct. We are in this together. Shall we do the honors for each other?"

"You sure made me spew in a hurry. But I don't know how to do that for you."

"I will show you." She set the baby down again, sat on a convenient mossy rock, leaned back, and spread her legs. "Wet your finger."

He looked around. "No water."

"With your mouth. Saliva is a fine lubricant."

Oh. He put his finger in his mouth, wetting it thoroughly. Then he kneeled and peered into her open crevice. The sight made his erection swell valiantly. "What now?"

"Slide your finger along the channel to the end."

He put the tip in her cleft and slid down to her hole, poking into it. As the warm flesh surrounded his finger, she reached across, touched his penis, and made it geyser. She certainly had the touch.

"Now the other direction," she said.

He drew his finger out and slid it to the other end of the channel. There was a small hooded knob there. "That is the clitoris," she said. "Stroke it, very lightly."

He did so, fascinated. First it swelled under his touch. Then she stiffened, breathing faster, and her body quivered. Then she closed her legs on his hand, pinning his finger there, while she writhed with orgasmic pleasure. Her climax took longer than his, but seemed no less intense.

"Kiss me," she said.

He moved his face to hers and kissed her mouth, finding it despite the blob of a hood. Her face seemed normal in that darkness. She met him with considerable passion. "That was good," she said.

"But maybe we shouldn't eat more of the fruit."

"Until we get hungry? Let's face it, as with the fart food, we're stuck for it. Eat and abate; we'll get by."

They moved on through the warm jungle. Suddenly they came to a stone wall. Rather, it was a sheer cliff, rising a hundred feet or so into the sky. There was no way to scale it; it was, for them, an impassible barrier.

They followed it to the side, eating fruits as convenient. That led to another crisis of desire. This time they didn't bother to lie or sit down. Veil took hold of his penis and made it jettison its load, and he stroked his finger along her cleft as she stood holding her baby. Soon she clenched her thighs on his hand and shook with her orgasm.

"But you know, there is a more direct way to do this," she said.

"Yes, but—"

"Let's agree that in this circumstance sex has no meaning other than the relief of a temporary condition. Once we get out of this conducive garden, we can revert to normal relations."

That did seem to make sense. "Okay."

"To make it quite clear, we'll use the rear position. No kissing."

That seemed to make sense of a sort.

They walked until they came to another boundary. This one was the opposite: a cliff leading downward. It dropped into a dark gulf that seemed to have no other side.

"It must be that Eden is set into the side of a mountain," Veil said. "Perhaps cut away to make a broad ledge. Thus we can't go up or down."

So it seemed. "We should have known that they wouldn't let us simply walk away from it."

"There remains more to explore."

They cut back into the forest, eating as they went. In due course the fruit got to them again. "So how do we do this, this time?" Prior asked, his member standing.

"You will climax before I do, especially if there is no clitoral stimulation. You will have to slow down."

"I don't think I can."

"This may help." She took hold of his penis and pressed a nerve below its base. Suddenly his member went numb, but did not go limp.

"What did you do?" he asked, alarmed.

"It's merely a temporary nerve block to detune you enough to match my pace. Now slide it in and pump." She leaned forward and braced one hand against the trunk of a tree. The other held her baby.

Well, if that was the way she wanted it, he could oblige. Prior set his anesthetized member at her proffered crack and found the entry with his finger rather than the dulled end of his penis. He slid the tip in, made sure of the lodging, and pressed the shaft on after it. Soon he came up against her buttocks. He was all the way in, though he wouldn't have known from the sensation in his member.

He thrust, and felt some faint response. He pulled out, and pushed in, and got a little more. He repeated, pistoning constantly, and slowly, slowly, the feeling intensified. Then she reacted, her vagina clenching around him, relaxing, and clenching again. She was going into her orgasm, and that helped him, but he still had to pump hard to work it into a climax.

Her orgasm raged like a seizure, exploding around him. She rode his pole, squeezing its length, milking it, seeming almost to suck at it. Maybe there was some suction, as he pulled back his stroke. She worked on him as her orgasm ran its course and faded.

At last he came. He pumped harder yet, sensation returning, and finally, almost painfully, spewed out his substance. It felt as if he were putting a gallon of hard cider into her, though he knew it was merely a spoonful of apple juice.

"Well, that wasn't easier," she said. "Maybe we can find another variant, next time."

They came to a glade that might be in the center of the garden. A single tree stood in its center. "That would be the Tree of Knowledge," she said. "Of whose fruit we must not eat."

So it seemed. "It's getting late. We need to find a place to sleep."

"Anywhere will do," she said. "There are no hostile bugs or creatures."

They gathered moss to make a bed, and settled down. The urge was on them again. "Maybe if you start before me," he suggested. "So you won't have to numb me."

"Good idea. Get behind me, but don't enter until I tell you." She lay on her side, her bottom presented. He saw that she was nursing her baby. Probably that was what she had to do, to keep the child quiet, but merging it with sex was weird.

He lay behind her, his groin not touching. He reached around her hip, found her crevice, and stroked her button. He was getting better at it, and soon she reacted, her body shaking. But she didn't tell him to enter. Only when she seemed to be well into her orgasm did she gasp "Now!"

He positioned his member and shoved. The first thrust got him all the way inside her, and it was like diving into a storm at sea. Everything was happening so violently that it was hard to tell how much of what he felt was his orgasm and how much was hers. But he must have gotten there, because his organ went limp and he had to withdraw it.

"That was better," she said. "Some fine tuning, and we'll have it."

So it seemed, again.

In the night they woke with a mutual urge. "I'll start myself," she said. "Be ready when."

He lay behind her, stroking her fine bottom in the darkness, waiting impatiently.

"Now."

His penis was ready. He rammed it into the rounded alcove, feeling her channel flex around it, and spurted almost immediately. She was right: the timing was good, and her clenching enhanced his jetting.

"But what about when we don't get hot together?" he asked.

"Good thought. Actually we don't have to climax together. When you feel the need, just enter me and do it; I'll understand. When I have the need, I'll nudge into you, and you enter, and there should be enough stiffness to enable me to finish mine."

"Good enough."

They slept again. He had eaten more fruit than she, and as a male was faster to react, so he was the first to wake. He found her posterior in the darkness and set his member carefully in. She remained asleep. There was something special about that, and he proceeded to a powerful orgasm. Then, sated, he slid out and returned to sleep.

At some point he felt her bottom nudging his groin. Oh. He grabbed his penis and held it out, touching her flesh. It wasn't even hard, but it wedged in. Then, as she embraced it internally, it stiffened, and held while she worked herself off. That was another interesting experience, and gradually the urge built up, and as she finished he went off too, though not strongly.

As dawn approached, he woke to find himself embedded in her again; she must have guided his member while he slept. Her flesh was warm and slick around him, but this time he didn't build to a climax. He held as firmly as possible while she did. Then, as she subsided, the urge came on him, and he started thrusting on his own. It didn't work very well, because she was lax after her orgasm, but she held still while he worked his way through it.

They got up. There was a small stream nearby, and they took turns scooping up handfuls of water for splash baths. Then they looked around.

"We've got to get away from this fruit," he said.

"I agree. Sex should be fun instead of forced. We need to let it rest."

He looked at the central tree. "I wonder."

"Let's do it."

They went to the tree, picked two of its ripe pear-like fruits, and bit into them.

"All is observed," a voice came from the tree. "This has been part of the show."

Oops. "You mean what we've been doing, even in the dark?" Prior asked.

A holographic picture formed in the air before them, as if made in daylight. It showed Veil stirring, holding her baby in front, backing into Prior, reaching back to catch his penis and guide it in to the cleavage of her bottom. It continued, taking them through the full sexual sequence. Somehow the

camera had gotten in close enough to show the details of the action, including her pink vulva lips as his somewhat flaccid member was moved along the
channel and crammed somewhat bendily into the hole. That was answer
enough.

"We should have known," Veil said tightly. "Put the animals in a setting,
feed them aphrodisiacs, and watch them perform for the circus crowd."

"Now you know," the tree said. "You will no longer be useful as innocent entertainment. Knowledge destroys naturalness. You are therefore ex-
pelled from Eden."

"We'll be glad to go home," Prior said. Somehow he doubted it would be
that easy.

Chapter 16–Gulf

Veil opened her eyes, wary of what she might find. Her caution turned out to be more than justified: she was in a bleak stony wasteland. Micro was beside her, his eyes still closed. They had been drugged again, and dumped in what appeared to be the gulf they had seen before. They remained naked, as was Chance.

There was a sound: an ugly snuffling or oinking. Something was coming. "Micro," she said urgently.

He woke. "Where are we?"

"In the gulf, I think. Something's coming."

Micro stood, somewhat unsteadily, and looked about. "Damn."

"What is it?" she asked, getting to her own feet, holding Chance.

"Pigs. Big ones. They smell us and are coming this way."

She looked desperately around. There was some scrub brush, but nowhere to go to.

"I'll try to distract them," he said. "You get away from here."

"And leave you to be overrun?"

"Better than both of us getting savaged."

It became academic. The pigs saw them and charged. They were huge brutes, a boar and a sow, standing two thirds as high as a person. It would be difficult or impossible to outrun them. "Stand still," Veil said. "They may not bother stationary targets."

They stood still. The pigs charged up and stopped. They put their snouts to the human crotches and sniffed, just like unmannerly dogs. Veil was terrified, but remained absolutely still, holding Chance up out of danger, as the boar nudged his snout up between her thighs. The sow seemed to be doing something similar to Micro.

The boar jammed harder. Veil lost her balance and stumbled. She managed to turn, flinging out her right hand to catch her fall as she shielded Chance with her left. She landed clumsily on hands and knees, her baby safe.

And the boar mounted her from behind. She couldn't scramble away because his forepart was on her, holding her down, while his corkscrew penis rammed into her posterior. It was all she could do to hold her position, so as not to collapse and crush her baby under her. All she could do was scream, and even that was more like a gasp, as she couldn't get enough of a breath.

The boar pizzle twisted like a screw being driven into a tight hole. It was small considering the size of the animal, but was distending her vagina awkwardly. She heard an urgent grunting. Then the semen came, like water from a firehose, flooding her aperture and pressuring out to slide down her legs.

Something moved. Blearily she saw a figure, maybe the other pig. There was a swishing sound, and a horrible smell.

The boar oinked and fell to the side. Veil was left on knees and one hand, her head spinning, her bottom soaking. What had happened?

A hand reached down to help her up. "Are you all right?" It was Micro's voice.

"What happened?"

"I farted."

"Come again?"

"The magic fart. My power. The sow was about to chomp my testicles, so I let her have it in the snout with a stunner. Then I came to stun the boar similarly. Did I get it in time?"

"Almost," she said, with a bit of a smile. What else was there to do? "I did get raped by a pig."

"I'm sorry. If I'd reacted faster—"

"I am familiar with sex, including the forced variety. I haven't freaked out. But I must say I'm angry."

"If I'd realized, I would have stunned them faster. I—I don't yet know all my powers."

"I'm not angry at you," she said. "I was caught offguard too. It's the damn rapist hog I'm mad at."

He considered. "We'll need food. Suppose we butcher it and eat it? Another magic fart will kill it."

Veil looked around. "I can gather some flint and make a knife, if you gather some wood for a fire. But I'm not sure how we'll light it."

"I can handle that."

She took him at his word. Carrying Chance, she foraged for the special stones she sought, while she saw him squat by the boar's head and blow out a visible cloud of vapor. The boar stopped breathing, while the sow struggled to her feet and fled the scene. He did have a remarkable nether talent.

She found several stones ranging from volcanic glass to chert, and cracked or chipped them until she had a crude blade. Meanwhile Micro fetched in several armloads of dry branches and twigs. He formed a small pyramid, then squatted, aiming his rear at it. What was he up to now?

A jet of flame shot from his anus, igniting the fire. Veil was so startled she dropped her stone knife. Those farts were truly magic!

She carved off a huge haunch. Micro came to help her, using a second crude knife she had made. "You're no helpless female," he remarked.

She didn't want to reveal the source of her expertise with knives, so demurred. "Merely kitchen skill."

They set the severed haunch on the fire. Soon the odor of roasting pig permeated the environment. "We seem to make a good team," Micro said.

"We do," she agreed.

In time they carved the roast and fed well. She nursed Chance, and set him in a comfortable declivity to nap. "One thing about this meat," Micro said. "It doesn't supercharge us sexually."

"That's a relief," she agreed. "I have nothing against sex, but I do prefer to indulge in it when I choose, rather than as an aphrodisiac forces the issue."

He nodded. "Actually I like it any time. But that fruit made me hungry for more too soon."

She saw his penis stirring. There was still some of that fruit in his system, as it was in hers. Despite recent events, she felt the urge. Nursing the baby sometimes had the effect. "If you wish to do it now, I'm amenable."

"But you just got—"

"Raped by a pig," she repeated. "I did get somewhat uncomfortably stretched. Therefore I ask you to be gentle."

He looked as if he was trying to demur, but his penis was thickening. Penises had little regard for finer instincts. "If you're sure. I don't want to hurt you."

"Let's do it this way," she said. "You lie supine and I will mount you. That way I will be in control, and can avoid discomfort."

"Great!" he agreed, and lay on his back on the ground, his member rising stiffly against his belly.

She straddled him, her thighs spreading outside his. She lifted his penis and fitted it carefully into her vagina as she lifted her body. She let herself down on him carefully. It was all right; the boar had stretched her, but Micro's normal sized member did not. Her buttocks came to rest on his groin, the connection complete.

"Oops," Micro said. "We're facing each other."

She had forgotten. "Perhaps this is no longer for purely sexual relief."

"I guess not," he agreed. "I like you a lot."

She remained there a moment, making sure. This was nice, but she needed more stimulation. "If you wish to fondle my breasts, you may."

"But they—you—"

"I nurse my baby," she agreed. "Is that a turnoff?"

"No! I mean, your breasts must be tender."

She smiled, knowing that he could not see the expression. She reached down and caught his two hands, lifting them to her breasts, which were very full. "They are, so stroke rather than grab. Do you wish to kiss them?"

"I, uh—"

She leaned down until her breasts were near his face. But she would have had to disconnect below to put them *at* his face, so she didn't. "Another time, perhaps."

He licked his lips. "Okay."

She sat back up, and he fondled, keeping it gentle. That helped, but still wasn't enough to work her up. "I will seek my own satisfaction," she said. "You will achieve yours in the course of that, I think."

"Sure. It's great just being in you."

She put her finger down and touched her clitoris, as she had when they had abated their drives the prior night. She titillated it, and felt desire spreading from it to her vagina. The clitoris was analogous to the man's penis, the most ready source of sexual response. Men, and many women, thought that female orgasm derived mainly from the vagina, but that was not true. It accounted for the difficulty many women had achieving orgasm; they were depending on the wrong stimuli.

She worked herself up, then went into the throes of her climax. At the height of it she felt Micro's member spurting; she had brought him off by her motions, rather than his thrusting. That had spared her most of the aggravation of the flesh caused by the pig. She was also satisfied to have erased that foul intrusion by overlaying it with a normal sexual event.

"You're great!" Micro gasped. "You didn't have to do it, but you did it for me."

"Perhaps," she agreed.

"I think I love you."

Such a reaction was fairly common with men during sex. "I care for you too," she said. Then she lifted off him, and used some dry moss to mop herself clean.

"No, really," he said. "You *are* my ideal woman."

"But you haven't seen my face."

"I admit it will be a shock if you turn out to have a face like a crone. But you're competent, and nice. I'm glad I came to rescue you, even if I'm not succeeding very well."

She was touched. "I selected you because you seemed to be the least objectionable of the candidates. But you, too, seem decent and competent."

"Well, I want to be, for you."

"But I do have my baby."

"I'm getting used to that. I don't have any experience as a father, but I'm willing to learn."

That was a significant hurdle being overcome. There were others. "Yet at such time as we return to our own culture, your amazing farts will not be of much use. I happen to be a woman of some means. That may deter you."

"Well, I sure never planned to marry for money. But if that's the price of you, maybe I can do good works, volunteer stuff, so as to have some self respect."

"Perhaps you can," she agreed. She did like him, as she came to know him. They could surely work something out.

He fidgeted. "Um, could I—kiss you?"

He was still feeling the emotion. "You may." She stepped into his arms.

He kissed her, his lips finding hers within her shroud. Then he kept his face close and whispered in her ear. "I think we're still be watched."

"I agree," she whispered back. "We're still entertainment. But how to we escape observation?" For surely the swine, trained to rape, were part of it.

"We go somewhere they don't expect."

"I agree," she said. Then they parted.

They carved more of the roast pig. Veil fashioned a crude basket of branches and twigs, and Micro hefted it. "I'll carry this, and we'll have food for several days," he said. "But we'll have to find water."

"Maybe downhill," she said.

They walked downhill, and in due course came to a small stream. They drank thirstily; the water was sparkling clear.

"Let's camp here for the night," Micro said.

He had something in mind? They foraged, and thus time fashioned a small lean-to of deadwood. They made another fire, ate more roast, performed natural functions downstream, and as darkness closed, lay in the lean-to, embracing for more sex. Actually it was a way to talk privately.

"I see the stream flowing away," Micro whispered. "But I don't see where it comes from. There must be a spring—or a cave."

"A cave system!" she whispered back.

"They might have trouble putting hidden cameras in there. We might be able to hide."

She wasn't sure of that, but it was better than nothing. "They can see us in the dark, and would know where we go."

"I thought about that. I can make an obscuring fart, so they can't see us."

She laughed, in a whisper. "How did you ever develop such a talent?"

"I didn't. I have a—a device."

"Ah, so you came to this realm prepared."

"Yes."

"Then let's go seek our cave," she said. "While they think we're indulging in sexual intercourse in the lean-to."

"It may stink some. Try not to cough."

She held Chance close and waited. She heard the faint hiss of escaping gas. There was an odor, not unpleasant, and the air around them seemed to thicken somewhat. The fart was taking hold.

They climbed carefully out of the lean-to and made their way upstream. There was just enough starlight so they could see; she hoped their accompanying cloud of mist prevented them from being seen.

Their guess was good: the stream emerged from the steepening slope of the edge of the gulf. Over the millennia it had widened its channel, and there was room for them to walk beside it.

But there was no light at all in the cave. They would quickly get lost in it.

Then Micro farted again, and this time the mist he issued glowed, faintly illuminating the cave. Truly, his farts were magical!

They followed the meandering stream channel upward, navigating dark pools and rapids as necessary. They were bound to reach the surface some time, and then, with luck, they would be free of observation and could try to return to their own realm.

There was a figure ahead. It seemed to be a woman, clothed in diaphanous gauze, of unearthly beauty. "Come to meee," she called.

"I don't trust this," Veil said.

But Micro was already walking toward the figure. He embraced her, kissed her, then bore her to the floor of the cave, which in that region was a cushioned bower. He was having sex with her already!

Then he wrenched up his head and looked back at Veil. "I'm stuck—in a—perpetual orgasm," he gasped. "She's a—a sexual vampire! I can't quit." His effort of free will exhausted, he returned to his long kiss.

A vampire! Veil figured it out: some vampires sought blood. Others were like deadly succubi, using pheromones to take over a man's testes and prostate, forcing him to keep generating and ejaculating the seminal fluid on which they fed. Until the victims expired.

She had to stop this. But how? Once the vampire got a man's member into her hole, she clamped on it so securely that if she were hauled away by brute force, she would rip off his penis in the process. She could not be persuaded to stop; she was a feeding mechanism. The accompanying kiss was the mechanism to feed in the pheromones, keeping him charged.

Veil reviewed her information, seeking an effective approach. Then she thought of something. It was truly weird, but just might work. She set Chance down. Even the baby had an erect penis in the present of this sexual monster.

She approached the vampire and put her face down by the thing's head. "I'm going to kiss you," she said to it. Then she took hold of its hair and wrenched its face away from Micro's face, breaking the kiss. Before the connection could be reinstated, she put her own mouth on the vampire's mouth.

But there were two differences. First, she was not a man, so the phero-mones did not affect her the same way, though they did make her clitoris twitch. Second, she was not inhaling, she was exhaling. She blew her air into the lungs of the creature. She breathed in through her nose, and blew more air out through her mouth. When some leaked out of the vampire's nose, she pinched it shut with her fingers, and went on inflating the body. The creature tried to struggle, but was locked on Micro and pinned under both him and Veil. It had very little play.

Veil continued to pump air into it. The vampire was not a regular person; her flesh was elastic, and almost boneless. It had no urethra or colon, only the business aperture, so there was no place to let the excess air out. The pressure was blowing it up like a balloon. It swelled, becoming fat, then rounded. Veil kept breathing, forcing ever more air inside.

At last the internal pressure was too great. Micro's intruding penis was popped out as the rubbery hole inverted. He rolled to the side, and lay there, staring upward. He was out of it for now.

Veil removed her mouth and let go of the vampire. Air whistled out of its mouth. The figure skidded along the cave floor, propelled by the escaping gas, then disappeared down the cave, involuntarily flying.

She focused on Micro. "Wake! We have to get out of here."

He lay there, moaning. A tired dribble of goo leaked from his subsiding penis. The pheromones had not yet cleared his body.

She got another idea. "Fart!" she said. "Magic fart. Fart out a nullifying gas. I know you can do it."

There was a small hiss as his colon got busy. A sweetish gas spread around them. It quelled her clitoris, and soon the man's penis shrank. But he remained too tired to move.

Well, that anti-pheromone gas was probably enough to keep the vampire away. She recovered Chance and lay beside Micro. "You're safe now," she murmured soothingly, holding his head against her breasts.

He recovered slightly. "You saved me!"

"A little late," she agreed.

He laughed weakly. "Just as I saved you from that pig a little late."

"So we're even now."

"I love you."

"You don't even know who I am. I don't know who you are. We can't speak of love." Yet her heart was yearning toward him.

"My name—my name is Prior Gross," he said.

Veil froze. She knew that name. This was the man she hated. The discov-ery was like a bucket of ice water, chilling her dawning affection for him. What a despicable pass!

Chapter 17—Escape

Prior emerged from his orgasmic horror to find Veil cradling his head on her soft bosom. He loved her; he knew it now. The succubus had not been fooling about this being his ideal woman.

"We don't even know each other," she was saying.

"I am Prior Gross," he said.

She was silent. Probably the name meant nothing to her. "I fetched a magical instrument called The Spire, so I could rescue you. That's what makes the magic farts. By myself I am nothing. So I can't blame you for lacking feeling for me."

"I have feeling," she said. "Strong feeling."

"That's good," he said, relieved, and sank back into sleep.

He woke later, significantly recovered. He didn't feel much like having sex for the next decade, but the rest of him seemed healthy.

Veil and her baby were sleeping beside him. He let out another illumination fart and looked around. The cave was quiet except for the trickle of the stream. They had gotten this far; they could surely make it the rest of the way to the surface.

He went to the water and scooped up a double handful to drink. He felt depleted, but the water seemed restorative.

A figure appeared, walking beside the water. The vampire! "Spire!" he said. "Blow her away!"

The Spire responded with a blast of gas. The vampire smelled it and fled.

Veil stirred. Her body was smudged with dirt, but she was a lovely creature. Even her baby was handsome for his age. He still knew very little about her, but was sure he wanted to spend the rest of his life with her, and not just because she had saved him from the vampire.

He went to help her up. She brushed away his hand. "I'm not helpless," she snapped.

Prior retreated. "Sorry."

She looked at him with an unfathomable expression. "You really don't know me," she said.

"I really don't," he agreed. "Just that I love you and want to spend the rest of my life with you."

She paused before speaking again. "We must make our way out of here. I want you to tell me about yourself as we do."

"Sure." And as they made their way, he told her of his larger background, encountering a succubus, discovering that his smegma had anti-VD properties, and having it stolen by a lady doctor.

"Who did that?" Veil asked sharply.

"Her name was Tantamount Emdee," he said. "Lovely creature, and I liked her. But that changed when she stole my penis. Oh, she sent me to her sister Oubliette, who made me a versatile prosthesis. But I wanted my real member back. So I went on a quest to find the Cherry Tree. I fought five demons, and won the Spire, the Cosmic Dildo, that jets anything it chooses to."

"That's where you got the magic farter, then."

"Yes, at the time. I left it with Tantamount for a year, spouting my formula of smegma, so she could have all she wanted."

"She must have been delighted."

"At first," he agreed. "Not later, when it flooded her out of her house."

"That was your revenge for the theft of your penis?"

"Yes."

"You must be very satisfied."

He considered. "I guess I was, at first. Not now."

"Why not?"

"Well, I got my penis back. I didn't really need to do that to her. It was pointless and unkind. If I ever see her again, I'll apologize. But her sister says she wouldn't talk to me."

"She wouldn't?"

"Oubliette made that very clear. Anyway, I don't know where she went."

"So you might as well forget it."

"Yes, if I can."

"Why can't you?"

He shrugged. "I did her wrong. I know it now. I can't make it right, but at least I could apologize, for what little it's worth."

They continued on up the stream cave. At length they reached the surface, where the stream encountered a blind gully and tunneled its way down into the gulf. It was still night, so they settled down to sleep until dawn. Veil cuddled her baby and turned away from him.

But then she did something odd. "Micro, I mean Prior, I have to catch up on a natural function. Will you mind Chance for a while?"

Prior was astonished. She had never let him touch her baby before. He sat up. "I'll try. But I don't know anything about babies. Suppose he cries?"

"Cuddle him," she said, and put the baby into his hands. Then she disappeared into the darkness.

Prior held the baby, who remained blithely sleeping. There was something nice about being trusted like this, though the little boy might well scream in protest when he discovered he wasn't being held by his mother.

There was an unearthly scream close by. Prior jumped, and the baby woke yelling. Something must have attacked Veil!

Prior found himself on his feet and hurrying toward the sound. "We'll help her, Chance," he said, trying to cuddle the baby without quite knowing how. There was faint light as dawn thought about coming; he could see well enough to avoid holes and rocks in the landscape. "Veil! Veil!" he called. "Where are you?"

"Over here," she answered.

He saw a dim shape. "Where's the animal? I'll stop it with a magic fart."

"No need. That was me."

He stopped where he was. "You?"

"My primal scream. It releases tension and helps me sort out my feelings."

He was relieved and annoyed. "I thought it was a beast attacking you. It scared me and woke Chance."

"Chance is quiet now."

So he was, Prior realized. His desperate reassurance had somehow worked, and the baby was resting quietly in his arms. "Uh, so did you get your business done?"

"That was my business."

"Then you can take Chance back now."

"No you keep him. We have to talk."

"I don't understand."

"You will, in due course."

They returned to their campsite and sat facing each other in the gloom. The baby was satisfied to return to sleep against Prior's shoulder. "What do we need to talk about?"

"Tantamount Emdee."

"I already told you about her."

"Not enough. You like her, don't you?"

"What do you mean?"

"What I said. You say you love me, but it's her you're thinking of."

He was amazed. "You're jealous of her?"

"Do I have reason?"

He started to protest, but was overcome by a confused rush of feeling. "I—don't know. I did her wrong, and she hates me, and I have to try to apologize, but I have to admit she's been on my mind some."

"So I have reason. You have unfinished business with her."

"I guess so," he said. "I do love you, but she's there in my background. I wish she didn't hate me."

"And if she were to stop hating you, you'd go back to her."

He laughed somewhat weakly. "There's no 'back' to go to. We were never together. We had one bout of sex, then she drugged me and stole my penis, and later I got back at her. Now I'm sorry. She never cared for me. She's not a caring person."

"How can you be sure of that?"

"Well, she cares about her research. She has all these ideas about making sex safe for the masses, forwarding science, and so on. Maybe she has a boyfriend; I don't know. She's smart and talented and dedicated. I was just a—a means to an end. So there's nothing there."

"There's enough to interfere with us."

He pondered. "I guess there is. I'm sorry. But you know, Veil, you're available and she's not, so—"

"The hell I am! You think I want to be someone's second choice?"

He nodded. "I guess not. Damn."

"So what are you going to do?"

"What *can* I do? I'll see you safely back to our realm, then I'll go find Tantamount and try to apologize. Then I guess I'll be on my own."

"I guess you will," she agreed. "What of the Spire?"

"I'll take that to Tantamount's sister Oubliette. She wants it, and it likes her. She's a great woman."

"You like her too."

"Yes. But she's even farther out of reach than Tantamount. She tried to help me win you."

"She what?"

"The thing about the Spire is it can make a woman desperately eager for sex, when it's set for that. Oubliette told me to touch you with the Spire."

"The bitch!"

"No, because you're my ideal woman. The Spire would make you want me. I wasn't able to touch you with it, and really, that's just as well, because that would not have been love, just passion. As it happens, you can make up your own mind, and that's best."

"Even if it means I don't marry you?"

He smiled in the dim light. "Best for you, not for me. That's the way it has to be. I really fouled it up."

"Perhaps." She looked around, her long dark hair flaring as her head turned. "We seem to have used up the night. We need to plan the rest of our escape."

"Yes. I figure I can fart us to food and lodging as we travel."

"No. Don't use the magic fart. That would be a dead giveaway, and they'd recapture us."

"But we have nothing, not even clothing. How can we make our way?"

"There are other contests. Farting is out, and I don't go for defecation. So it will have to be urination."

"Pissing?"

"There are contests for volume, color, and distance."

"Well, with the Spire I could—"

"No Spire."

"But I'm not that good a pisser."

"Fortunately I have a fairly tight bladder. I should be able to get some distance."

"I wouldn't ask you to—"

"We're not where we came from. Here women can urinate as freely as men."

Prior looked at her, out of sorts. "But your hood is as much of a give-away as the Spire. Neither of us can—" He paused, astonished. "Your hood is gone!"

Her mouth dropped open. "Oh!" She sounded oddly dismayed.

He peered at her face, but it wasn't yet light enough to get it clear of shadow. "Not that it matters. I'm sure I don't know you anyway.

"It matters," she said. "You'll know soon enough. I'm Tantamount."

Now his own jaw dropped. "But she doesn't have a—" He glanced at the baby, on his shoulder.

"And Chance is your son. Why did you think I was so angry?"

"But—but I never—"

"You certainly did. You seduced me with the Spire, and deliberately impregnated me. Not to mention burying my house in smegma. I had to give up my practice and hide, lest my reputation be destroyed."

Now he remembered. He *had* done that.

"I suppose it's too late to apologize," he said.

"Way too late," she agreed with controlled fury.

Chapter 18 – Trap

Well, now it was out, Tantamount thought as she worked her hair into a halter. Now that the secret was gone, she could afford to be comfortable to that extent. Of all the men who might have come to rescue her, this was the worst. But she was stuck with it.

One thing that really bothered her now was that she should have recognized him when she numbed his penis. His artificial member fitted very well, and there was no obvious juncture where it connected to his living body, but she was a doctor specializing in penile malaise. She should have caught on immediately that his member was artificial. She had been distracted by their situation, and had never thought to inspect it. The more fool, she.

"Well, I'll still do my best to get you out of here," he said. "Then you'll be free of me."

"Not so fast, you jerk. You can't just kiss off your son. You have legal responsibilities."

"My son," he echoed, as if just realizing. "He's quiet when I'm holding him. Does he realize?"

She shrugged. "You like holding him?"

He considered only briefly. "Yes."

That was one point in his favor. She had tested him by having him hold Chance when she did her primal scream. The baby had firm notions about who was all right and who wasn't.

"There was one thing I couldn't decipher," she said, as they ate the remaining roast pig Prior had hauled up through the cave. "Why was I kidnapped? At first I thought it was random, but I did wonder why they took a woman with a baby, surely a drug on the fresh maiden market. Then they arranged to notify you. That didn't make sense either, as long as you were anonymous. But now it is clear that this was set up from the start. The question is why. My sister evidently caught on, and thought it was a good match, the canine, but she didn't set it up. Who did that?"

"I don't know. Someone with a sadistic sense of humor. Putting you together with the man you most despised, and watching the action."

She nodded. "The ancient Romans had some similar entertainments. On the other hand there's the analogy of *The Magic Flute*."

"The what?"

"It's a literary reference. Naturally you wouldn't know." She was punishing him with her contempt.

"I'm an ignorant guy," he agreed, accepting it.

"It is an opera by Mozart, dating from 1791. The Queen of the Night gives a magic flute to a young prince so that he can rescue her daughter from the palace of an evil high priest who has abducted her."

"I'm the prince," he agreed, laughing weakly. "You're the kidnapped daughter." He shook his head ruefully. "Some prince!"

"But you were the one with access to the magic fart."

"The Spire," he agreed. "But this can't be an old opera."

"That depends on the whim of whoever set this up. There does seem to be a certain devious logic."

Chance woke and began to fuss. "I guess I'd better give him back to you," Prior said. "He's been great." He held the baby out.

"He's hungry," she agreed, taking Chance and putting him to her breast. "How does it work out, in the opera?"

"The prince goes to the castle of the high priest, protected from danger by the music of the flute, and discovers to his surprise that the man is not evil, but merely protecting the girl. The prince gets to know the girl, and likes her a lot, and she him. So the prince undergoes the ordeal of the search for truth. This prevents him from speaking to the girl, who thinks he doesn't love her."

"So much for the parallel."

"Parallels can be figurative as well as literal. We met each other anonymously, here in Fartingale, so had our misunderstandings."

"Like my thinking you could love me," he said.

"I confess to being severely stressed with respect to that. I was coming to like you, before I discovered your identity."

"That's the opposite of the opera."

"Opposites are parallels too. Here is what I am faced with: you are the father of my son. I don't love you but I do love Chance. I want what is best for him. So I am obliged to consider you seriously."

"This is hell for you."

"Yes. I am trying to fathom who hates me enough to do this to me."

Prior spread his hands. "I really am sorry. I do like you a lot, love you even. I'll do anything to make it right, if I can. I just don't know what that is. So—whatever you decide."

"Thank you," she said tightly. "First I want to escape this awful culture and return home. Thereafter I'll decide."

"Fair enough," he agreed. "But maybe you'd better let me use the magic fart."

"No. I think urine is our best bet, and I'm the one to do it. Now that my hood is gone, I'm essentially anonymous. That will help."

"Except for Chance," he said. "They'll be alert for a woman with a baby."

She put her hand to her forehead. "Oh! I forgot about that. You're right."

"Maybe I can use the magic fart after all. I can made a little cloud that conceals the baby, making him invisible, if I'm carry him. Then we'll look like an average young couple."

"That might work. We'll have to act like it, kissing and such."

"I'm sorry."

"Don't be," she snapped. "It's a necessary act."

"Not for me."

She paused. "You really thought of me during our separation?"

"Yes. You're such a smart, beautiful, motivated person—all the things I'm not. Now I understand why you took my penis. It was for the benefit of mankind."

"Don't praise me for that! I let the ends justify the means. My sister told me that, and now I realize it's true. I did wrong you."

"We were pretty mean to each other."

"We were indeed." What was getting to her was that she found herself softening toward him. They had offsetting wrongs, and with that cancellation, what was left was an ignorant but decent guy, and her need for legitimacy. She didn't want her son to be a bastard.

"Let me see what I can do," he said as Chance finished nursing. He took the baby back, and there was the squeak of a narrow fart. A trail of vapor floated up from his posterior and clung to his upper section, surrounding Chance.

And Chance disappeared.

"But can he breathe?" she asked, alarmed.

"Sure. Take a breath and see."

She put her face to the cloud and inhaled. The mist was faintly sweet, like dilute perfume, and made her feel satisfied and sleepy, but not out of breath. It was a rather special magic. She put her hand in and found Chance, nestling peacefully.

"I have to acknowledge that the Spire is apt," she said. "This will do. Very well, let me see whether I'm fit to pee, as it were." She found a rock as the light brightened, sat on, it leaned back, and let fly a long jet of urine. "Measure that."

Prior paced it off, from her feet to the wet landing spot. "About six feet."

"I doubt that's good enough. These folk are competitive pissers. But with practice and a full bladder I'll improve. Let's go find a clothing shop." She was privately amazed to hear herself talking like this, but this did seem the best way to travel anonymously.

"We'd better tank up," Prior said.

"Agreed." Prior lay on the ground by the steam and sucked in water, man style, while she scoped handfuls up to sip, woman style. They both drank until their stomachs were full. This was uncomfortable, but she, at least, needed the ammunition.

They walked across the terrain, following the stream upstream. Water was usually a good place to find human habitation. After an hour they came to a small settlement. A sign identified it as Piss Creek. Good; a urination contest should be quite in order. Her bladder was already filling.

She took Chance back and nursed him, then returned him to Prior. Not having to carry his weight made her walking easier.

"Here's our situation," she told Prior. "We were out walking and lost our clothes in the stream; they just disappeared into the ground. We were part of a tourist tour, and missed our transport. We need to get some clothing."

"They won't just give it to us."

"Correct. So we'll piss for it."

They came to the central privy, always a social center. It was posted with ads: MULTI-COLORED TURDS, GUARANTEED. EMPOWER YOUR FARTS: FLOWERY SMELLS, GREATER VOLUME, MELODIOUS SOUND, IMPROVED VELOCITY. MASTER THE POWER OF PISS: THE FAMILY THAT PEES TOGETHER, SEES TOGETHER. While she read the notices, Prior spoke to a likely man, telling the story Tantamount had suggested.

"Nothing's free," the man said sourly. "Where's your money?"

"Lost that too. We'll have to piss for it."

The man nodded. "We're always up for a good pissing, here in Piss Creek. Folk who piss together, have bliss together. What stakes?"

"Clothing for each of us, versus a fast fuck with my wife, who will be the contestant."

The man looked at Tantamount, seeing her shape. "My wife's got spares, and my son needs a good fuck."

"She's not going up against a man," Prior said quickly.

"Naturally not," the man agreed, though evidently he had had it in mind. "My daughter will take her on."

It was playing out pretty much the way Tantamount had planned; her research in the Tower now stood her in good stead. Soon the villagers gathered for the spot show; pretty women were more fun to watch urinating than men.

The man's wife showed off a good used farthingale dress that looked as if it would fit, and a pair of pantaloons. The son and daughter come out.

"First pissing," the man announced. "For the dress."

Oops—they wanted to contest separately for the items, instead of making it a package deal. They were stuck for two contests.

The daughter, who was a halfway comely teen girl, removed her dress, sat on the pissing stool and let fly with a good stream that cut off abruptly. The spectators applauded. Trust the villagers to know how to do it well. It was necessary to have a sufficient amount to maintain a steady flow, however briefly, and the girl had done that.

Tantamount took the stool, held her breath, compressed her bladder, and forced out a powerful stream. It splashed just beyond the girl's effort. The villagers applauded again.

"You won it," the man said, handing Prior the farthingale. Now for the pants."

The daughter let fly with another jet, the same distance as the first. But Tantamount, her pressure diminished, fell short. She had expended too much urine the first time, her inexperience costing her.

"Well, now," the son said, stepping forward, his member stiffening.

"Hey, we didn't say public," Tantamount protested. She knew she was stuck for the fuck, but there were limits.

There was a sigh of regret among the villagers. But they went along, allowing Tantamount to take the young man into the closed privy. She put her hands on the seat, presenting her bottom.

"Hey I want it from the front," the boy protested.

"You can't feel my breasts from the front," she pointed out. "This way you can reach around me."

"Say yeah," he agreed. Without further argument he stepped up behind her, put his stiff penis to her cleft, reached around to grab her breasts, and rammed home. He jetted on the first thrust, being young.

That was it. One advantage of doing it with a teen boy was that it was fast. He was out in a moment, and she grabbed some toilet paper and wiped herself dry.

But they still needed the pantaloons, and she had little urine left; she had let too much flow in the contests. "Let me consult privately with my husband," she said as they returned to the plaza.

The villagers smiled. Women paid off their bets, but often preferred to have follow-ups with their own men, to erase the feel of foreign intrusion.

Prior joined her in the privy. "Give me Chance," she said.

"Oh." He obliged. She nursed the baby as she talked. "I need more urine."

"That will take time."

"No. I want it now, so we can win the pants and be on our way. You have it."

"I'm no good at power pissing."

"I need you to give it to me."

"I don't understand."

"Put your penis to my urethra and urinate with sufficient force to transfer it to my bladder."

He stared. "You can't be serious!"

"You do want clothing?"

"Yes, but—"

"We don't have time to debate this." She took his penis and lifted it as she sat on the potty hole. "Do it."

"I don't think it's possible."

"I'm a doctor, remember? This would be much easier with a catheter, but we don't have one, so will simply have to make do. Hold it tight to the mark and urinate, hard."

"I can't. I've got a hard-on."

True; his penis had swelled with her manipulation, and that blocked off the avenue. He had recovered from the vampire depletion. "Very well, abate your lust," she snapped, and directed his stiff member into her vagina. She clenched on it, then used her hand to draw his bottom forward so that he entered her without delay. In a moment he caught the fever and thrust on his own, and in another moment his orgasm sent his semen surging into her. Good; that was out of the way.

She drew out his softening penis and set it against her urethra, but the fit wasn't tight. "Hold Chance," she said.

He took the baby back and stood there, his diminishing penis at her cleft. She used both hands to hold it there, actually forcing the lubricated tip part way into her urethra. "Urinate. Now."

Still he hesitated, his reactions not cooperating.

"Piss!" she snapped, slapping his bottom.

That jolted him into action. The urine started. It squirted wastefully out around the edges. She mashed the rounded head against her vulva lips and pressed the tip farther in. It was a messy connection but the leakage stopped. She tried to relax her own channel, so as not to oppose the reverse flow. Still it balked, the pressure equalized. Then she got smart, and tried to urinate herself. That opened the channel with the pressure higher on his side. Gradually, the urine coursed down through his tube and up hers, and made its way to her bladder. She felt it slowly filling. The sensation was weird but not unpleasant. She was thankful that as a woman she had a short urethra, facilitating the transfer.

"Good," she said. "Keep the pressure on. Squeeze it all out, into me."

He did, and the flow strengthened, now that the channels had been opened. There was a lot of it, because he had not urinated recently. She felt her belly distending uncomfortably, but this was exactly what she wanted.

"It's like spurting," he grunted. "Only with piss."

"You are sending your substance into me," she agreed. "There's a parallel. Keep it coming."

He bore down, forcing it out. "This is weird. I'd be coming now, if I hadn't just come."

"Lean down so I can kiss you."

He did, carefully so as not to press on the baby. She kissed him ardently, surprising herself. "I like it when you come through for me," she told him. She felt his penis twitch in response; indeed he would have gotten an erection if she hadn't just taken his edge off. This was a whole lot like sex. They would have to try it some time just for fun. Would it be possible to reverse it again, and have her urinate into him? Suppose they tried it when he had a full erection? This was an aspect of male sexuality she had never had occasion to explore. She was interested as a scientist, and perhaps as a woman too.

Finally he ran out; he could pump no more. She released his penis as she clenched her urethra closed. Urine spattered out and on them both. She cleaned them up, quickly. "Now we go out and conquer," she said. "Keep Chance concealed."

"Oh," he said evidently bemused. "I never did that before, exactly." He issued a small fart that rendered the baby invisible again.

"Obviously." She took his arm and urged him outside.

"We consulted," Prior said, gesturing at his limpening penis. The villagers nodded understandingly.

"He recharged me," Tantamount said. "Now I'm really ready to piss."

The daughter let fly a third time, having rationed herself to keep pressure up. Then Tantamount jetted, readily outdistancing her.

The villagers applauded again. "He really did recharge you," the man said, handing over the pantaloons.

"He's more of a man than he looks," she agreed. "Now we'd like some food to travel on."

"We've got food," the man said. "But my son's fucked out. You really took care of him. Will you take me on?"

"Yes, if your wife agrees."

"I want to see her piss again," the woman said.

So it was agreed. The daughter pissed once more, making the same mark a fourth time. Then Tantamount did, matching her third mark. This time the applause was considerable; the villagers were impressed, because her volume was much greater than the daughter's had been. Only the man looked disappointed;

he had wanted that fuck.

"Come with me," the wife said, leading Tantamount into her hut. She made an efficient bundle of assorted fruits and breads. "A good fuck can satisfy a man, but I never saw it help a woman to piss better. I'll trade you for your secret."

"What do you offer?"

"Information of likely interest to you."

"Give it."

"You are being watched, your actions recorded. My guess is you're a Tower Maiden."

"Damn!" Tantamount swore. "I thought we'd slipped that noose."

"There's no escape, just new settings, as they wring the last bit of entertainment from you. Ordinary folk aren't in on it, but I was a Tower Maiden in my youth, and I learned how it was. They let you think you're free, and a selected paying clientele gets to watch. So they know what happened in the privy; I don't."

"I took his urine," Tantamount said, and explained the process.

The woman whistled. "That's a new one! I'll tell my daughter, but I don't think she'll go for it unless there's a really big prize on the line."

"I thought our prize was anonymity," Tantamount said.

"I'd like to make another deal, to explain to the others what we talked about," the woman said. "Not the pissing secret." She lifted a small bottle of wine, as if pondering whether to add it to the bundle.

"That fuck for your husband," Tantamount said immediately.

The women smiled. "That will do. You're a lovely woman. He's a good man; he deserves an occasional nice piece."

"You're a very understanding wife."

"The Tower experience broadens one's perspective." She put the wine into the bundle.

"It certainly does," Tantamount agreed fervently. In this land, sex was an open commodity. "I'll make your man glad."

They returned to the public privy. "Honey," Tantamount said to Prior. "I made another deal. For a bottle of wine." She opened the bundle to show it.

"What deal?" Prior demanded, playing the part of the possessive partner.

"That fuck for her husband."

"The hell!" Prior exclaimed as the husband's face lighted.

"Taste the wine." She opened the bottle and proffered it to him. "Agree," she murmured.

He tasted the wine. "Damn, that's good. Okay, but make it quick."

Tantamount took the husband into the privy. "How would you like me?"

"How'd you do it with my son?"

"I bent over," she said, demonstrating. "So he could fondle my breasts at the same time."

"I don't want to step in his tracks. Give it to me front face."

"Hold me close," she said, stepping into him as he doffed his pantaloons. She lifted one leg high so he could guide his penis in, then clung tightly, wrapping both legs around his body as he stood. He put his hands on her bottom, squeezing her buttocks as he held her up.

"Hoo!" he gasped, loving it. He thrust, lifting her body, then relaxed and thrust again. The play wasn't great, because she was supported in large part by his pole within her, but it was enough. Soon he was pressuring out his fluid. "God's fart!" he swore blissfully.

She knew he had had his best climax in years. She kissed him as he faded. "Your wife bought it. She said you deserve it."

"I'll thank her every day!"

She dropped her feet to the floor and disengaged. She cleaned up again, but let him drip. "Go show your neighbors," she said.

They went out, and the man showed off his spent penis, advertising his enormous satisfaction, while Tantamount assumed an air of innocence. The villagers applauded again, understanding everything, and the men (plus a few women) looked appropriately jealous. They would remember this visit a long time.

Soon Prior, Tantamount, and Chance were on their way, walking the path that led to the next village. "Something I wondered about," she said. "What made my hood fade out?"

"It must have had a time limit."

"I don't think so. It seems we're still under observation."

"We're what?" he asked, startled.

"The wife was a Tower Maiden in her youth. A lot of the local women were, considering there's a new one every week. She told me, and I believe her."

"So we're still monkeys in a cage."

"We still are. We'll have to keep performing, assuming they don't know we know."

He laughed ruefully. "After that sex vampire, I thought I wouldn't want sex for weeks, but you got me hot in a minute. You know how to make me spout. If you want to."

She avoided that. "So the reason for the hood fading out was to let us think we had escaped. Unless there was some other trigger."

"I've got it," he said. "When I spoke your name."

"My name!" she agreed. "That would of course be it." She paused, thinking it through. "But you didn't actually know my identity in the cave."

"The program's not smart enough to know the difference. It figured I spoke your name because I knew you. That washed out the hood, because it was supposed to make no difference then."

"So it would seem."

"So we're not out of it yet. Whatever happens, I have to say that you're a great woman, and you proved it yet again in the village, doing what you had to to get us clothing and food. Whatever you need of me, you can have, even if it's just urine."

She smiled without having to force it. "Thank you."

They moved on, eating the food, drinking the wine, nighting at villages. They might be under observation, but there was no interference. Would the Tower authorities allow them to walk right out of Fartingale?

In the evening, in a nice room in an inn she had won by expending more of Prior's piss, her head tingling with a bit more wine than she should have taken, facing the prospect of a joint bed, she came to a conclusion. "I believe you will do."

"Do what?" he asked.

"You're a decent man, down deep. I can't say I love you, yet, but I do like you. My hate for you was evidently a function of my feeling *for* you, because you had seemed to dismiss me with contempt. It seems best simply to recognize this and accept you. I could do worse."

"Accept me?"

"When we return home, I will marry you."

He gazed at her. "Oh, Tantamount! You really are my ideal—"

Then things changed.

Part 4:
Fart Off

Chapter 19—Challenge

"—woman," Prior concluded. But the woman and baby were gone.

Then a picture appeared. It showed a horrendous demon with a nine-inch penis as thick as a young tree trunk. "A salutation, shithead," he said. "Do you recognize me?"

Bemused, Prior wasn't sure. "One demon looks much like another, to me," he said. "Where's Tantamount?"

The demon fuzzed and shifted into the image of a limb from a tree, with a single bright cherry. "Now do you know me, turdass?"

"The cherry tree!" Prior exclaimed. "The First Branch."

The demon reappeared. "You got it at last, pukemouth. I'm ba-a-ack."

"But I abolished you," Prior protested. "I fucked you into oblivion."

"Get this straight, twat-head. You had the incredible luck to get your perverted little weenie into my ass and send me into limbo for a year. Now my time is up and I have reconstituted. By demonic law I can neither re-challenge you nor indulge in another fuck fight with you. None of us can. But that doesn't mean I'm willing to let that outrage pass."

"All—of you demons—are back?" Prior said, horrified.

"With a vengeance, feces-face. We spent our time in limbo planning how to fix you once we got the chance. We realized that we would have to make you come to us. That meant we would have to have something you wanted, even if you didn't know it yet. So we set you up with a special Tower Maiden and gave you a chance to get to know her."

That explained everything. They had abducted Tantamount and let him know it, without naming her. She really was his ideal woman, as he now knew. They had arranged it so that he would discover this. The moment she committed to him, so that he knew there really could be a future with her, they had pounced. She had never been the real target; *he* had been. She was the one thing that would make him come to the vengeful demons. She had served their purpose admirably.

The demon nodded, aware of the progress of Prior's thoughts. "Now here's how it's gonna be, fuckass. We can't challenge you, but you can challenge us. We can't fuck you, but we can fart you. So you are going to challenge each of us to a farting to the death as long as you last, which won't be long because I will vaporize you before my sibling branches have the chance, much to their displeasure."

Prior knew he had been supremely lucky to have beaten the five demons, there on Mount Icecream. He knew better than to tackle them again. He would have to find some other way to rescue Tantamount from their possession. "Forget it, twiggy. I'm not getting into a hexagon with any of you."

The demon frowned. "Oh, that's too bad, pantywaist. Are you sure I can't persuade you to change your ignorant little mind?"

"Quite sure," Prior said.

"Not even if I do something foul to your girlfriend?" The demon reached out of the picture, caught hold of something, and hauled Tantamount into sight by her hair. Baby Chance was still in her arms.

"Let her go!" Prior said. "She's not part of this!"

"Ah, but she is, stink-guts. She is your inspiration."

"She's my fiancée," Prior agreed. "But you have no quarrel with her."

"Here's how it is, putrid prick. She's going to ask you to challenge us."

"No I won't!" Tantamount cried. "Don't do it, Prior!"

"So why should I?" Prior asked, though he was now distinctly nervous. These demons were not nice folk.

"Because," the demon said with relish, "I just might encourage her with some fucking heat."

"Heat?" Prior asked blankly.

"Like so: a small demonstration." The demon hauled the woman in to him, forced her legs up, and inserted his thick member into her flinching vagina.

"Raping me won't accomplish anything," Tantamount said scornfully. "I've already been raped by a pig. You're just another pig."

"Give it a moment, honey," the demon said, shoving the full nine inches in with an obviously satisfying effort. Tantamount winced but did not protest.

Then she began to look uncomfortable. Then she struggled to free herself, but the demon held firm. "Oh, it's hot!" she cried.

"You don't say." The demon faced Prior. "I can heat my member to red hot," he said conversationally. "That makes no difference to you, since I can't fuck with you. But it just may make a difference to her. I think we're about a hundred and twenty degrees now."

Tantamount screamed in pain. Prior realized that he hadn't thought this through well enough: Tantamount wasn't just a way to bring him to the demons, she was a way to make him do their will.

"Or higher," the demon said. "I'll just cook her innards until you see the light, diarrhea-snot. Take your time; this is fun."

Tantamount screamed again, in obvious agony.

It was too much. "I'll do it," Prior said.

The demon cupped an ear. "Eh? Did you say something?"

Tantamount's mouth stretched in a rictus of torment.

"I challenge you!" Prior yelled.

The demon nodded, and allowed Tantamount to scramble off his steaming member. "I'll just have to roast this pig another time," he said, as she collapsed into a huddled mass. "Your appointment with me is tomorrow at noon, at Castle Demon. Be late if you wish; your gal here is a nice hot fuck."

Prior knew he would not be late.

Chapter 20 – Tease

Tantamount huddled pitifully. It was true she was hurting, and had been made to scream, but not completely true. She had realized that the demon intended to make her scream, and that he had the capacity to do so, so she had obliged sooner rather than later. Thus she had avoided suffering actual heat damage to her vaginal tract, though even so the pain had been awful. There was no question: she was in the monster's power. She was the lever to make Prior do what he didn't want to do: risk his life by fighting the demons a second time.

She didn't want him to do it. But she knew he would, as long as she was hostage to his performance. She wished she had just kept quiet about her decision to marry him; then the demons wouldn't have pounced. She had really brought this horror on herself.

But all was not yet lost. If she could escape the demon, Prior wouldn't have to do battle. She would simply have to use her feminine cunning.

"This is your room, bitch ass," the demon said. "Make yourself comfortable. You will be my mistress, once I abolish your boyfriend, so keep your hole tender."

She didn't argue, knowing it was useless. It was surely true: if Prior died, she would remain indefinitely in the demon's power, and what else would he want from her other than sex? Every act of copulation would be a further reminder of his victory over his enemy. She understood that demons liked possessing human lovers; it was a mark of status, since few humans agreed to such liaisons willingly. Not when the demons were the ones holding the power.

She surveyed the room. There was a fancy double bed in the center, a basin and large chamber pot in the corner, and what appeared to be plenty of closet space. There was also a table with an assortment of fruits, breads, pastries, and drinks. And even a television set in another corner, next to a crib. This had evidently been set up for her occupation, awaiting her acquisition.

"It will do," she said.

"It had better, sweet cunt." The demon faded out.

She went to the table and sampled the food. She had to eat, so as to have milk for Chance. She sipped a glass of blue lemonade; it was surprisingly tasty. But almost immediately her stomach went to gas; this was fart food. It seemed the demons liked farts too. Or maybe it was simply another aggravation they were inflicting on her.

She ate, nursed Chance, and turned on the TV set. It offered the usual fare: news features, weather, and feculent fiction. She might as well have been back in the Tower.

She put Chance down to sleep, and used the pot. No need to store urine now; she would have no need of it. She was almost sorry to let go of the last of the fluid Prior had provided her. He had adapted well enough to the necessity, a point in his favor.

She washed up and went to bed. She blew out the lamp. She needed her rest.

Two hours later she woke, went to the crib, picked Chance up, and nursed him in the darkness. Then, carrying him, she made her silent way to the chamber door. There was a faint glow to the walls, enabling her to see her dim way. She explored the hall and adjacent chambers, searching for she knew not what.

She found it: a small rolled carpet. This was a magic castle, in a land where magic was common, at least for those who could afford it. She spread the carpet on the floor, sat cross-legged on it, and whispered "Lift."

It rose from the floor. Sure enough, it was a magic carpet. She had hardly dared hope, but had had to seek any possible avenue of escape.

"Down," she said, and it descended to the floor. She rolled it up again and carried it to her room. She opened the big window wide, then spread the carpet and got on it again, holding Chance. "Up and out, carefully," she said.

The carpet obligingly rose and floated slowly out the window. The starry night was above and around. She was free! But this was only the beginning; she needed to get well away from here, so the demon would not locate her and fetch her back.

She pondered briefly. "Nude-on-Toilet," she said, identifying the village Prior had passed through. It was near the path leading away from Fartingale. If she got there, the demon might never find her. Prior was bound to pass that way when he left, so she could intercept him.

The carpet accelerated smoothly, climbing and flying through the darkness. She saw the lights of a nearby village, and the dark outlines of trees. Glorious!

The flight became dull; the village was several hours distant. She slept sitting up, as the carpet was not large enough for her to stretch out comfortably.

She woke as it descended toward a village. She saw a statue of a bare woman sitting on a potty: this was Nude-on-Toilet!

"The house of Smellie," she said, hoping the carpet was knowledgeable enough to know it. Evidently it did; it landed before one of the huts in the village.

"Wait here," she told the carpet as she got off, knowing she would need it again. Just to be sure it stayed, she lifted a corner and kissed the cloth. "I like you." The carpet made a shiver of pleasure. It would stay.

She held Chance and knocked on the door.

After a moderate delay, a hooded figure opened it. "Yes?"

"I—am a friend of—of Micro. I believe you know him."

"Oh, yes! Come in."

Tantamount entered. The woman's comprehensive hood reminded her of her own recent masking. Then she remembered: Smellie was recovering from magic facial surgery. "Micro helped you."

"Yes!"

"May I see?"

The woman drew back the hood. Her face was beautiful. "It's still healing," she said uncertainly.

"It's a success. You are lovely."

"Really?"

"Really. You are now a beautiful woman."

"I'm so relieved." Then Smellie got practical. "Who are you, and why are you here?"

"I was the Maiden in the Tower. Micro rescued me."

"Oh, yes, he wanted to do that. He said you were his ideal woman."

"So I turned out to be. But then the demons pounced, and are using the threat of harming me to make him fight them, so they can kill him. I must escape. Will you help me?"

"How can I help you?"

"By hiding me until he realizes they have no hold on him. Then he'll go home, and will surely pass this way." It sounded simplistic as she said it, but it was all she could do. Prior would surely look for her, and the demons would track him as he did, so she had to be excruciatingly careful.

Smellie nodded. "I will do what I can. But it is too soon for me to ply my trade. My face is not yet healed; it hurts when anything touches it. I can't even kiss a man."

"As it happens, I can. Bring your men here, and promise them rapture in darkness. I will deliver that." Thus would she earn her keep: anonymously whoring. This misadventure in Fartingale had certainly changed her circumstance.

They discussed it, and concluded it was feasible. Then Tantamount set

Chance down on the bed, and something weird happened. The blanket rose up and wrapped itself around him.

Startled, Tantamount reached to take her baby back, but the blanket constricted, making Chance cry. "Forget it, bitch," the blanket said. "I will crush your brat to death."

"The demon!" she exclaimed in horror.

"The First Branch," the blanket agreed. "Now it is time to go home. We wouldn't want to disappoint your idiot man, would we? He expects to do battle with me at noon."

"My escape—it was just a tease," Tantamount said.

"It was a demonstration, whore girl. You can't escape as long as I have your brat. Do you concede that, or shall I throttle him now?" The blanket tightened around Chance's throat.

"I concede it!" she cried.

"I'm so sorry," Smellie said.

"And you, fart face, will not speak of this."

"Never," the woman agreed, cowed. What else could she do? The demon could throttle her too.

"Now sit on me," the blanket said, shifting to the magic carpet form. "We have a way to go."

Meekly, Tantamount picked up Chance and sat cross-legged on the carpet. It lifted and plowed into the wall—and through it without resistance, giving her a momentary scare. A demon trick. It sailed up into the brightening sky.

Something goosed her. "Oh!"

"Sit still, slut slot. I'm giving you a ride; I'm going to soak my pecker comfortably on the way. Do you have a problem with that?"

Tantamount realized how readily the demon could drop Chance off, to fall and be smashed on the ground far below. "No problem."

The center of the carpet rose up, forming the demon's phallus, and poked into her reluctant vagina. "Like that cute story you told the impotent jerk, even the sheets wanting to get into her," the demon said. "You'll be riding my motherfucking horn for the next hour, young mother. Relax and enjoy it, cuddle cunt, while you feed your brat. Fuck and suck, ha-ha." Each syllable of the laugh drove the cloth phallus farther in.

She couldn't relax, as the demon knew, but refused to give him the satisfaction of protesting. She was stuck for his teasing.

Chapter 21—First Branch

Prior spent a restless night, hating what he had brought on Tantamount. He was the reason she had been abducted and made a Tower Maiden; he was the reason she was now being tortured. It really, truly, was all his fault.

But he loved her. He would do what he had to do.

He had no trouble finding his way to Castle Demon. It was not far off, and everyone knew where it was, and avoided it.

The castle itself was like a giant tree: a cherry tree, with five massive branches. That was the code name of the demons who had been assigned to guard the Spire; he had defeated them and taken the Spire, and thus earned their enmity. Could he beat them again? What choice did he have? He couldn't let Tantamount remain in their vile hands. He had no doubt they were forcing her into sex already; any threat to her baby—*his* baby—would be enough. Just as any threat to her was enough to force him to challenge. They had planned this trap most cunningly.

"Okay, I'm here," he called. "First Branch, I challenge you to a farting off."

The demon appeared. "To the death," said. "You have to say that, or I can't kill you."

"There's a choice?"

"Of course. Most contests are merely to unconsciousness."

"And that won't do?"

"Put it this way: your girlfriend needs impaling. She will get it in an hour, if you don't arrange to prevent it."

"You're raping Tantamount," Prior said flatly. He knew the demon was trying to rattle him.

"That, too. She has a most conducive hole, and I expect to be reaming it for some time, as I did this morning. But this is more specific."

Prior didn't want to ask, but had to. "How so?"

"I'm so glad you asked. Are you a student of history?"

"Not much."

"I'm thinking of the Assyrians. They won many battles, and liked to impale their enemies on tall stakes. The point of the stake was set into the victim's asshole; then the stake was erected and set in the ground with the man on top. His own weight slowly drove the stake deeper into his rectum and his guts, until at last he expired. Admirable folk, the Assyrians; I can't think why others didn't like them."

Prior did not like the direction this was taking. "What has this to do with Tantamount?"

"Behold." The demon gestured.

A stout wood stake appeared, sharpened to a point above. Suspended over it was Tantamount, holding the baby in a sling. Her arms were extended up over her head, her wrists tied by a thick loop of rope. The rope passed over a pulley and descended to a big old fashioned clock that had the current time: noon. The loop was wound around a wheel that was evidently on the same axle as the minute hand of the clock; in an hour it would rotate a full turn, releasing about a foot of rope. She hung there unmoving, though her eyes showed she was conscious.

"Now let's complete the setting," the demon said. He went to the stake, reached up, caught the woman's legs, and pulled them down around the stake. The rope gave, allowing this. "Now let's see your pretty little pucker, sweetie." He parted her legs and guided her hanging body so that the point of the stake just touched her cleft. He drew her body down a little more, so that the point nudged into her vagina. "I see you know better than to kick or struggle, dearie," he said. "Because that will merely cause the rope to slip faster, dropping you onto the stake. Absolute stillness is best; then only the passage of time brings your descent. Nevertheless, it could become uncomfortable after half an hour, and worse after an hour, as the penetration moves from half a foot to a full foot. At some point your lovely wet cunt will run out; then the prick will deepen it in its own pointed fashion." He turned to Prior. "Have I made the situation clear, smegma brains? Within the hour one of us is bound to win, and that person will rescue the woman, with luck before she suffers significant harm. If the contest should extend beyond an hour, that can not be guaranteed. But you are welcome to take your time if you want to."

"It won't take an hour," Prior said grimly. "Let's get on with it." He had no certainty of defeating the demon, but obviously had to try. Win or lose, it had to be fast.

"Done." The demon gestured, and a pentagram appeared: a five pointed star. "The combat will take place within the figure; if you wish to take a break, merely step out." He stepped in.

Prior doffed his pantaloons and stepped in, naked. Instantly the demon was on him, wrestling him to the ground. "First I owe you for that candle fuck." He got Prior on his belly, lay on top of him, and angled his ramrod penis into the crack of his posterior. "An ass fuck doesn't count for this, but bear with me; it's for personal satisfaction. It wouldn't be the same after you're dead."

Prior struggled, but was helpless. He couldn't get his hands or feet under him; the demon's weight kept him flat. Meanwhile that phallus was driving at his rectum, trying to force the aperture.

He looked up, and saw Tantamount, already lower on the pole. The demon was happy to take his time, but Prior wasn't. He had to finish this soon.

Time, Spire, he thought urgently.

I THOUGHT YOU'D NEVER ASK. the Spire gouted. Then it issued a small thin little squeaker of a fart.

"What a pipsqueak!" the demon said. "You call that a fart? That hardly shook my pecker hair." He sniffed. "This wouldn't stun a butterfly! It's laughable."

"I'm going to beat you," Prior gasped.

"Not with that puny little effort. The very idea is hilarious." The demon laughed again, harder. "I thought we'd have at least the semblance of a contest. What a joke!"

"I'm winning," Prior said. "You're finished, branch."

"Ho ho ho! What a ludicrous threat. I haven't heard anything that rich in centuries!"

Overcome by humor, the demon laughed so hard that he rolled off Prior and curled up on his back on the floor, hardly able to get a breath between guffaws. Prior got up, dusted himself off, then squatted over the demon's face and let out another small fart.

The demon inhaled. A look of shock crossed his ugly features. "Oh, I'm done for! How could this happen?" Then he popped out of existence.

Prior ran across to Tantamount. Only about fifteen minutes had passed, but that was enough to set a good three inches of the stake into her.

"Don't touch me!" she gasped. "Any jog will drop me on it. Pull from the other end."

He ran to the clock. He was about to take hold of the rope between it and the pulley, but she stopped him again. "Wind the clock hand backwards. That's safest."

He did so, and slowly the rope rewound and drew her up off the stake. Once she was clear, she pushed herself to the side with one leg. "Now lower me, slowly."

He did so, and soon she stood on the ground, bringing her hands down. He rushed to embrace her.

Chapter 22 — Demoness

Tantamount turned eagerly to accept Prior's embrace. "What happened?" she asked. "The demon was winning, and I feared for you. Then he started laughing and didn't stop. The joke couldn't have been *that* funny."

"No joke," he said, pausing to kiss her. "I farted laughing gas."

"Laughing gas!" she exclaimed, laughing herself. "But that's an anesthetic."

"Yes. He thought he was laughing of his own volition, so he didn't even try to fight it. That was his mistake."

"You're wonderful!" She kissed him passionately. "Let's find a bed, while we have time. I'm so relieved to be free again."

"Forget it, mortal man," a sultry voice said. It was a dusky demoness in an elegant dress, bold of breast, stout of thigh, classic of feature, with a necklace of fifty severed shriveled human penises. "You must win her from me. Tomorrow at noon."

"The Second Branch!" Prior exclaimed.

"But we should have a day to ourselves, between bouts," Tantamount protested. She was feeling downright romantic, after the horrors of the night and her near brush with impalement.

"No. You are in my power now." The nails of the demoness's fingers extended like the claws of a cat, digging into Tantamount's flesh. "Hostage to his performance tomorrow."

Then the scene changed. They were in a lush bedroom suite. This was obviously the second level, the residence of the Second Branch.

Maybe she could learn something useful. "You look too svelte to be in a business like this," Tantamount said. "You have an hourglass figure."

The demoness dropped into an easy chair and crossed her legs, the left ankle over the right knee, so that her well-fleshed thighs showed all the way to the cleft. "True. But a very small slit. Look." She reached to her crotch with her two hands and pulled her vulva lips apart.

Tantamount looked more closely. It was true; the vulva was hardly more than a crease, and the vagina seemed to be a pinpoint hole that a hypodermic needle would have had trouble penetrating. "How do you ever manage to have sexual intercourse?"

"That, my dear, is the point: in a normal combat with a male, my anatomy is virtually impenetrable. Of course I could loosen it if I chose, but I will hardly choose to do so tomorrow. I remain angry at your boyfriend."

"Because he defeated you in fair combat?"

"It wasn't fair!" the demoness snapped. "He changed weapons in mid engagement. He screwed on his pipe-cleaner model, then beat me up until I could no longer resist. He raped me!"

Tantamount had to laugh. "Rape a sex demoness? That's a hyperbolic exaggeration."

The demoness nodded, putting her lifted foot down and straightening her skirt so that her genital region no longer showed. "True. But it was a considerable annoyance. Tomorrow I will repay him in kind."

"You don't look strong enough to hold him down for a killer fart."

"I'm not. However I have a strategy that should prevail. I would have used it last time, had he not annoyed me to the point of rage so that I couldn't think straight."

This was interesting. "What did he do?"

"He bit my breast," she said indignantly. "He chomped my nipple, hard, repeatedly. Then in my distraction he tied me up and drilled my hole with his thin rod. It was an outrage."

"But as a demon you shouldn't have felt pain, should you?"

"We don't need to feel pain, but turn it on for important encounters, as it's an excellent guide to damage. But it was the barbarism of the act that got to me. No man chomps a breast as lovely as mine!"

"It does seem barbaric," Tantamount agreed.

"So you will understand why tomorrow you will be fitted with a miniature toothed animal trap that will close on your right nipple after a certain length of time has passed. You will lose the use of that breast for nursing if that trap trips."

Ouch! But the demoness would do what she chose to do. "I do understand."

"Very good. Now make yourself at home. I want you to be pretty for tomorrow." The demoness faded out.

It did make sense, Tantamount thought as she nursed Chance. The demoness had a grudge, and this would not only hurt Prior back, as it were, the same way as he had hurt her, it would make him appreciate the horror of Tantamount's predicament. What was to stop the demoness from destroying the other nipple too? Chance was not yet ready to be weaned, and anyway, she liked nursing him; it provided the kind of closeness she had never before had with another person.

Fortunately Prior had the Spire, and it had proved its effectiveness. He would find a way. She hoped.

She washed Chance and herself, and put on one of the exquisite gowns she found in the closet. It fit her perfectly, as the wall-sized mirror confirmed. Demons did know how to do things when they wanted to.

The demoness reappeared. "Would you like to join me for dinner?"

"Do I have a choice?"

"There is no need to be defensive. We both know our situations, and what will happen tomorrow. Tonight we can set that aside and be social, if you wish. You do have a choice."

Tantamount realized that even demons might like to socialize on occasion. "Truce for the evening?"

"Truce," the demoness agreed, and smiled. The room actually brightened; demons could make things literal when they chose.

Dinner was in a dining hall like that of a major hotel, but there were no waiters. Instead the platters floated in on their trays and settled before them as required. It turned out to be an excellent meal, complete with quality wine and delightful dessert. Tantamount was quite satisfied. So was Chance, sitting in his convenient high chair.

"I must say, you are a quality entertainer."

The demoness made a wry moue. "The males insist on it, on occasion, between bouts of sadistic sex. I am expected to conjure the food and clean the dishes. Woman's work."

"I'll help with the dishes."

The demoness paused, considering. "Very well."

They repaired to the kitchen, where the used dishes were piled on counters. Tantamount got to work, sorting and scrubbing, and the demoness helped. It was pleasant working together.

"I had understood that demons did not need to eat," Tantamount said.

"We don't. But we have few natural pleasures, and food can be one such. We spent several centuries having to eat nothing but ice cream; I was glad to get away from that. The Third Branch didn't eat; he had neglected to form an alimentary tract, so could not process food well. But I could eat, and prefer it to sex, for an obvious reason."

"The males have monstrous penises, and you have a very tight vagina," Tantamount agreed, rather understating the case. "I'm surprised you can manage sex at all."

"Demon flesh is elastic, and the males enjoy the challenge of a tight closure. They do hammer it in, taking my grimacing for pleasure. Some demons are amorphous, adopting whatever form they prefer at the moment; we

EEGS are less so."

"Eegs?"

"Expressly Endowed Golems, created expressly to guard the Spire from molestation. It was a great shame when we failed that mission; now we mean to win it back. That will save us from abolition by EGG, the Eldest God of the Galaxy, who made us and the Spire, at such time as he discovers our dereliction."

"So it's not just vengeance against Prior."

"Correct. But vengeance is one of the demon pleasures."

Afterward, the demoness accompanied her to her room. Tantamount nursed Chance again and put him down in the crib for the night. She wasn't concerned about him being taken from her; the demoness could do that at any time if she chose. She did not seem to be into sadism for its own sake.

"Do you ever?" the demoness inquired, opening her gown to show her beautiful breasts.

This was a new dimension, yet not completely unexpected; the demoness had been surprisingly friendly. "Once I tried it with my sister, when we were teens in med school, just to see what it was like. I'm heterosexual."

"So am I. But males can be such jerks."

"Agreed!" Tantamount removed her gown, hung it up, and stood naked. The demoness was already bare on the bed.

They made love, stroking each other, kissing, and fondling wonderful breasts without biting. The demoness was an experienced and effective lover, not at all violent or insensitive. She used her tongue to caress Tantamount's clitoris into virtual ejaculation, and reacted similarly to attention to her own miniature. But mainly it was the full-length embracing and intertwining, the ultimate closeness of two beautiful bodies. It was delightful.

"If it should happen that you lose your man tomorrow, and come into my power permanently," the demoness said, "I hope your bitterness will fade in time and allow you to do this again."

Tantamount was tempted. She realized now that demons were people too, with some similar feelings. If Prior lost, she would be the continuing captive of this creature, and a positive relationship would surely be preferable to a negative one. Certainly it was a far better prospect than captivity by the First Branch would have been, with his delight in power and humiliation. "Perhaps so, in time."

"I would like to learn caring. You could surely teach me, despite my limited capacity for it."

"I can try."

The demoness nodded, and faded. Tantamount was left undisturbed for the remainder of the night.

Chapter 23 –
Second Branch

Prior reported to the castle promptly at noon. It was now only four branches high, having settled one level.

The demoness appeared, ravishingly beautiful. But he knew better than to give her any leeway; he had to go for as fast and certain a victory as he could manage.

"We meet again," the Second Branch said. "I believe you know better than to try that laughing gas on me; my sense of humor is negligible. There is also no need for you to attempt sex with me. This is a different kind of encounter."

"I'm aware of that," Prior said tightly. "Where's Tantamount?"

"Your delightful woman? She remains in good health." She gestured, and Tantamount appeared, lovely in a close-fitting gown. Her baby was at her left breast, but there was something obscuring her right breast. It looked like a small reptile.

"True?" he asked her.

"I have not been mistreated," she said. "But this is a demon lizard whose teeth will slowly close on my breast as time passes, crushing the nipple and destroying its effectiveness for nursing. It will be exceedingly painful."

"This is what she told you to say?"

"Yes. But it is also true."

He had no doubt of it. "Let's get to it, bitch," he said to the demoness, and stepped into the pentagram, naked.

The demoness joined him, her gown evanescing. She embraced him and kissed him firmly on the mouth. Startled, he braced for a bite, but it turned out to be a straight kiss. Her perfect breasts pressed into his chest, and her groin touched his, causing his penis to react. Her body lifted so that she was his height.

"Hey—I thought you said no sex!"

"Perhaps I changed my mind. I understand you are a good lover. If you press hard and persistently, maybe you can penetrate my tight little pussy."

His penis was stiffening. "We're supposed to be fighting! What kind of trick is this?"

She ran her hands down along his back, cupping his buttocks. "One of us will surely perish by the end of this engagement. Why not glean a bit of pleasure along the way?" Her bottom shifted, allowing his erect member to lodge in her cleft, which was warm and slick.

He couldn't help himself. He thrust, and the tip of his member did manage to nudge into her aperture. It wasn't quite as taut as Tantamount's urethra had been, and was yielding slightly to his urgency. He thrust again, and got it in another inch. Her tight hole was stretching to accommodate him in a way it hadn't at their prior encounter. Apparently she could let a man in if she chose. But he hardly trusted this. "What's the catch?"

"How can there be a catch?" she inquired, kissing his ear. "To win this contest, one of us must get a posterior close to the other's face. This is not feasible while we are sexually connected."

His body kept thrusting despite his distrust. He jammed in another inch. Then the orgasm overtook him, and he sent his semen into her close chamber.

"Smartly accomplished," she murmured. Her firm vagina loosened further, and his pumping member slid in to full depth as it completed its fluid delivery. "You are indeed an apt partner. I am discovering my own climax." Her body heated, her vagina clenched, and she breathed harder. "Oh, yes, yes!" She found his mouth again for a passionate kiss.

"You didn't even bite," he said after a moment.

"I was tempted, believe me. But I wanted the fuck more than the bite, at this moment. Of course I could still form teeth in my cunt and bite your pecker off."

Prior froze, appalled.

She laughed. "But it's against the rules for this sort of engagement. Real cunts don't have teeth, so mine can't either, or I forfeit the match. Had you going there a moment, didn't I!"

"You did. I'm sorry I had to do that, then. Biting you, I mean. This is much nicer."

"Thank you. Sometimes it is indeed possible to mix pleasure with business, however fleetingly."

He was, amazingly, almost getting to like her. Then he looked past her flaring hair and saw Tantamount wincing. "The biting lizard!" he exclaimed. "You're stalling so it can hurt her!"

"Curses, foiled again," she said, laughing. Suddenly all pressure ceased and he felt his penis dribbling into space. Her center section had dematerialized.

Yet it had been one fine fuck. Furious that he had fallen for this diversion, Prior grabbed her—and his hands passed through her body without resistance. "Huh?"

"I am doing what I should have done a year ago," she said. "Spot dematerializing so that you can't manhandle me. But I'm glad we were able to connect before things got serious; there's something special about mortal sperm."

"You really wanted the fuck?" he asked as he grabbed again, with similar lack of effect. "You weren't lying so as to stall me longer?"

"Yes, actually. I knew it would not be feasible after our match was done, so it had to be at the outset. I thank you for a nice event. But now, alas, I must dispatch you." She caught his ears and yanked his head down toward her crotch. Prior heard a fart.

He yanked back, getting clear. "No you don't, bitch!"

"Yes I do, man thing. You can't pin me, but I can pin you when you get tired." She put her hands on his shoulders and leaped up in the manner of a cheerleader, her legs swinging forward. She caught his head between her plush thighs.

He found himself staring into her open cleft, from which a driblet of his seminal fluid leaked. It was a fascinating view; the hole had not yet quite recovered from the stretching he had given it. By similar token, his face was close to her cutely puckered rectum, which now loosened enough to blow out a small but potent fart.

Danger! He held his breath, put his two hands on her knees, and pried them apart. They dematerialized—but that cost them their purchase on him, and she fell down, barely righting herself before hitting the floor.

"Nice ploy, man thing. You made me waste a good fart. But I'll get you in the end, ha-ha."

Meanwhile the toothy lizard was slowly biting down on Tantamount's nipple. He had to finish this soon.

He grabbed her again, and his hands passed through her again. It looked as if he were punching through her breast and out her back, then hooking down to goose her bottom from the inside. Meanwhile she was maneuvering to get that bottom into his face again.

She tripped him. Surprised again, he fell backward to the ground. She leaped on him, her breasts on his crotch, her thighs parting to frame his head. He saw her rectum loosen; she was about to fart, and this time she had him more securely pinned. Because wherever he tried to push her off, she had no substance. She was solid only where she chose to be, and that was in her ass.

Spire, I'm in trouble, he thought.

GOT IT, the Spire gouted. It let out a windy fart.

The demoness held her breath; Prior felt her soft breasts stop heaving against his belly. But this wasn't the final fart; it was a fixative fart, nullifying her ability to spot dematerialize. Then Prior put his hands on her legs, pushed her over, and got out from under. Quickly he squatted by her now-upturned face and issued the coup-de-fart.

She was still holding her breath. There was a slight wind; it was likely to dissipate the gas before she breathed it. So he put his fingers on her ribs below her breasts and tickled.

"Eeeek!" she giggled, then took a breath, perforce—and popped out of existence.

Prior stood, relieved yet paradoxically also saddened by his victory. The demoness could have been a lot of fun, had she not been his enemy.

He went over to Tantamount. The lizard's teeth were just starting to prick the flesh of her breast and nipple. He reached for it.

"Don't touch it!" she said. "It's primed to chomp hard when touched. That's why I didn't dare."

He pondered briefly. "Get down," he said. "I'll have to fart it off."

She sat on the ground. He aimed his rear at her breast. "Hold your breath." Then the Spire let fly with a small addendum.

The lizard dropped off, stunned.

"Oh, Prior!" Tantamount said. "Thank you!"

He laughed. "I fart on you, and you thank me."

"And now I'll kiss you." She stood, stepped into his arms, raised her face—and disappeared.

"Tomorrow at noon," the Third Branch said grimly.

Chapter 24 –
Third Branch

The Third Branch demon was huge and muscular, but his penis was oddly stubby. "Now what am I going to do with you, cutie mortal, all night while I contemplate my vengeance on your puny man?"

"I suspect you already know," Tantamount said with resignation. They were in his apartment, which was relatively spare; evidently this demon wasn't much for residential comforts. She was holding Chance, and knew that again her baby was hostage to her performance.

"I'll fuck you, of course. You have never had a phallus like mine before."

"I haven't seen one like yours before," she said. "On a humanoid." She refrained from mentioning animals.

He laughed, not at all insulted, and his stubby member jiggled in and out. "Then I will demonstrate. Bend over so I can get at your hair-pie."

She thought of resisting, but knew he would have his way with her regardless. Her recent experience with the demoness had shown her that it was possible to get along with these beings, if she was careful. Sex was nothing, really; she was fully experienced there, especially recently. She turned her back to him and bent forward, presenting her bottom as she glanced back at him.

The demon put forth a gnarled thumb and poked her vulva. "A bit small, but it will do for now." Then he brought his penis around and lo, it telescoped in the manner of a stallion, becoming much larger. He put the tip to her crevice, slid it up and down a couple of times, then set it at her vagina and pushed. It was now larger in diameter than her orifice, but that didn't bother the demon; he simply shoved it in, dilating the opening. The member was still expanding, forcing her tube to expand too. This was, she thought, like birthing a baby, only in reverse, taking an oversized object in.

Then he came, and his hot fluid pressured into her, distending her even more. A baby wasn't the proper analogy, she realized; a fire hose was. It squeezed out around the member and dripped to the floor.

He let it soak a moment more, then withdrew it. "Like that," he said. "Every half hour or so should do it. I haven't had a mortal woman in a long time; I have some catching up to do."

"I should think you would want to rest, so as to be fit for your duel tomorrow."

"This is how I relax, babe. That and flying."

"Flying? You have a magic carpet too?"

He laughed again. "Come here, honey cunt, you and your tyke. I will make another demonstration."

"That isn't necessary."

"But I enjoy it." He reached out and drew her in. He turned her around so that she faced away from him, his brawny arms around her waist. A thick strap appeared, which he passed down between her legs and up behind her and fastened somewhere.

There was a roaring sound, a gust of wind, and a peculiar odor. Then the demon lifted her, carrying her with him as he leaped toward the ceiling. No, he was flying up, somehow propelled. The strap between her legs jerked taut; she fidgeted, getting it less uncomfortable.

They flew out through a window in the ceiling, then rose above the castle. The roaring sound continued. She looked nervously around. She saw a jet of flaming gas below them; the demon must be wearing a power jet.

No, the flame was issuing from between his legs. From his rectum! This was a phenomenal extended fart!

"You are jet propelled," she said.

"That I am, luscious tush. Want to know how this came about?"

Actually, she did; she had never imagined something like this. "Yes. It seems to be contrary to ordinary physics. The human system can generate only so much gas at a time; nothing on this order."

"Humans are puny. I am a demon. I am not bound by mortal limitations."

The castle was now far below. "Of course," she agreed quickly. "How foolish of me to forget. You are more than human." She was flattering him; dialogue was cheap.

"I was not always thus," he said expansively. "For most of my existence I had no asshole at all."

"Is that possible?" she asked, evincing girlish wonder.

"We golems craft our own bodies, to a considerable extent. But once they are set, they are difficult to modify. Second Branch made her cunt too small, and was stuck with it. I forgot to include an asshole. That didn't matter, as I didn't eat, so had nothing to shit. In fact it was an advantage—until that turd Prior Gross showed up."

"Prior Gross," she echoed dutifully. "You have a history with him?"

"He raided the Cherry Tree to steal the Spire, the Cosmic Dildo. We defended it from such mortal molestation, but he cheated."

"Cheated? How can that be?"

"The rule of combat, there, was fuck or be fucked. I was about to fuck him in the ass, but first I thought I'd bite off his stupid phallus. I put my face there—and he fucked me in the nose."

"The nose!"

"The left nostril. He rammed it up there and shot off his wad before I could even sneeze. All because I had no asshole. What a humiliation!"

"I can imagine," Tantamount said, suppressing laughter.

"So when I reconstituted this time, in Fartingale, I fixed that omission. I reamed out an ass like no other hole, and backed it up with a gut that could generate a virtual hurricane. And lo, I could fly!" He swooped around dizzyingly, carrying her and Chance along.

"Magic gas," she said. "How brilliant."

"You trying to false-flatter me, mortal piece of ass?"

She gambled on the truth. "Yes."

"I like it. Sure, I know you'd rather see me farted to oblivion, but you're one appealing cunt and I'm satisfied with your game. So keep on playing it and we'll get along."

In due course he brought her back to her chamber in the castle. "Now am I going to have to torture you to make your boyfriend fight?"

"No," she said quickly. "I will play the game."

"Okay. Give me another fast fuck."

She bent over, holding Chance, and he rammed into her vagina again, overflowing it with cream. It was less uncomfortable this time; either she was getting adapted, or he was less forceful. Then he disappeared, leaving her to clean up and forage for food.

But true to his word, in half an hour he was back. Wordlessly she bared her bottom and bent over, accepting his fornication. This continued through the night, but she was able to sleep between times. Certainly it was better than being tortured.

In the morning she fixed herself breakfast, pausing to take the demon's equine member in again, washed, nursed Chance, and accepted another wash of semen from the demon. It had become a familiar routine she worked around, and not difficult considering that that was all he demanded.

By noon she had been breached ten more times; the demon was indefatigable on his schedule. Other than that he was tolerant and even generous; she had whatever she requested for herself and Chance. It really was no worse than it would have been with the hyper-sexed human contestant.

"You're a good sport," the demon told her at noon as his foaming member slid out of her overflowing vagina. "No evasion, no fussing, and you pretend you like me. You are also quite pretty for a mortal."

"Thank you," she said as she nursed Chance, who was on a roughly similar schedule.

He touched her with his hand, and suddenly they were outside the castle, facing Prior. "Are you going to fight me, man thing, or do I have to ram the guts out of your woman?" The demon swung his telescoping member around toward Tantamount, who obligingly flinched.

"I'll fight," Prior said grimly.

They stepped into the pentagram and grappled. The demon was bigger and stronger, and in a moment he had Prior down and pinned. He oriented his rear on Prior's face and let out a blast that practically vaporized the man's head. Tantamount screamed.

But when the smog cleared, Prior was still lying there, unscathed. He stuck out his tongue at the demon.

Bewildered, the demon turned around, brought his ugly visage close to Prior's head, and peered into his face. "How come you're still breathing, man thing?"

"Because that isn't really my face," Prior's voice came from the vicinity of his crotch.

"Huh?"

"It's my posterior. I let out an illusion fart to change my seeming orientation. You farted at my ass, idiot."

"Oh, no!" The demon jerked back, but too late; Prior's fart caught him in the mouth and nose and he breathed it all in before he got clear. He vanished.

Tantamount ran gladly to hug Prior. But a dusky, sultry, shapely greenish demoness appeared between them. "Tomorrow at noon," she told Prior.

Then Tantamount found herself in the suite of the Fourth Branch, facing a tigress.

Chapter 25–
Fourth Branch

Prior stared at the castle that was now just two branches high. On the new ground level was a chamber whose walls were transparent, like those of the Maid-in-Tower tower, and inside was Tantamount facing a tigress.

The animal advanced on her, snarling. Tantamount retreated, backed into the bed, and fell on it as the tiger pounced. She held Chance protectively to her bosom and tried to kick the animal away with her legs. But the tiger wedged its head between them and gaped its jaws to take a huge bite of her crotch. Then, as Tantamount screamed, the tiger's tongue came out instead and slurpingly licked her vulva.

The tiger's head turned toward Prior and nodded as the walls turned opaque. He knew what it meant: the Fourth Branch was a shape changer, and was toying with Tantamount so that Prior could see. If he did not show up for the fight tomorrow, that crotch bite could readily become real.

"I'll be there, never fear," he said, and turned away. He had defeated the demoness before by getting a good hold on her and hanging on while she madly shifted shapes. He had gotten his penis into her slit, but then she had turned frigidly cold, cooling his necessary ardor. He had prevailed only by a trick: he had faked an orgasm and pissed into her, pretending it was semen. Obviously that wouldn't work again, despite his recent practice pissing into another woman.

"So how am I going to take her this time?" he asked the Spire as he walked to the local inn where he had farted for room and board.

IMMUNITY, the Spire gouted, and explained. It seemed feasible.

The innkeeper met him at the door. "No more contests," he said. "You've proved you can fart anyone else under the table. Give me something I can use, you goldbricker."

That gave Prior an idea. "I'll give you a real gold brick," he said. "Put out your hands." He turned around and dropped his pantaloons.

"You're going to shit in my hands?" the innkeeper demanded, outraged.

"I'm going to shit a gold brick," Prior said. "If you don't want it, someone else surely will." He oriented his bottom. *Spire, do your stuff.*

The Spire did. From it, seemingly from Prior's anus, issued a golden colored mass. It was a moderate turd—of solid solidifying gold.

"Will that do?" he inquired as he covered his ass.

The innkeeper stared at the mass in his hands. He could tell by its heft that it really was gold. "Oh, yes, for the next month!" He hurried away.

Prior ate and rested well. In the morning he repaired to the castle ahead of time.

Tantamount came out to meet him, dressed in a slinky gown rather than the standard farthingale. He much preferred it, and not just because it showed her figure off to advantage. "Oh, Prior, she said, rushing into his embrace and kissing him. "It was awful! She changed into a tigress and threatened me!"

"And licked your vulva," he said.

"You know?" she asked amazed.

"She kept the walls translucent so I could see. She wasn't threatening you so much as warning me."

"Oh, of course."

"How come you're out here alone?"

"Believe me, she's watching. She knows I can't escape; she's got Chance."

That figured. Tantamount would not go anywhere without her—their—baby. So the branch knew it was safe to let her out for a while. Yet it seemed unusually generous of the demoness to give him even this much joy of the woman he loved. What was she planning?

Still, whatever the catch, he was glad of it. "She didn't—do anything to you?"

"No, just frightened me. Actually none of them have been really bad, except maybe the First Branch, who let me think I was escaping." Her body moved seductively against him.

"How could you think that?" He stroked her shapely bottom.

"He let me sneak out and steal a magic carpet. I flew to your friend Smellie in Nude-on-Toilet, and she agreed to help me. Then it turned out the carpet was the demon; I had not escaped at all. He made me sit on his spike all the way back."

"His spike?"

"His big phallus formed in the center of the carpet and penetrated me. I had no choice. So I nursed Chance. The demon called it suck and fuck."

"Oh." He hated to admit it, even to himself, but that sounded sort of sexy.

"The Second Branch was actually nice to me. The Third Branch demanded sex every half hour, but apart from that he left me alone. The Fourth Branch left me alone, after that first scare. We had an interesting dialogue, and I learned some things. The door was open when you came, so I came out to meet you. But she couldn't let Chance come with me."

Prior nodded. "I can't figure why she's letting us have this time together. There's bound to be a catch."

"I think she wants me to distract you so you aren't properly prepared for your encounter with her."

Prior looked at the watch he had won in a farting match. The hands looked like penises, and the numbers were the spread legs of eager women. "We still have five minutes until noon. Is it okay to—?"

"Yes, Prior, yes!" she breathed, melting against him. Then she tugged him to a soft section of the ground and drew him down with her.

He had her skirt up and his eager member in her without delay. She kissed him, facilitating it. She was hot and slick, completely ready for his entry. "Oh, Tantamount!" he said as his passion surged.

"Oh, Prior!" She wrapped her bare legs around him, clasping him close.

He thrust, and thrust again, climaxing powerfully, and she spasmed with him.

Then, as the last of his semen flowed, she wrapped her arms around him, tightened her legs, and suddenly squeezed him so tight that the gas in his colon ripped out in a loud fart.

"What?" he gasped, surprised.

"Got you, lover," she said, and morphed into the demoness.

"It was you all the time!" he exclaimed, dismayed.

"Yes, idiot. And now you have no fart for me." She disconnected, slid out from under him, spun in place, spread her legs, and let fly a deadly fart to his face.

Prior's gaze went blank as his body went limp. She had caught him right when he was inhaling.

"You thought I would just let your wench out to give you joy? You should have looked that gift ass in the mouth." She peered at him. "You're down but not out; I'll have to finish the job." She got to her feet, straddled him, squatted right over his face, and let a second fart directly into his mouth.

He put his two hands on her two buttocks and shoved her forward. Off-balance, she flopped down on him, her face plowing into his crotch. "You faker!" she cried.

He blew out a formidable fart. It caught her in the face before she could turn it away. She tried to hold her breath, but he stabbed her crack with a finger, reaming her hole and forcing a gasp. She had to inhale—and she was gone.

He sat up as she dissipated into mist and floated away, like a cloud of spent gunpowder.

Tantamount—the real one—came from the castle, carrying her baby. "Oh Prior, I thought she had beaten you!"

"Not quite," he said, standing up. "The Spire made an immunity fart so that I could withstand her effort for a while, and of course it never runs out of gas, so I was armed when she thought I was farted out."

Then, womanlike, she was angry. "But did you have to fornicate with her like that? You looked as if you really enjoyed it."

"I did," he said. "I thought she was you. I forget about her being a shape changer. Until the end."

"Oh. I forgot she assumed my likeness. In that case, I forgive you." She reached out to him—

And the Fifth Branch interceded.

Chapter 26—Fifth Branch

Tantamount found herself and Chance in the top stage of the castle, which now was the ground level. Before her stood the dread Fifth Branch, the final and most formidable demon guardian of the Spire.

This was definitely male, a full-grown eeg seven feet tall with a two foot long perpetually erect penis. It was reminiscent of a crossbreed between a griffin and a goblin, with more than a dash of devil, with snaggle tusks projecting from where its mouth wasn't, a hooked beak without nostrils, saber-claws on its hands and feet, barbed wings, and a spiked tail. It had metallic upthrusting animal ears with serrated edges, and bright red eyes that looked painted on. Overall, it was the most horrendous creature she had seen in some time.

He—this grotesque thing was obviously male—stepped toward her. She retreated, affrighted. The monstrous phallus jetted a taffy-colored string of gism that splatted across her free arm and hip. She tried to brush it off, but it clung elastically, binding her arm to her side.

Tantamount was not stupid, particularly about penises. She realized that this was a weapon of restraint, so the demon could render her helpless without otherwise harming her. She was imprisoned here anyway. So she got smart, and negotiated.

"Demon, don't tie me up! I need to be free to care for my baby." She lifted Chance with her other arm. "I know I am in your power for a day, as I was with the four other Branches. I got along with them, and I can get along with you. Leave me free, within this chamber, and I will do whatever else you want, without trying to fight you."

The demon paused, considering. Then the massive phallus swung grandly around, like a nuclear cannon, to orient directly on her.

"Please!" she cried. "I'm pretty sure all you want is sex, and it looks impossible, but maybe it isn't. The Fourth Branch was a shape changer; she was teaching me how to do it, and I was learning a little. I can't change into a tiger or a bird, but I think I can modify my body somewhat, slowly. Maybe I can make my vagina big enough to accommodate you, so you can have sex with me. I'll even pretend to like it. I'll kiss you and make ecstatic groans. I doubt you have had full sex with many mortal women. Just let me be free."

The phallus made a correction of azimuth and shot out another gout of fluid. It splatted on the taffy that was pinning her arm—and the taffy dissolved, freeing her. The demon had understood and agreed!

"Good enough," she said, giving Chance a last nursing and setting him down in the nearby crib for a nap. "Let me focus. I can't do it instantly, but in a few minutes there should be progress." She concentrated on her vagina, willing it to grow.

It worked. She felt the tube of it expanding, displacing other organs of her body, lengthening and thickening. It swelled up into her abdomen, into her midriff, and pushed up between her lungs, past her heart, and on to the base of her throat. She felt queasy as her body adjusted, making way, but things continued to function. As the demoness had explained, shape changing was topological; aspects could be stretched or compressed without changing the essential nature of the body. Of course it could be a challenge to assume the eight legged form of a giant spider; that required greatly extending some toes to resemble legs, and not all the eyes were operative. But a change from the likeness of one human being to another was elementary. This was in between: an adjustment of the size of one portion, and shifting of position of others.

The demon waited patiently, his member never slackening.

Finally she had it. She glanced at the full length mirror, and saw that her outline was unchanged; she retained her hourglass configuration. It was only the inside that had changed, and that at this point was a mere flattened tube. "I believe I'm ready, to whatever extent is possible," she said. "At any rate, it will have to do. Now you can have sex with me."

The demon stepped forward, put his hands on her hips, lifted her up into the air, drew her in, and set her crotch on his member. She felt the hot tip of it nudging her cleft, and hoped she had made herself big enough. He let her weight drop, slowly, and that carried it down on the huge hot pole. She thought of the impalement stake the First Branch had set her on. But now she was ready for it, she hoped, and this one was rounded, not pointed.

She felt the phallus pushing in. Her flesh stretched around it, like an elastic condom, giving it room without any to spare. The great dome of it distended the aperture, denting it inward. Could she stretch enough? It seemed to be sticking.

Then there was a jet of warm taffy, or maybe petroleum jelly, and her hole became slick with lubricant. The phallus slid in, like a piston, following the greased channel, opening it up. She glanced down and saw that the member was half a foot deep, but at least three quarters of the shaft was still to come, as it were. She wriggled her torso, spreading the juice, and slid down farther, passing the halfway mark. Her belly was swelling with the size of it, sacrificing her wasp waist, but there was no pain; maybe the lubricant had an anesthetic property too.

The demon continued to lower her, and his member shoved on up inside her. She felt it passing her intestines, her kidneys, her liver, her heart, her lungs. Her breasts became more prominent, forced outward by the mass in her chest. Then, just as it reached the limit and threatened to block her throat, she felt the base of the phallus come up against her vulva. It was all in!

She sighed with relief, and felt her lungs shifting around the giant pole within her. She had accommodated the colossus. Two feet long, five or six inches thick, a genuine monster, encompassed. It was a singular victory.

But the climax was still to come. What horrific eruption was likely to come from such a gargantuan member? She rested in place, her legs dangling, feet not touching the floor, awaiting the culmination.

The phallus heated and swelled a bit more, readying its delivery. She felt a tremor down in the scrotum, maybe only a two on the rectum scale, but suggestive of the blast to come. It rumbled in the channel, and the organ became yet more turgid. At last the fluid surged out with such lava-like force that she was lifted a foot, sliding up the shaft. Then she settled again, pneumatically, as the flow diminished, and her weight pressed it out to drool onto the floor.

But that was only the half of it. The moment the turbulent elixir struck her inner flesh, the wondrous delight of it radiated outward through her body, transforming it into a vessel of transcendent joy. Her heart and lungs seemed to function more efficiently, her breasts fairly glowed with enhanced sex appeal, and her head became marvelously clear. As the substance coursed downward, her guts and kidneys shared the joy, and her vagina became a column of rapture.

"Oh, demon," she gasped. "I never had an orgasm like that!" She lifted her face and managed to reach his face, kissing him on the tusked chin. "I didn't have to fake anything."

But all things had to end, and though the phallus remained rigid, the pleasure slowly faded as the ejaculation lost its freshness. The demon put his hands on her hips and lifted her off, inch by inch and foot by foot, until her crevice cleared the divine pediment.

She staggered to the bed and flopped onto it, driblets of the demon's semen still leaking from her cleft. She lay there, recovering from an experience that had become far more rewarding than she had expected. She had taken in quadruple the ordinary length, and had quadruple the pleasure.

She slept, delightfully exhausted. At one point she woke, discovering

Chance with her, nursing. The demon must have brought him, and made no further demand on her. It just might be that the experience had been as fulfilling for him as for her, and he needed no further contact.

In the morning she got up and washed, dressed, and ate while nursing Chance. This apartment, like the others, was well appointed; everything she needed was there.

She poked an exploratory finger into her vagina and found that it had reverted to its normal configuration. That was just as well; she didn't need a two foot long vagina when not having sex. However, she suspected that she would be able to lengthen it again more rapidly at need; she had established the template.

The demon reappeared. Oops, she might have reverted too soon. She put Chance down and indicated her body. "Do you wish another session?"

He shook his head no. It seemed that once was enough, and he was just checking in on her. "I'm fine," she said, realizing that he was the strong silent type, having no actual mouth orifice. "You are a good host."

He nodded, and turned away. But she found she couldn't leave it at that. She went after him and stood before him. "Lift me up so I can reach your face."

He did so, and she kissed him on the mouth region, between the tusks. "You were great last night, Branch Five. We really must do it again some time." She had found that it paid to flatter the demons, but what she said was true. It had been a truly transcendent experience.

He set her down and departed. She had the rest of the morning to herself.

At noon Prior arrived, ready for the final challenge. Tantamount related to him, of course; he was indeed the right man for her, apart from being the father of her child. This whole business of the tower and demon combats had satisfied her. In time she would surely come to love him. But she was sorry that the demons had to be dispatched. They were not evil, merely trying to do their job, which was to recover and guard the Spire. Even the mean-spirited First Branch had that useful magic carpet form, and he hadn't abused her once she accepted his persistent phallus. In fact it had been an interesting way to travel; his penis, like the others, had radiated a certain pleasure into her body.

She was allowed to bring Chance out and witness the event. Apparently once she had committed to indulging him, the demon trusted her and gave her full freedom. That suggested an underlying decency she appreciated.

Prior and the demon entered the pentacle. They grappled. The demon lifted the man up and shoved his face at the end of the perpetually erect phallus. That would be where he farted from, of course; the demon had no other orifice. She saw that Prior couldn't get his posterior into place; his whole body was in the air.

The demon's fundament quivered as he readied his emission. Tantamount held her breath. Prior needed to break this hold in a hurry or he would be farted into oblivion.

Prior put his mouth on the slit of the penis. What was he doing? That would wipe him out the moment the gas emerged.

Then the demon staggered and disappeared. Prior dropped to the ground, managing to land on his feet.

"What happened?" Tantamount asked, astonished.

"I put the Spire in my throat," Prior explained. "I farted before he did."

Amazed, she had to laugh. So obvious, yet she and the demon had missed it. "Oh, Prior, you're so clever!" She ran up and kissed him. "Now we can go home and get married."

"Not so fast."

She turned. There were all five of the Cherry Tree Branches standing around them.

Chapter 27–Three Curses

Prior stared. "But I abolished you!" he said somewhat dully.

"Listen, shit for brains," the ugly First Branch said. "After the way you hoodwinked us on Mount Icecream, we resolved not to be caught that way again."

"Yet despite your unprepossessing appearance," the shapely Second Branch said, "we found you to be a satisfying sexual partner, so we decided to salvage you."

"So we made a plan," the grotesque Third Branch said, his stubby telescoping penis jiggling. "We resolved that should we discover ourselves to be on the verge of defeat, we would invoke an escape mechanism."

"Thus avoiding destruction," the voluptuous Fourth Branch said, shifting rapidly through several animal forms. "Thus we deceived you by decamping rather than dissolving."

The monstrous ever-rigid phallus of the Fifth Branch, the full grown eeg, twitched. It spurted a thin line of taffy as it wiggled. The taffy landed on the ground and spelled out a message in script: *In short, we cheated.*

"But that's not fair!" Prior protested.

"Yeah?" the first Branch asked belligerently. "So what are you going to do about it, loser?"

"I'll put you away again," Prior retorted with obviously false bravado.

"All of us at once?" the Third Branch inquired with a warty nosed sneer.

"Yet it need not be an arduous confinement," the Fourth Branch said with a truly lovely smile. "My sister and I will use you for frequent sex, and our brothers will have similar use for your girlfriend. All you have to do is agree."

"I hope you *don't* agree," the First Branch said. "Then we'll have a pretext to rape both of you until your holes turn inside out."

Prior looked at Tantamount. "This is awkward," she said. "But faced with their reneging, I must say that it is not hard to get along with them, if you don't fight them. They are fair minded, for demons, and if you give them what they want, they are tolerant and even generous in other respects."

"But all they want is sex and the Spire!"

She nodded. "What is your point?"

"I can't abide letting them win by cheating. It just isn't right."

"Your sentiment becomes you. But unless you have a way to enforce your victories, we must be practical."

Prior sought better advice. "Spire, what can we do?"

"I doubt the Spire can help you now," the Second Branch said. "It is our purpose to keep and protect the Spire. It is our reason for being." She smiled and stroked her luscious outline. "Really, Prior, we are offering you a reasonable alternative. We'll even allow you to have some sex with your girlfriend when we aren't using the two of you."

"Voyeurism can be fun," the Fourth Branch agreed, making her voluptuous flesh quiver.

Meanwhile the Spire made a small gout in Prior's mouth. **YOU CAN'T OVERPOWER THE CHEATING EEGS. THE ONLY CHANCE IS THE MAGIC FART.**

A magic fart? We've been using them all along.

THE MAGIC FART. THAT WILL SUMMON EGG. BUT THAT'S DANGEROUS.

I don't care what it is or who it calls. If it solves this problem, I'm for it. Loose the Magic Fart!

YOUR FOOLISH WISH IS MY COMMAND. AIM ME AT THE SKY.

Prior tilted his head back and opened his mouth so that the tip of the Spire had access to the sky.

"Look out!" the Third Branch cried. "He's really going for the Magic Fart!"

All five demons pounced on Prior. But the Spire was already loosing the Fart. It powered out of his mouth like the hiss of a jet engine, making a lurid burning column in the sky, expanding as it went.

The demons landed on Prior and bore him to the ground. The First Branch had one arm, the Third Branch the other arm, and the Fifth Branch his legs. The sultry Second Branch's tight cleft was in his face, and he felt the cool plush bottom of the dusky Fourth Branch on his crotch. They had overpowered him. But the Fart had been loosed, and was on its way to summon EGG.

"Piss, poop, and damnation!" the First Branch swore. "The thing is out. It will accelerate to E=MC cubed."

"It will scorch Earth's atmosphere and warm the globe five degrees," the Second Branch said, her petite vulva quivering with horror. Indeed, the ambient temperature already seemed warmer. "And that's before it gets its second wind."

"It will blow the corona off the sun as it passes," the Third Branch said. "Before it gets its third wind."

"And finally lodge in the very center of the galaxy," the Fourth Branch said, taking Prior's stiffening penis into her eager vagina. "Which it will solidly plug."

"Which should get the attention of the Eldest God of the Galaxy," Tantamount said. "Now if you demons will kindly let my man up, maybe we can make ourselves presentable for his arrival."

The demons hastily let Prior go, though not before the Spire had tickled Second's vagina with a thin jet of laughing gas, making her giggle, and Fourth had evoked a driblet of pleasure from Prior's captive penis.

"Now you were giving us the choice between cooperation or rape," Tantamount said to the demons. "What will you offer us to intercede for you when EGG comes?"

The demons were obviously shaken, fearing the wrath of EGG. "Absolute servile loyalty and service," First said.

"Sex, whenever and however either or both of you want it," Second said.

"And information," the Third Branch said. "Beginning with this: you are in danger too, but there is a way out for all of us."

"Ask for the Punishment of the Three Curses," Fourth said.

Fifth squirted script. *And apply your curses to others, not yourself.*

Tantamount turned to Prior. "Does that make sense?"

"Does it?" Prior asked the Spire.

YES, IF USED INTELLIGENTLY.

Then all became perhaps moot, as an incredible effulgence formed around them. This coalesced into a giant scintillating man, flanked by a woman so luscious it was difficult to gaze directly at her. The five demons fell to the ground, groveling. This was evidently EGG, the Eldest God of the Galaxy.

"Welcome, O EGG," First quavered.

"And Favored Concubine of the Moment," Second breathed.

"**Cut the crap. Who abused the Spire?**" EGG demanded, assuming a less effulgent aspect.

"I did," Prior said, as boldly as he could manage. "I demand the Punishment of the Three Curses."

EGG considered. "**That could be interesting. Very well, name your curses.**"

PHRASE YOUR DESIRES NEGATIVELY. the Spire warned.

"**Shut up, dildo,**" EGG snapped. "**You have proved to be more trouble than you're worth. I'll abolish you after destroying this human miscreant and the errant eegs.**"

That gave Prior the hint. "My first curse is on the Spire itself, for obeying an unworthy mortal human man. Abolition is too good for it. Instead it should be forced to serve the lowliest of creatures, a mortal human woman.

That will truly make it wish it had never been made. Send it to Oubliette Emdee, to answer to her every ridiculous whim."

EGG nodded. "𝕴 𝖑𝖎𝖐𝖊 𝖙𝖍𝖆𝖙. 𝕯𝖔𝖓𝖊." And the Spire was abruptly gone from Prior's throat.

"My second curse is on these five expressly endowed golems, who failed to properly guard the Spire," Prior continued. "Destruction is too good for them, also. They should be reduced to at least as lowly service as the Spire. Bind them to another mortal woman, to perform exactly as she orders, no matter how degrading. To this woman here, Tantamount Emdee."

EGG nodded again. "𝕴𝖙 𝖎𝖘 𝖋𝖎𝖙𝖙𝖎𝖓𝖌. 𝕯𝖔𝖓𝖊."

The five demons crawled to Tantamount's vicinity. "We are duly appalled," Third whispered.

The Favored Concubine frowned, not entirely fooled.

Prior took a breath. So far so good—but could he save himself? He had to gamble. "My third curse is on you, EGG."

EGG inflated, and small lightning jags radiated from his eyeballs. "𝖂𝖍𝖆𝖙?"

"Because it was your inattention that allowed the eegs and Spire to go astray," Prior continued doggedly. "You must do penance by renouncing any further vengeance against any of these parties, returning Earth to normal temperature, restoring the sun's corona, and unplugging the galactic black hole before it blows the galaxy apart. In addition you must spend a few hours away from your Favored Concubine." Here the Concubine frowned danger-ously. "You must treat a mortal woman as you would the Concubine, though she be not a hundredth as beautiful." The Concubine's frown faded. "And grant that mortal wretch a nice legacy: fulfilling her most foolish wish."

"𝕷𝖚𝖉𝖎𝖈𝖗𝖔𝖚𝖘!" EGG exclaimed.

But the Concubine touched his arm. "It is fitting," she murmured dul-cetly.

Before EGG could protest further, Prior continued: "The woman is Smellie, a whore of the village of Nude-on-Toilet."

EGG nodded. "𝕯𝖔𝖓𝖊." He vanished.

That left just the Favored Concubine. "You're rather clever," she mur-mured to Prior. "And you're cute. One day I may come to you for a tryst." Then she too vanished.

That was it. "Well done, Prior," Tantamount said. "There are indeed worthwhile qualities in you I did not properly appreciate before." She turned to the demons. "Prepare the castle as it was, for our use this night, and stand by for further directions."

"We hear and obey, O honored mistress," the First Branch said, bowing. He had clearly figured out the new pecking order.

The castle appeared, as it had first been, with five stories. "Come, dear,"

Tantamount said to Prior. "We have a night to celebrate."

"Just us, I hope."

"Just us for now. In the future, you may divert yourself with the demonesses and the succubus too if you wish, and even the concubine if she shows up, while I am with the demons. So we don't get bored with each other. Fair enough?"

An open marriage, with her as the centerpiece. What more could he ask? "Fair enough."

"But it may take us some time to get bored," she said, kissing him.

It was more than a night in the castle, blissful beyond belief, but in due course they got on the magic carpet and flew to Nude-on-Toilet. "Look at that!" Prior exclaimed as they passed the village statue. "Now it looks just like Smellie!"

Smellie's house was fancier than it had been. She came out to welcome them, now a lovely woman, as the demons made themselves scarce. "Micro! Veil! You'll never believe what happened."

"We saw the statue," Prior said.

"Yes, I had this strange wonderful visitor, and we spent a remarkable night together. I swear, pleasure radiated out from his divine member! Then in the morning he departed, and I discovered the statue. They had made me the new Mistress of the Village. My utterly foolish dream came true after all! Can you imagine that?"

"Actually, we can," Tantamount said. "You are a deserving person."

Smellie eyed Prior. "Ordinarily I would insist on being your host tonight; it's one of my duties. But with a woman that beautiful beside you, you won't be interested."

"No problem," Tantamount said as she nursed Chance. "We'll both be with him tonight, for the sake of variety."

And as Prior found himself delightfully in bed with two beautiful and attentive women, an odd thought occurred. He recollected the Magic Fart. "I hope EGG remembered to unplug the galactic black hole."

"It could get complicated, if he forgot," Tantamount agreed. "There could be a cosmic stink." Then she and Smellie set about making Prior forget about everything but the two of them.

Author's Note

I wrote the original novel, *Pornucopia*, in 1969-70, but for some reason it took almost twenty years to get it published. I wrote the sequel, *The Magic Fart*, in 2002-03, expecting less of a problem with the marketing. Avenues exist now that did not exist then, such as the Internet.

My challenge was to write a book as naughty, dirty, and fun as the first. Close to half my life passed between the novels; could I still write as effectively as a senior citizen? I had saved stray notions in the interim, and used them, but for the most part it was contemporary writing. Readers will have to judge whether I succeeded in matching the level.

Readers may note that there are a number of inset stories within this novel. This is a technique I observed in the classic Arabian Nights stories, and I liked it and have used it in some of my novels. In this case, it was perhaps the only way to present some of the stray notions I had, that weren't exactly jokes but also weren't exactly complete stories. I hope they contribute to the larger flavor of the novel.

Will I write another sequel? I doubt it; I have pretty well squeezed out the otherwise untouchable notions, and should now be satisfied to write less naughty fiction. But it has been fun.

About the Author

Piers Anthony is one of the world's most prolific and popular authors. His fantasy Xanth novels have been read and loved by millions of readers around the world, and have been on the *New York Times* Best Seller list many times. Although Piers is mostly known for fantasy and science fiction, he has written several novels in other genres as well, including historical fiction, martial arts, and horror. Piers lives with his wife in a secluded woods hidden deep in Central Florida.

Do you want to learn more about Piers Anthony?

Piers Anthony's official website is HI PIERS at **www.hipiers.com**, where he publishes his bi-monthly online newsletter. HI PIERS also has a section reviewing many of the online publishers and self-publishing companies for your reference if you are looking for a non-traditional solution to publish your book.

Printed in the United States
119364LV00011B/71/A

9 781594 260087